WORK OF ART

ISBN: 978-0-9893919-4-8

Cover Photography: David Johnston
Cover Design: Jada d'Lee
Cover Model: Michael Senich

Editors: Angela Borda, Janine Savage of Write Divas and Janell Parque
Interior formatting: Robert Reid at 52 Novels

To all the artists…

Thank you for bravely
Showing us what you see
When you close your eyes

I see the world differently
Because of you

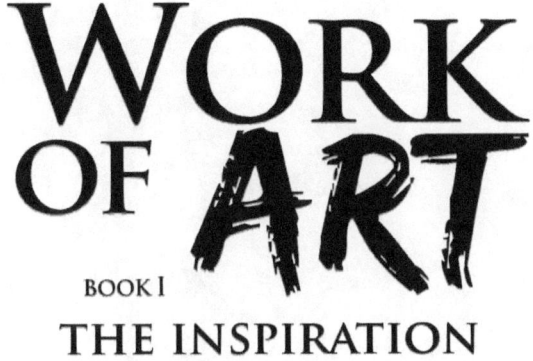

WORK OF ART

BOOK I

THE INSPIRATION

RUTH CLAMPETT

Chapter One / The Artist Emerges

We are living in a storm where a hundred contradictory elements collide; debris from the past, scraps from the present, scenes of the future: swirling, combining, separating, under the imperious wind of destiny.
~Adolphe Retté, La Plume 1898

"Get the hell away from me, Dylan. I'm not going to kiss that faux-art collector's ass!"

I look up just in time to see the blur of a man charge into our exhibit pavilion. In his fury, he slams the wall I'm facing with his fist, and I jump up as the row of paintings quiver and settle askew.

The second man, who I assume to be Dylan, is right on his heels, and he glances at me, rolling his eyes as he follows the raging artist into our private viewing room.

Not wanting to miss the drama, I jump up and position myself at the edge of the entrance, just as my boss, Adam, slowly stands and addresses the two men.

Adam has a regal air accentuated by his black turtleneck and tailored wool slacks. His silver shock of hair contrasts with his tan rugged face. Something in the way he carries himself makes him a formidable presence.

He steeples his fingers and turns to his left to study the large abstract painting of wide black slashes across a crimson field. A sudden hush falls over the room.

"Max, Dylan, the show's just begun and you're already at war." He pauses and then smiles at Dylan. "I warned you not to have him at the show. Maxfield doesn't suffer fools gladly, and there are plenty of fools here who think they know art."

Dylan's dark eyes narrow in frustration as he grumbles, "We can't exhibit at the most important art show of the year and *not* have our star artist here. Collectors want to meet the artists before they invest."

"Invest! Fuck, I hate that word!" the artist curses as he throws his head back. "This is about someone buying a work of art to make it part of their life. There should be passion about a relationship with their art. Investing is for buying goddamn real estate or government bonds!"

Although I still haven't seen the artist's face clearly, I notice the muscles ripple across his back as he crosses his arms across his chest. He's tall, over six feet, with strong broad shoulders and a tangle of hair so dark it's almost black.

He turns back to Adam. "So Dylan serves me up on a platter to this tiny, irritating woman with her face pulled so tight it's about to snap. She kept scraping her fake fingernails up and down my arms and going on about how she loves my work, while I'm trying to keep my breakfast down.

"As if that isn't brain-numbing enough, her flaming yippy designer whips open a leather bag and starts pulling out fabric swatches."

"Why couldn't you've just called me over? Mrs. Stanhope's husband owns the world's largest chain of sporting goods stores and a chunk of New Jersey. They spend millions on art every year!" Dylan practically shouts.

"I don't give a fuck who she is. The nervy bitch told me she wanted me to repaint *Dreaming of Daybreak* to match her bedspread!"

I gasp in horror, and the room suddenly goes quiet as the three surprised men turn around to regard me. "That's outrageous. What an insult!" I say angrily, giving the artist a sympathetic glance, but gasp again when I realize this stunning man is examining me intently.

Published pictures haven't done Maxfield Caswell justice. His eyes are the most extraordinary shade of blue-gray, and his face the perfect chiseled combination of angles accented by full lips. The edges of those lips curl up and his eyes spark as he regards his newfound ally.

"And you are?" Dylan challenges me, probably for stepping out of my lowly station in the business of art.

"Gentlemen, this is Ava," Adam says, giving me a warm smile. "She's new to this side of the art world and has much to learn."

"Sounds like she knows more than either of you." Max slowly moves toward me. I lower my eyes and feel a blush burn across my cheeks. He gently takes my hand. "Ava, such a lovely name," he murmurs. "I'm Max Caswell, and I don't create art to match bedspreads."

"Of course." I smile, realizing one of the most important emerging artists—according to the last issue of *Newsweek*—is holding my hand. I can feel the energy surging around this magnificent man, and his energy flows into me, igniting a fire somewhere deep inside. I realize I'm not breathing, and for a moment, I don't remember how.

I'd read an exposé on Maxfield Caswell in *Art World News*, which romanticized the fiery, mercurial disposition of the young artist. Well, clearly they weren't far off the mark, but they neglected to mention how incredibly charming he is.

As I glance down, I'm hyper-conscious of my conservative attire of a tailored shirt and sophisticated black fitted skirt. I sense the irony that my intention of choosing a work wardrobe to look professional also makes me blend in. If I hadn't boldly defended this artist, he wouldn't have noticed me.

The longer he gazes at me, the more aware I become of the absurdity of my instantaneous infatuation. This man is a sensation in the art world, and women like me are expected to fawn over him. I may be a mere gallery assistant, but I don't intend to join his fan club. Yes, his art is exhibited around the world, but I plan to make my mark one day too.

Lay off the romantic novels, Ava, I think to myself. *Do you seriously think the prince of the art world will sweep you off your feet?* But I look at Max and he's smiling like he has plans for me.

"Adam, would you mind if I borrowed Ava? I want a break away from all of this, and I sense she's just the one to calm me." He looks down and winks, and I shift uncomfortably. As Max takes my arm and begins leading me out of the room, I look back, and although Adam looks extremely displeased, he quietly nods. My sheer curiosity keeps me from insisting I stay.

"Do you always get your way?" I ask him with an arched brow as he pulls me along.

He shrugs with a crooked smile. "Pretty much. Grab your coat."

I take my purse as well, wondering what I've gotten myself into.

Although the aisles of the exhibition are crowded with people, Max seems to clear a path as he quickly leads me away from the scene. I can feel people's eyes on us, I assume due to Max's striking good looks and dramatic presence. I realize he must deal with this on a daily basis, and I shudder as I think about that much attention. He picks up speed, and I become entranced by the blur of colors and light from the paintings and sculptures we pass.

"Where are we going?" I ask, as we explode out the exit and into the crisp cold air of New York City.

The sights and sounds of the city are upon us, the jagged skyline of buildings against the vivid blue sky. Even though I've been here before, I'm overwhelmed by the sensation; I take in the swirling sound of traffic and voices, the flash of lights and swarm of people walking past. I'm intrigued by the mystery of where this man's taking me. I close my eyes for a moment, and when I open them, I realize Max has stepped forward, hailed a cab and now holds the door open.

"Your coach, madam." He smiles as I slide inside.

I'm feeling a bit disoriented, as if I've stepped into a nineteen-forties romantic comedy and Cary Grant has charmed me into an adventure.

As he leans forward to give the driver directions, I catch his scent, a mixture of soap and a subtle musk of some fragrance I don't recognize. My insides clench. *Damn, he's good-looking.* I focus on the strong line of his jaw and the rough texture of his unshaven stubble. Despite my intent to keep a clear head, I have an urge to scrape my teeth along that jaw, and I press my legs together.

He flops back on the seat and laughs. "We've escaped, Ava! We're free!"

I laugh, surprised to see him so happy. "You're a bad influence, Mr. Caswell," I admonish him with a teasing tone. "I'm supposed to be cataloguing paintings right now, not gallivanting off with you." I tip my head and gaze at him through my eyelashes playfully. Two can play the flirting game.

"Well, to hell with that. Gallivanting is the order of the day. Only the best for my defender and savior." He lifts my hand to his cheek and pulls it slowly across his face, lightly brushing my hand with his lips before setting it in my lap.

He's good at this stuff. My heart's fluttering, and I turn away to gaze out the window, embarrassed.

The cab lets us off on a side street in the Village, and we descend a short flight of stairs and enter a small Italian restaurant with dark wood-paneled walls and soft lighting. A weathered fresco of the hills of Tuscany is painted on the far wall. There's a gentle muted blend of voices floating through the air, as if the patrons in the restaurant are whispering.

As we step further into the restaurant, the host greets us warmly, and it's apparent that Max has charmed everyone who works here long ago. They fawn over him like a long lost brother and treat me like his adored queen. I don't even notice him order, but the servers quickly bring us a bottle of Ruffino Chianti and platters of bruschetta, calamari and antipasto.

This is a break? I think to myself. It's much grander than I expected and I'm secretly delighted.

Max settles, stretches his strong arms across the top of the booth and watches me intently as I sip my wine and smooth my napkin over my lap.

"So, I've never seen you at the show before, Ava. How long have you been working for Adam?"

I hesitate, not sure how much of my story to edit. "Adam offered me a job seven years ago when I was in a tough spot, and he and Katherine ended up bringing me into their family. As a matter of fact, while

I finished up my degree at UCLA, I lived in a guesthouse on their property."

He arches his eyebrows and strokes his chin with his long fingers. "Interesting. So what do you do at the gallery?"

"For several years I've helped Sean Kenary run their print studio, but recently Adam's been getting me involved in various aspects of the business. This is my first time working one of the shows."

"I wondered why I hadn't seen you here before. Well, they must think a lot of you."

"Believe me, the feeling is mutual. I'm not sure what would've happened to me if it hadn't been for them. I owe them a lot."

He looks at me intently, and I worry he's wondering about what I didn't say.

"And what did you study at UCLA?"

"Art history with a focus on contemporary art, and a minor in literature. Literature because of my passion for reading, both classic and current authors, but I also have a particular interest in writing about art."

He nods and, judging by his expression, he's impressed. I'm surprised that he's interested to learn these details about me. Maybe it's an act, or he isn't as self-absorbed as I'd surmised.

I decide to change the topic by asking him about his current work. He explains his recent exploration of the influence of technology versus organic inspiration in his work. I hate to admit it, but he's even sexier when he's talking about his passion. It's hard not to be enchanted by him.

"Do you live in L.A. full time?" I ask, trying not to be obvious, while he pours more wine in my glass.

He smiles. "Yes, and there's a large group from L.A. at the show this year. It seemed as if half the passengers on my flight here were artists and dealers." He lifts his glass and takes a sip of wine. "I'm staying through Wednesday, but most people are leaving Tuesday after the show closes. How about you?"

"We're on a later flight Tuesday evening." I feel a surge of disappointment, wishing I were booked on his Wednesday flight.

Before I know it, we've almost emptied the bottle of wine, and the effects have softened all my edges. I'm probably sounding less sharp, but Max doesn't seem to notice. He's still engaged in the conversation, and he definitely looks relaxed as he studies me.

"You know, Ava, you have the most beautiful green eyes."

If he were indeed Cary Grant, at this point in our film he'd reach over and slide my glasses off, loosen my ponytail until my hair cascaded around my shoulders and then let out a low whistle at the way he's transformed me.

I take a sip of wine and push my glasses up the bridge of my nose. "Are you going to take my glasses off?"

Max gives me a puzzled look. "Why would I do that?"

"I thought dashing guys like you always took the glasses off girls like me."

He raises his eyebrows. "Actually, I think the glasses are sexy. You're rocking the serious art dealer look. It's hot." He leans closer. "I like to imagine that professional women who dress like this wear smoking lingerie underneath it all."

I blink, picturing my demure cotton panties with the tiny bow. I give him a saucy look to throw him. "Wouldn't you like to know?"

He narrows his eyes seductively as the corners of his mouth curve up. "I knew it."

He looks very pleased, and I wonder if he knows how much he's provoking me. I gaze at his full lips and wonder how they would taste.

He leans forward, places his elbow on the table and rests his chin in his hand. His head tips one direction, then the other. I feel as if I'm being studied for a portrait.

"What?" I ask, before taking another sip of wine.

"You're really something, Ava."

"So are you." I run my fingers down the stem of my wine glass and hope he doesn't ask me to explain. Instead he elaborates.

"You're smart, beautiful and sexy too."

Is he kidding? I'm doubtful due to the intense look he gives me. I should know better, but damn, this man knows how to unravel a woman. My face is on fire and the flush moves across the top of my chest. I gaze at him while trying to control all the impulses surging through me.

My mind wanders and I imagine he's leaning back against the booth, his head tipped toward the light while I slowly undo each one of his buttons and pull his shirt open. I start by pressing my lips just under his jaw and slowly burn a trail of kisses across his chest, and down his abdomen. He tangles his fingers in my hair as he holds me gently, his soft moan encouraging me on.

"Ava?"

My eyes snap into focus when I realize he's speaking again.

"Will you come to my show tomorrow night? You must know Jess. She'll be there. You could come with her…or of course, you can bring whomever you wish. It's down in SoHo at ArteHaus."

"I'd like to go. I'm sure I can come with Jess or even Adam."

"Give me your phone," he says, holding out his hand open. "I'll give you my number and you can call if you can't arrange it with anyone, and I'll send my car."

A thrill shoots up my spine. *Am I really going to do this?*

I hand him my phone, and when he's done entering his number, he pulls out his phone and asks for mine. He's smooth as silk.

I'm programmed in Max Caswell's phone, I giggle to myself. I wonder how many other girls are on that microchip?

He takes another sip of his wine and looks back up as he slides his phone away. "So what's your passion, Ava? Working in the art field, or is there something else?"

His question and earnest look surprise me. Is there more depth and empathy to him than I realize? I take a sharp breath, realizing this is the first time in my entire life anyone has asked me this question; not just what I want to study in college or do for my career, but what my passion is, what my heart tells me to do. Dozens of thoughts slide through my mind.

"When I moved to California, my intent was to survive and prove I could take care of myself. I was so lucky to meet Adam and Katherine's son, Brian, who led me to the gallery business." I smile, remembering those early days getting to know the Kesters. "It's been very exciting to work in the art world. It's one of my great passions. But it can be discouraging too, as you know, especially with the Mrs. Stanhopes of the world. It's eye-opening to learn it's merely a business to so many."

"Unfortunately, a majority of the people," he agrees.

"I've loved the experience of getting to know the artists. And seeing how people create sparked that feeling in me to create something too. I'm not an artist, but I do have a gift with words, so now I spend a lot of my free time writing. I recently was accepted into a writing group, so it's helping me develop my craft and share my work with my peers. It's nerve-racking, but fulfilling at the same time."

"That's cool. It's so easy to get off-track when real life gets in the way, but always remember, there's nothing more important than following your passion."

As he smiles, he skims his fingertips back and forth across the tabletop and I watch, mesmerized. What if it were my bare skin instead?

His face is so alive, so handsome, and the way he's looking at me makes me feel as if I'm the most important person in the world. As a result, I've lost my will to fight my attraction to him.

There are certain moments of clarity where you can feel your world shift, and that's how I feel in this moment. This complicated man has pushed me off a cliff. The free-fall is terrifying yet exhilarating because I feel a crack opening my heavy heart. I've never felt so wide-awake. It's dangerous and joyful and wicked and deep—the realization that I'm under the spell of Maxfield Caswell—and there's not a damn thing I can do about it.

Chapter Two / Paint by Numbers

Art is the only way to run away without leaving home.
- Twyla Tharp

"Are you going to get in trouble?" Max asks with a mischievous grin. The waiter delivers the check, and Max picks it up immediately so there's no question who's paying. The interruption has succeeded in snapping us back to reality before I have a chance to share any more of my story.

"Trouble, why?" Has he been reading my mind? The idea that he knows my illicit thoughts horrifies me, but then I realize he doesn't and instead studies his watch with a frown.

"We've been here over two hours."

"Good God!" I exclaim, sliding out of the booth. "Adam's going to kill me. I need to get back."

"Slow down, Cinderella," he says with a laugh. "I won't let our carriage turn into a pumpkin or anything. We'll get a cab and I'll call Adam and make up an excuse."

The restaurant staff showers us with a medley of warm good-byes as we make our way out the door.

It takes a few moments for our eyes to adjust to the bright light after the dim restaurant. The bustle of traffic and people rushing past only amplifies the stunned feeling. I notice a group of exceptionally thin and good-looking people talking to our left. I assume it's a bunch of models from the agency just down the street, although I can't be sure.

As we step toward the curb, one of the women turns toward us. Max looks at her, and they both immediately gasp and share wide smiles.

The tall beauty runs over. "Max!" she squeals as she wraps her arms around his neck.

He hugs her, swinging her off her feet. "Katya! It's been forever. Where've you been, beautiful?"

She stays in his arms while they talk and she runs her long fingers through his hair. Meanwhile, his fingers are clasped together behind her back, holding her in place. It's intimate and makes me uneasy. I feel like leftovers from an all-you-can-eat buffet.

During the time I'd spent with Max, he'd aimed a glowing spotlight on me. Now it's shifted to *Katya* and I'm left standing in the dark. It's abrupt and startling, as if I'm not even here, and I feel myself slowly seeping into the cement of the gray, grainy sidewalk. I feel like I've been played, and I'm so humiliated I want to disappear.

A vacant cab turns onto our street, so I flag it down and open the door.

"Hey, Ava, I'll see you back at the show," Max calls out.

I nod, not looking back until I'm seated and the door is closed. The beautiful couple is still talking animatedly, and I can't believe how crestfallen I am, considering I only met him hours ago.

As the cab rolls toward the exhibit hall, I admonish myself for believing his flirtation meant something. Some men make a hobby out of charming women.

It's possible he does it automatically, so effortlessly that he doesn't even realize the wilted egos he leaves behind. I stoically try to remind myself that, even if Max were interested in me, we're so different. What could we have together but an impossible mess?

Adam's involved with clients as I approach our exhibit, so I quietly slip into the viewing room to put my things away. I'm grateful he's doing so much business because it's distracted him from my absence for over two hours. The rest of the afternoon stays busy as we prepare for Jess's appearance.

Jess is my favorite of our artists. She's tough as nails and doesn't give a crap about what anyone thinks of her or her art. Her current work, oversized canvases featuring textured paintings of street musicians and dancers, is painted in a loose style with bold strokes and color, full of energy and tension. Collectors either love Jess or hate her, which makes for entertaining openings and appearances. What I wouldn't give to have a tenth of her attitude.

Samuel, the DJ for our event, has arrived along with the three street dancers we've hired to perform. I jump in to direct the bartender where to set up. In all the excitement, I realize there's no time to go to the hotel and change into my dressier outfit.

"Ava! My favorite bitch!"

I turn crimson as Jess storms toward me laughing, her blonde hair spiked like little daggers around her head. She's wearing tight black leather pants and a dramatic long jacket with graffiti painted on the back.

"Girl, how the hell are you?"

As Jess grabs me in a bear hug, I look over her shoulder and see her entourage in tow.

"Jess, I'm so glad you're here." I sigh happily, feeling grateful because this party will take my mind off the events earlier in the day. "Are you pleased with how things look?" I wave to the artwork. "Anything need to be moved? Is the lighting okay?"

"Yeah, it looks good. And Adam tells me he's already sold five paintings. It's all good." She steps back and looks at me. "But what about you, sweet Ava, I thought you were going to pretty up for my show?"

"I know I promised, Jess, and then I went and forgot my stuff at the hotel. I'm sorry."

She calls over her girlfriend. "Laura, Ava forgot her fancy threads at her hotel. What can we do with her?"

Without any hesitation Laura leads me into the viewing room and shuts the door behind Jess. Laura's a makeup artist for film, and working magic is her job. She opens her black canvas tote and pulls a series of items out.

"Take off your shirt." Laura yanks a small black tank top encrusted with rhinestones out of the bag. "The embellishment is Jess's logo from her website. It'll be perfect."

I remove my shirt, revealing my white lace bra.

She shakes her head. "The bra will have to go too."

"No way."

"Look, this shirt is tight and will hold you in. Besides, the rhinestones will cover your whole chest area, so it won't be a big deal, Ms. Modesty." I lift my eyebrows and break out in a cold sweat. Jess undoes my bra clasp before I can say anything, and Laura pulls the bra away. Her eyes get big. "Oh baby," she moans playfully. "So gorgeous—are these real?"

"Lay off, Laura, you're going to freak her out."

I blush, but before I can fully process her reaction to my breasts, she drags the tank over my head and down to my waist.

"It's tight all right," I say trying to deal with the idea of wearing something so provocative.

"Skirt's too long." Laura grabs my waistband and yanks the knit skirt up so it's mid-thigh and she folds the excess waistline down over my hips. She reaches again into the Mary Poppins bag.

"Here, put these fishnets on those long legs. That'll look hot, especially with the pumps you're wearing."

To finish the effect, she whips out a makeup kit and applies a smoky color around my eyes and a dark berry stain to my lips. Finally, she takes my hair down and, in a fury, works gel through the chestnut strands until it's a tousled, wavy mess.

"You're good to go," Laura says as she steps back to review her work. The whole thing has taken less than five minutes.

"I can't go out there like this. I look slutty."

Laura laughs. "You wish. Your natural look is like an elegant porcelain doll; you couldn't look slutty if you tried. You definitely look fuckable though, but in a Four Seasons, Dom Pérignon kind of way."

Jess smiles widely. "Now you're talking. Come on—let's do this thing!" She heads out the door, ready to party.

If Adam's reaction upon seeing me is any indication, I must really look different.

He does a double take. "Wow, Ava, you look stunning."

He turns to Laura. "Is this a good idea? Everyone's going to be looking at her instead of the paintings."

"Oh yeah, right." I moan and get my client list and folder in an attempt to focus on my job.

I instruct Samuel to start the music, and as the Kings of Leon's "Sex on Fire" blasts through the speakers, the guests start arriving. The bartender's serving up mojitos in graffiti-scrawled glasses, along with beer and wine. Soon the crowd loosens up and gets comfortable, the perfect vibe for buying art.

Adam is the master of the soft sell, cleverly talking people out of buying the work until they're begging him for it. He then turns them over to me for the less glamorous chore of arranging payments and delivery. I don't even mind this part of the process tonight because the vibe's so festive. The dancers interact with the clients, and Jess holds court like the queen she is. The photographer gets shots of her with the significant guests and other artists who have come by to say hello. A few of these will surely be published in *Art World News,* if Adam has anything to say about it.

With all the important business taken care of, I finally allow myself to relax. Adam stashed away several bottles of champagne for this moment, and he gives me a full glass to toast Jess and our event, which is clearly a success. The first glass goes down easily and I give myself permission to drink a second. As the champagne slides down my throat, I feel the warmth unfurl in my body. I'm almost in my happy place when I glimpse a tall well-built man at the bar. He has his arm around one of the art groupies who follow these events. When he shifts his face to whisper something in her ear, I feel a jolt.

Max.

Frustration twists in my gut.

Although he's the last person I want to see, I decide to not let him ruin my evening. I wander over to the DJ and request "Solar Midnight" by Lupe Fiasco.

"Time for some fun, Samuel. I need to relax." We've become friendly through the functions I've hired him for. He smiles broadly, his white teeth contrasting his smooth ebony skin.

"Let it go, girl! And I hope you don't mind me saying…you look *very* fine tonight." He dazzles me with his smile once again, and I slip behind his music station so we can chat and dance around. His dreadlocks sway as he takes my hand and twirls me around.

I throw my head back and laugh, my mood quickly improving. The music has a driving funk vibe and our bodies move easily together. Samuel knocks the volume up again and the crowd reacts. Several people move to the dance floor for the performers.

Samuel leans in and whispers in my ear, "Ava, babe, who's that dude talking to Adam? He's staring at you like he wants to eat you for dinner."

Adam and Max are across the room discussing something and they look very serious; all the while, Max stares intently at me. I turn back to Samuel and continue to move to the music, but out of the corner of my eye I can see Max come toward me like a leopard stalking its prey. I try to pretend I don't know he's there, but the energy from his intensity makes my heart pound.

Max stops in front of the soundboard. He watches my every move and, with each second passing, his countenance grows darker. I have no idea what his expression means. The music's too loud for conversation, so he grabs my hand and pulls me out from around the table until I'm in front of him. His eyes move all the way down to my feet and then back up. He smiles. *Of course the racy look appeals to him.*

"Look at you, Ava. This is the second time today you've surprised me, and we just met. What other secrets are you hiding?"

Don't even go there, Rico Suave. I cross my arms protectively over my chest. "Hey, Max, it's nice of you to come to Jess's show." I figure the polite professional route is the best way to handle him.

"Jess is an old friend, and we were at art school together. But don't change the subject." He unfolds my arms, slowly sliding his hands down to mine. "How else can you surprise me tonight?" His expression is blatantly seductive.

"Surprise?" I press my lips together. *He's messing with me again.*

"Yes, you were dressed like a lawyer earlier, and now you look like a rock star."

I roll my eyes. "Oh, you can thank Laura for that. I had nothing to do with this." I wave my hands across my body. "Jess seemed to think I was underdressed for the event, so Laura restyled me."

"I'll thank Laura later." He laughs and looks up. "We're being watched. You know, Adam just told me to stay away from you." He watches me carefully for my reaction.

"I see you take direction well."

"Why is Adam so protective of you?"

"He and Katherine are like parents to me. They know I can take care of myself, but they still look out for me."

"That's all well and good, but I definitely don't like being told what to do."

"Somehow, that doesn't surprise me. So did Adam give you a reason why you should stay away from me?" I'm curious.

"Maybe I'm trouble."

"Indeed." I give him a dubious look.

"But the question is, am I the good kind of trouble, or the bad kind?"

"Or possibly both?"

"Hmm." He takes my hands again and begins to slowly walk backward, pulling me toward the dance floor.

I really don't want to dance with Max, but then again, I do. He rests one hand on my hip and slides the other up my arm to my shoulder, his fingertips lightly grazing my neck as we dance.

Of course, the bastard's a great dancer, moving slowly, seductively. As I move in tandem with him, my natural hesitancy dissolves. The beat of the music pulses through me as he pulls me closer. I try not to look at him because, every time I do, his vivid gray eyes look not just at me, but into and through me. It's unnerving and incredibly arousing.

Damn, the alcohol must be getting to me. I want to press against him, but I don't dare.

He slowly twirls me around as the music crests, and he pulls me back with just a sliver of space between us. My breath hitches, but I feel another hand on my shoulder.

"Ava, I need you," Adam says firmly, looking unhappy and fighting to be heard over the loud music. "Mr. Barenholder wants to make a change to the installation." He steps back and waits.

I look at Max. "Excuse me," I murmur.

As I follow Adam, I begin to regain my composure. Dealing with this difficult client will bring me back down to Earth.

Mr. Barenholder lives in a museum-like mid-century home with terrazzo floors and walls of glass. It's perched on a bluff overlooking L.A. As spectacular as it is, his house seems barely lived in and always feels cold. Jess's painting, which he's now decided should hang in the foyer, will liven things up, but we have to go over every detail at least three times. Every meeting with him is fraught with anxiety. By the time I finish the final notes with Mr. Control Freak Extraordinaire, the crowd disperses and Samuel packs up his gear.

Suddenly, I hear Jess's voice coming from the viewing room, and she sounds pissed off. Concerned, I move closer to the doorway to listen.

"What are you fucking doing, Max? You're so goddamned transparent. She doesn't need to be your next conquest, your thirty-one flavor fuck, so just leave her the hell alone."

"What, you too? Why does everyone seem to feel the need to protect Ava from me? She seems very capable of making up her own mind. Besides I'm not fucking with her. I just danced with her, for God's sake. You make it sound like I'm about to drag her by her hair to my cave."

I sway and lean into the wall to steady myself. They're talking about me. I consider walking into the room to speak for myself. Once I assure them I'd never be interested in someone like Max, there'd be no reason to argue. But my feet are glued to the floor, and a feeling I don't understand holds me back.

"Oh yeah, just dancing, and I paint by numbers," she says sarcastically.

"Does she have a boyfriend? Is that what this is about?"

"I'm not going to even answer that," Jess says.

"What, is this because you *like* her? I bet you want to get into her pants."

"Fuck you! That's so *muy macho*. You think a lesbian can't have a friendship with a straight woman, that all I care about is getting between her legs. I love Ava because she's extraordinary in every way. She's a loyal friend, and she deserves the best. That's why I've made sure she wasn't around at events when you were these last few years." Jess fumes and lowers her voice. "You know it's not just Ava I'm worried about. I'm worried about you."

"You have no reason to worry about me." He sounds offended.

"Yeah well, you just seem to be all over the place—partying too hard, a parade of vapid women. It's like you believe this fame bullshit. What really matters to you these days, Max?"

He doesn't reply.

"I just wish you had someone to help you navigate all of this, someone to enjoy the success with. I haven't seen you with anyone you cared about since Chlo—"

"Stop! Don't go there. Just don't go there."

"All right, I'm done. You know, the irony is, the guy you used to be, that sensitive brilliant guy I roomed with our first year at Pratt, he's someone that would've been perfect for Ava. Is that guy still in there?"

"Stop," he moans, sounding like he's in pain now.

"I hope so…I really liked that guy." And with that, she sweeps out of the room and turns in the opposite direction of where I stand. I quickly walk over to Samuel and grab my third glass of champagne. I guzzle the contents and the fine bubbles tickle my nose. I don't turn around to see Max leave the room.

"Are you all right, girl? You look whiter than usual," Samuel says, concerned.

"Uh, Samuel, do you mind if I catch a ride with you? I want to get out of here and my hotel's just a few blocks away." I twist the edge of my shirt nervously. He agrees and I let Adam know that I'm leaving.

It rained while we were in the hall, and the cool air feels good against my face. All the streetlights glow, their colors reflecting in the wet asphalt. My mind swirls with everything I've heard. I jump up into the van next to Samuel and we take off.

"So, who was the guy?" Samuel asks playfully.

"Do you mean Rico Suave?"

"Yeah, Rico. He sure seemed to have a thing for you. Are you dating?"

"Hardly. We just met today, and no, I'm not interested."

Samuel's eyes widen as he shakes his head. "Could've fooled me. That was some pretty powerful chemistry burning between you two."

"Oh, you're such a romantic," I say, trying to keep it light.

He pulls up in front of my hotel and I give him a goodbye hug. "Thanks. I'll call you tomorrow to settle things up."

I watch him drive off before I stop at the hotel bar and order a glass of wine to take up to my room. Alcohol seems like the best way to take the edge off my tangled mind. It's been one hell of a day, and right now all I can think about is the hungry look in Max's eyes right before Adam pulled me away.

Chapter Three / Fascination Street

Art is what you can get away with.
~Andy Warhol

As lovely as it is for the hotel bartender to give me a wink and fill my wine glass almost to the brim, the combination of that and the three glasses of champagne in my petite frame is a bit much. Perched on the edge of my hotel room bed, I'm clad only in my fishnets and black tank as I hold onto my knees, hoping to correct the tilt the room has taken in my head. I focus on the framed print in front of me, and chuckle. Normally I hold hotel room art with great disdain, but right now, I find it completely fascinating.

I wonder if the person who created this blend of colors and stack of rectangles felt as serious about their art as the artists who are represented in the best galleries. Who's to say the Rothko hanging in the Museum of Modern Art this artist knocks off is any better?

"Good God, Ava, You're sooooo drunk." I slur, flop back on the bed, and lift my right leg up in the air to admire the fishnet tights I'd been embarrassed about earlier. I rub my hands up and down my thighs and turn my legs in the light. At first the texture captivates me in my drunken stupor, but the more I rub my hands over my legs, the better I feel.

As soon as my sexual feelings kick into gear, that damn Max pops into my head, and no matter how hard I squeeze my thighs together in protest, I can't get the image to leave. I remember the hot look on his face when I defended him against Dylan. It was more than simple attraction. It was as if our meeting was transformative and we were about to share a secret that would change our destiny.

I close my eyes, slide my hands up my inner thighs and picture him—long and lean, with formfitting black jeans over his strong thighs.

Oh, and his shoulders, his arms… I sigh. *He must work out…a lot.* I imagine those strong arms and shoulders holding me, and I slip my hand under the fishnets to relieve the pressure where I'm aroused.

As my hand moves back and forth and my breathing gets heavy, my phantom Max pulls me against his body, and looks at me with those burning blue-gray eyes.

"Ava," he whispers, brushing his full lips against my hair, close to my ear. "Dance with me." And as we slowly move together to the exotic music, I feel my arousal pulsing through my body.

My desire becomes more intense with each movement. He cups my ass, pulling me even closer, and his hardness presses against me.

My hand's working fast now as my climax builds. I desperately want him to kiss me, to feel his tongue slide against mine before he takes me. I look up, my lips parted.

What the hell?…

Music blasts from my cell phone and interrupts my delicious fantasy. It's a text, so I grab the phone with my free hand, the other still working under my tights.

Text from: Maxfield Caswell

My right hand speeds up again while my left clutches the cell phone. He's not just in my head now; his words are in my hand. I can feel the electrical pulse between us, knowing the phone is still in his hand while he's thinking of me. *Oh my God!* I touch the screen and read the tiny words across the screen.

You didn't say good-bye.

And with that I throw my head back into the pillow. He's on me, and in me, and it's so damn good I surge to a fierce climax, waves of fire flaming over my body and bright lights flashing through my head.

The new light of morning illuminates my room as I slowly wake and try to figure out where I am and why my head's throbbing. I shiver. I'm on top of the covers and spread eagle across the bed with one hand still wedged down the front of my tights. My left hand is stiff, and as I uncurl my fingers, my phone drops to the bed.

Wow, I really was loaded last night. I glance at the glowing red numbers of the clock on my nightstand. It's just before six o'clock.

I stumble out of bed, peel off the tights and tank top, and slide into my PJs. After brushing my teeth and gulping down a tall glass of water and two aspirins, I crawl into bed to get in a few more hours sleep. I hope I feel human when I wake up.

The next time I open my eyes, my room is much brighter. After room service coffee and toast, I decide to disregard my hangover and enjoy my free time this morning with a museum visit. Adam said I don't need to be at the exposition until one this afternoon. I put extra care into my appearance to make up for the out-of-control feeling last night, and as I approach the Guggenheim Museum in my tailored navy coat, high-heeled leather boots and sleek hair, I feel quite the New Yorker.

The current exhibit, *Paris and the Avant-Garde: Modern Masters from the Guggenheim Collection*, is right up my alley. I take the elevator to the top and start the corkscrew descent that defines Frank Lloyd Wright's unique design for the museum. The exhibit is heady stuff: Chagall, Gris, Picasso, Braque and, my favorite, Joan Miró. I'm delighted with Miró's *Carnival of Harlequin*. The whimsical shapes create a surrealist party, and I get lost in that little world. I take my time in front of each painting, savoring the experience of seeing the works of art I've studied in books come to life in front of me.

The feeling reminds me of the time my mom brought me to New York when I was in high school. She fell short in many ways, but she did try to share her love of music and art. She was always checking art books out of the library and teaching me about artists from different periods. Shortly after my dad died, she took some of the insurance money and we went to New York for a week. Every day we visited a different museum. The Guggenheim was in the middle of the trip and, after seeing the exhibit, we ate a fancy lunch in the restaurant on the lower level. That was a defining trip for me and certainly affected my decision to study art history.

I reach the bottom of the Guggenheim spiral with just enough time to catch a cab to the hall. Adam is already busy getting ready for the day and gives me a warm smile. I debate whether to ask him about his conversation with Max last night, but decide with a steely resolve to push him out of my mind. With only two more days left of the show, I won't be likely to see Max again for a long time.

We're busy with clients all afternoon and, right when it's time to wrap up, Jess and company breeze in.

"I thought we'd go by Zadi's event first, and then stop by Max's show." Adam gages my reaction, but my face reveals nothing. This had been part of the planned trip, and I've prepared myself.

"Am I okay in this?" I ask Jess, since my attire last night required substantial revision. She glances at my sleeveless knit sheath, which stops mid-thigh above my boots. A long pendant made from various antique Venetian beads knotted along a silk cord hangs around my neck.

Jess tips her head and smiles. "Only a figure like yours could pull off that dress. It's like a second skin. Is it cashmere? It looks so soft."

I nod and put on my coat, relieved to know I won't have Laura working me over tonight.

Zadi's show, *House of Shadows,* is at the International Center of Photography on 43rd Street, and it's already crowded by the time we arrive. Her large black and white photographs, still lifes, and interiors from abandoned insane asylums are positively haunting. I appreciate the emotion they evoke, but I certainly wouldn't want one of the prints hanging in my house.

I wander through the show, saying hello to some of my business acquaintances. There's a burst of laughter and loud voices at the front of the gallery. It looks like Jess has run into a few old friends from Pratt. She waves me over and introduces me to the impossibly hip group. Joe, who's heavily tattooed and pierced, commands everyone's attention.

"Hey Jess, Ba-roque Beat is set up in Times Square. Let's check them out." He turns toward me and smiles. "It's just too damn quiet in here."

"What's Ba-roque Beat?" I ask him.

"They're a group of performance artists led by our friend Alessandro, who also went to school with us. He's a performance artist and street performer."

I nod, realizing Jess has painted him several times in her current series. I'm happy to be included with the group, and we head to Times Square on foot, laughing and joking the entire way.

As we near the open area of Times Square at 6th and 42nd, I hear a thunderous pounding. We join the large crowd around a group of men sitting in a row with varied sizes of plastic tubs in front of them. They're beating the tubs in synchronization with large wooden sticks. In front of them is a man in a black body-stocking making the strangest shapes with his body.

Joe taps my shoulder and nods to the man in the body stocking. "Alessandro."

There are four other performers dancing around Alessandro to the tribal beat. It's electrifying.

Jess is already dancing and Laura laughs and joins her. Soon we're all dancing and howling, a misfit tribe on the primitive savannah of Manhattan.

Just when I think I can't dance another step, Alessandro's group finishes the song and two of his dancers move through the crowd with tubs to procure donations. Jess tosses in a twenty.

"Let's get over to ArteHaus before the booze is gone," Joe says.

"SoHo, corner of Greene and Broome," he barks at the cab driver as we pile inside.

As we head to Max's show, I give Jess a nervous look.

"Don't worry, babe. I won't let him anywhere near you," she says, assuring me.

When we step inside ArteHaus, I squint to adjust to the dramatic lighting. It's dark other than the brilliant spotlights focused on Max's large-scale paintings. The floor's vibrating with the throbbing bass of loud music. We move to the bar where the featured drink is a Flaming Dragon: a mix of herbal liquor and Bacardi rum that's set on fire to heat up the liquor before drinking.

"So hot going down and then you're on fire." Joe grins as he passes me one and downs his shot. My face flushes as the combination of flavors burns through me.

Joe pulls me over to a painting. "Fucking Max. I hate him."

The towering canvas is an intricate layering of paint, scratches, words and imagery that pull together cohesively. It's chaotic and your eyes can't stop moving from one area to the next. I finally settle my gaze on a small flat screen meticulously built into the canvas. It plays a series of serene images—the ocean, a grass field, a cerulean sky with puffy clouds. The jarring appearance of a documentary photograph of a man with a gun pointed at his head and his mouth twisted in terror stuns me. I inhale sharply and the image reverts back to a field of trees.

"Joe, how you doing, man?" I turn to see Max knock knuckles with Joe, followed by a raised handshake and slap on the back. I can't keep up with the moves that cool guys to do in greeting.

"You ass. I hate you. This shit is too damn good." He nods up to the painting.

Max grins. "Well, from you, that's a high compliment."

"You bet your ass, Romeo," Joe says laughing. "By the way, let me introduce you to the enchanting Ava Jacobs."

My cheeks go red.

"Oh, we've met," he says coolly.

He squints at me, lifting his sharply defined jaw. "You didn't reply to my text, Ava."

"You were expecting a reply?"

If he only knew what I was doing when he sent that text, I think, half amused, half horrified.

He raises his eyebrow, but Parker, the owner of ArteHaus, interrupts and apologizes as he pulls Max away.

Joe grins. "Ha! I like you, Ava. You're the first girl I've seen in a while not falling all over Max and trying to get in his pants, with the exception of Jess and her girl-power posse."

We move to the bar for another round of shots, and I only take a half shot, intending to keep my wits about me. We push through the crowd, looking for Jess, and spot her near the back of the gallery. Laura sits at a cocktail table while Jess talks animatedly to a handsome man wearing professorial glasses and a tailored suit.

Jess waves us over. "Jonathan, I believe you know Joe, and this is my good friend, Ava Jacobs. She works for Adam."

The man gazes at me, and he doesn't even glance at Joe.

"Ava, Jonathan's the publisher of *Art+trA* magazine," Jess says.

Impressive. My eyes widen as I smile warmly at him.

Jonathan steps toward me, and stretches out his hand. "Ava," he says softly as he slowly shakes my hand. His hand is strong, but his touch is almost a caress.

"Hey, Ava. Laura's been up since five, and she has an early shoot again tomorrow. I think we're going to call it a night. Do you want to hang out more or share a cab back with us?" Jess asks.

I hesitate. I want to stick with Jess, but I've always wanted to write for *Art+trA,* and who knows when I'll have this chance again.

"I can get a cab for Ava," Jonathan says.

I look up, surprised. *He must want to talk to me,* I think excitedly. He's not just handsome; his presence has an alluring sense of command.

"That's fine, Jess. I'll stay for a while."

Joe walks Jess and Laura out, leaving me alone with Jonathan. I feel very awkward, fearing this sophisticated man is out of my league. Can I hold my own with him in a discussion about art?

He turns to me and pushes his glasses up his nose before tipping his head.

"So Ava, what do you do for Adam?"

"A little of everything. I started out in the serigraph studio, but now I help in the gallery with clients. I particularly enjoy working with the artists and assisting them."

"Which area are you most interested in?"

"Actually, my real love is writing. So Adam's been having me handle some of the publicity writing, much to the chagrin of his PR agency."

"I can imagine," Jonathan says with a low laugh. "But Adam must really like your work." He pauses, and then addresses me with a professional tone. "If you're interested, why don't you send me some samples? There may be an opportunity at *Art+trA*, but only if Adam lets you freelance. I wouldn't want to upset him. He's an old friend."

My heart starts thumping with excitement, but I play it cool. "Actually, Adam encourages me to expand my horizons. He and Katherine are both generous that way." I step sideways to clear space for a waiter to pass. "I was under the impression that *Art+trA* was in New York."

"Our parent publisher is there, but we've always maintained a West Coast office. About five years ago, I decided to move to Los Angeles for personal reasons, so they accommodated my relocation. Although, I still end up spending a week a month in New York."

I nod, feeling encouraged that he's in L.A. I study his cheekbones and the way his eyes light up when he smiles at me. I realize that it's the first time I've felt this attracted to an older man. My mind races for the right question to ask.

"Do you like Caswell's work?"

"I'd like to hear what you think."

He's testing me and I don't want to disappoint him.

I clear my throat, gathering my courage and my thoughts. "You know, I wasn't a big fan of the subway series he did last year. The monotone pallet lacked the sensual use of color that's Caswell's trademark. The paradox with his choice of obvious imagery conflicted with the heart of his art, stripped-down simplicity, a kind of intangible atmosphere and an appearance that deceives, yet still tells the truth."

Jonathan arches a brow, and as he pushes back his glasses, I see a spark in his eyes.

I gesture to the painting in front of us. "In contrast, the work here tonight...the juxtaposition of the video monitor's harsh documentary statement contrasting the lush abstract landscape of the canvas is strict realism that gives way to loose drama."

"And..." Jonathan prompts me after my dramatic pause.

"I love it." I give him a big smile.

"Indeed." The edges of his mouth turn up as he nods, and I relax a few degrees, hoping I haven't made a complete ass out of myself. I want to please him. Jonathan's undoubtedly extremely smart and clever. He wouldn't be in the position he is otherwise. We wander from painting to painting as he shares what he thinks works and doesn't.

Jonathan pulls me into the third room of the gallery and links his arm with mine. It feels as if I've been claimed, and it stirs something inside of me. I focus on being a mix of charming and sophisticated, someone worthy of working for *Art+trA*.

Everything seems great until I feel like someone's watching us, and I look up and see Max stare at me, then at Jonathan, then back to me. He doesn't even smile, and I notice that there are about five art group-ies surrounding him. He's holding court with a collection of art babes as if he's the master of their harem. One hands him a shot glass and he downs the contents without hesitation. It doesn't appear to be his first drink of the night.

Max's angry look is strangely attractive. He's standing tall with tight black jeans and a black turtleneck sweater.

My violent attraction to him revs up and it pisses me off. *Why does he have to be so damn good-looking?* I turn back to Jonathan and smile as I study his intense blue eyes.

He follows my gaze and shakes his head. "Ah, Max. Up to his old tricks—the partying, the women, the attention. I've seen this all before with other young artists. Soon they lose their focus and the other stuff becomes more important than their art. It's the kiss of death in this business," he says with a condescending tone.

"Indeed," I mutter.

"I always thought there was more to Max. That's why I haven't given up on him yet. I've been working on a joint project with Taylor and Tiden Press to publish a coffee-table book about his work, but I'm not one hundred percent sure we should. If he doesn't get a grip, he could be obsolete in a couple of years."

Max moves toward us, as if he knew we were talking about him.

"So, Jonathan, I see you've met Ava. She's the belle of the ball to-night," he slurs.

I look up, alarmed.

Jonathan edges closer to me. "Yes, Max, Ms. Jacobs and I are having a delightful time getting acquainted and discussing your work."

"So what's your conclusion? Is it the best fucking art you've ever seen? And don't tell Jean-Michel Basquiat he inspired me 'cause he can kiss my ass too."

Jonathan gives him a disapproving look. "Hardly. Besides, Basquiat's been dead for over twenty years, but I can certainly use that memorable quote when we interview you for the magazine."

"Won't have time to do interviews. I'll be too busy entertaining my numerous fans," Max says loudly and sloppily waves to the girls in the corner.

My heart falls and I feel sorry for Max as he digs himself in a deep hole. Jonathan is too important a bridge to burn.

I pull Jonathan aside and whisper, "I'm so sorry for his behavior, Jonathan. Jess warned me earlier that Max got some very bad personal news today. He's a mess. I'm going to have Joe get him out of here. Can I contact you when I'm back in L.A.?"

"Are you sure? I don't like the idea of you dealing with him in that state," he says, his expression wary.

"But I promised Jess I'd look out for him." It unnerves me how ef-fortlessly I lie. *Why am I even doing it?*

Jonathan purses his lips and his eyes narrow as he glances back at Max. He pulls his card out of his pocket and hands it to me. "Will you call me tomorrow and let me know everything's all right?"

I agree, just as Max slurs a string of profanities.

I grab his arm tightly, step close, and I say between gritted teeth, "Stop it right now, Max. Keep your mouth shut and I'll get you out of here before you do any more damage."

He pulls back and eyes me with a suspicious look as he sways. "Did you just tell me to shut my mouth?"

"I certainly did," I snap, as I drag him toward the rear of the gallery and into the hallway leading to the back door off the alley. I push him against the wall and give him a long hard look.

"What, what, Ava? What in the fuck do you want?" he barks as his eyes narrow.

"I'm trying to help you, asshole. You're just too damn talented to go down in flames. Why would you say that stuff to Jonathan, of all people? Don't you care about any of this?" I wave my arms toward the gallery walls. I'm so frustrated, tears start sliding down my face.

The moment Max notices my tears, he freezes. I don't know why, but something about my reaction shuts him down, and his whole demeanor goes dark and introverted as if a heavy black cloth has been pulled over him. His defeated expression reminds me of a friend I had once who described her swings into severe depression like falling into a black hole.

That's it. I better get him out of here before he gets worse. "Okay, Max, I'm going to take care of this. Promise me you won't move. Just stay here."

There's no recognition, just a deep sigh and the blank, desolate stare, but at least he doesn't move.

When I rush to the front and find Joe, I plead, "I need your help."

"What's up, babe? I'm about to leave with Monique. The show's closing up soon anyway. Do you need a ride or something?"

"No it's Max. He's completely fucked up and I have to get him back to his hotel. Can you get a cab and bring it around back for Max and me?"

He looks irritated, but agrees and tells his friend he'll be back in a few minutes.

I angrily admonish myself as I quickly retrace my steps through the gallery. *What is it with your stupid caretaking tendencies? Like Mom wasn't bad enough, now you're looking out for a crazy artist you barely know.* I'm disgusted with myself.

As I finally rush into the hallway, I stop suddenly. One of the art groupies is on her knees in front of Max and she's moaning and rubbing her hands across his crotch. He's still in the same position I left him with the same dark expression, and unbelievably, doesn't even seem to react to what the skank is doing. I gasp loud enough that she jerks her head toward me. She licks her lips and gives me the evil eye.

In a raw, gritty voice she says, "Back off, bitch, he's mine."

Chapter Four / Reluctant Savior

Life beats down and crushes the soul and art reminds you that you have one.
    ~Stella Adler

I'm gone for what, a frigging minute, and he's already moments away from a blowjob. How'd this skank even find him? The temptation to spin on my heel and leave the sordid scene is overwhelming, but I remember Joe's probably waiting in the alley, so I resign myself to finish what I started.

Max still hasn't moved an inch, and his blank stare is even more haunting. I storm down the hallway, around the bitch on her knees, and grab Max's arm to pull him toward the back. Luckily, he doesn't resist, and the girl falls on her ass with the momentum of his movement. The shrill echo of her cursing follows us as I push him out the back door.

Joe's right there and finishes the motion, pushing Max right into the cab, swinging his legs inside and slamming the door shut. I give Joe a kiss on the cheek, whispering my thanks, and run to the other side of the cab and slip inside.

"Where to?" the cabbie asks.

Shit, where's he staying? "Max, what hotel are you at?"

I get no response from him, just the empty stare before he rests his forehead on the window. I push him forward and wedge my hand into the back pocket of his jeans. He doesn't even seem to care that I've practically grabbed his ass. But the effort is rewarded with his hotel room key and the sleeve with the room number written on it.

"Gramercy Park Hotel, please."

When we arrive, I ask the doorman for help getting Max out of the cab as I pay the fare. I get the impression this isn't the first time he's had to take care of the hotel guests in this way. He gets Max into the lobby, and luckily, Max walks steadily enough to steer him to the elevators and down the hall to his room. I note that there's a Do Not Disturb sign hanging on his door handle, and I hesitate for a moment, wondering what nightmare I'm going to face when I get him inside. I take a deep breath and swing the door open.

Once inside, I'm initially distracted by the décor: dark red walls and ebony antique wood furniture with heavy dark velvet couches and chairs.

No badly printed hotel art in this place, I note. Instead, an impressive collection of black and white photography hangs strategically throughout the suite.

I exhale with relief, noting there's no naked woman sprawled across the couch or bed. I lead Max to the bedroom and push him down to sit on the edge of the bed. He's despondent in his movements and still staring straight ahead. He's starting to freak me out.

I get a bottle of water from the bar area, and fish in my purse for the bottle of aspirin. I open the water and hand it to him.

"Drink," I command.

After he has taken some water, I push two aspirin in his mouth and command him to drink more. He complies, but when he's done, he leans forward, rests his elbows on his knees and puts his face in his hands while exhaling a long sigh of despair.

I stand back, wondering what to do next. I decide he needs sleep, so I kneel down and slowly pull off his boots. He doesn't help, but he doesn't stop me either. When I gently pull off his socks, he looks down and watches what I'm doing. I look into his eyes, and see heartbreaking sadness.

"It's okay. You'll feel better after you rest."

Realizing his turtleneck is much too hot to sleep in, I rise and peel the sweater over his shoulders. I look down and my breath catches.

His body's so beautiful, I think, staring at the definition along his chest and abdomen.

When I finally get the sweater over his head, his hair is a mad frenzy, and I resist the urge to run my fingers through it. I decide he'd better sleep in his pants, since I'm not going to take them off—for more than one reason. Our eyes meet again, and there's a curious expression mixed in with his sadness.

He watches me as I remove the layers of decorative velvet pillows from the bed before I gently push him back against the remaining linen pillow and lift his feet up onto the bed. I turn on the bedside lamp to the dimmest setting and shut off the overhead light. The room's dark now but for a faint glow from the lamp. I can no longer clearly see the expression on his face.

"Goodnight, Max," I whisper as I turn to leave. I'm halfway into the sitting room when I hear his voice.

"Ava," he calls.

I stop and hold my breath.

"Ava!" There's more urgency to his tone this time.

I step back into the doorway of the bedroom. "Yes, Max?"

His hand reaches out from under the comforter. "Please don't leave me, Ava. Please don't leave."

There's such agony in his voice. I've never heard anything so sad—a black arrow to my heart. Knowing he needs me to stay stirs up confusing emotions for me.

I stand still for maybe a minute, my mind racing…not sure what to do. It hits me that my experience with Max is no longer a 1940s romantic comedy, but a gothic romance novel. He's a tortured Heathcliff, but I'm sure as hell not playing his Catherine. He watches me silently, his expression falling with each second passing.

"Okay, I'll stay for a while," I finally reply.

"Please sit next to me," he says, as he reaches for me again.

I pull off my boots and hesitantly climb onto the bed, sitting back against the headboard. His back's to me and I can't see his expression, but I can feel his tension.

"Just relax," I whisper as I push the covers down a little. Instinctively, I soothe him by running my hand through his hair, down his back and over his broad shoulders. As I repeat the motion over and over, I can feel his body settle bit by bit with each pass of my hand.

He's silent for a few minutes, but finally turns just slightly toward me. "Thank you." His voice breaks with emotion.

"You're an angel, *my* angel." And moments later, his breath falls into a steady rhythm.

I continue to stroke him as he sleeps, realizing I may never touch him again like this, and I try to get my fill of the feeling of being connected to him. I marvel at his physical perfection. His hair's so soft, such a contrast to his hard shoulders.

I shake my head. *I'm in Max Caswell's bed touching him while he sleeps.* What a strange couple of days.

I rest my hand in the middle of his back and feel his heat beneath my fingers. *What happened tonight?* One minute he was Mr. Party and the next, a wounded soul. It didn't make sense, but I know nothing about this side of Max. I lift my hand off his back, and inch-by-inch ease myself off the bed. Luckily, he remains asleep as I tiptoe to the sitting room with my boots in my hand.

I sit for a moment on the couch and realize that I should leave him a note in case he wakes up completely disoriented. I find a pad and pen by the phone.

> *Dear Max,*
>
> *I'm not sure how much you will remember, but I brought you back to your room after your show last night. You were pretty out of it and needed help from a friend. I hope you don't mind that I was that person. Anyway, have no concerns—nothing unseemly happened, I just tucked you into bed and left.*
>
> *Drink lots of water, and hopefully your hangover won't be too wicked.*

Regards,
Ava

I notice a sketch lying on the floor. In fact, there are drawings lying all over the room— some on the floor, some scattered across the desk and end tables. I can't believe I'd missed them when I came in.

The drawings have the ragged edge from being torn out of a bound book. I set my pad down and take a closer look. They're all very loose-gesture drawings of a woman. There are loose sweeps of charcoal across the rough paper, some roughly blended. Then layered over are minimal cleaner lines from a dark pencil.

The woman is nude in all the drawings and it feels like the sort of thing done during a life drawing class. They're beautiful in their simplicity. I feel a pang of jealousy for whoever she is. She got to pose for Max here in his room. With that wave of jealousy comes the resolve to get out of his room and back to my reality.

I go back to my note and add a final line before tearing it from the pad and laying it on his bedside table:

P.S. I like your drawings very much. Who's the subject?

In the morning, I head to the exposition to oversee the guys packing up the art. I also go over all the details with the shipping company transporting our crates back to California. It's a relief to know the show's finally over and it's been a success.

On my cab ride back to the hotel, I ask the cab driver to drop me off in Central Park so I can take a leisurely walk in the brisk air.

As I wander down one of the many paths that wind through the park, I watch the nannies pushing their strollers, the old couples sitting on the benches and the young people with their lunch bags and sodas. A middle-aged woman takes a picture of her daughter standing proudly in front of the pond. A gaggle of school children in uniforms walk past while their teachers try to keep them on course. My love for

New York City swells up in my chest, and I vow to return soon, hopefully next time for pleasure, not work.

I decide to turn down another path when I hear my cell's ringtone. *Maxfield Caswell.*

I'm only half-surprised. He's probably calling to apologize for last night. I'm curious to see how he's doing.

"Hey, Max," I say casually.

"Ava." He takes a sharp breath. "What are you doing?"

"Um, walking in Central Park. Why?"

"I was wondering if we could meet for coffee before you leave. You mentioned you guys were flying home tonight."

I'm amazed he's remembered that detail. "Well...I just had coffee," I say, trying to be playful to lighten the mood.

"Okay, then tea. Where are you in the park? I'll grab a cab and meet you now."

I look around for a landmark, impressed at his determination. "I'll sit on a bench facing the pond at 61st Street, just in from 5th Avenue."

"Okay. I'll be there in about ten minutes."

I pace for a few minutes as my heart races, and I finally sit on the bench. *What's this about?* I wonder. He doesn't have to take me to tea. A thank-you call would've been sufficient.

Each minute feels like an hour. I finally look up just as he exits a cab on 5th Avenue. He strides toward the pond and flashes that gorgeous smile when he sees me stand up from the bench.

God, he's beautiful, I marvel, allowing myself one last swoon before I steel myself for what's to come. The only thing I'm sure of is I have absolutely no idea what's going to happen.

"Hi, you want to walk?" he asks casually as he approaches, pushing his hands into his jacket pockets.

I nod and we stroll silently toward the park exit at 59th Street and 5th. The trees are all edged with a brilliant green as their coats of spring leaves are just breaking through. I'm trying to imagine that this silence isn't awkward, but he gives me a break by finally speaking.

"Thank you for looking out for me last night," he says quietly, looking down at me.

I smile. "It wasn't a big deal. You didn't have to come out of your way to thank me."

"I know, but I thought we could talk."

"Sure." I realize that we're now heading down 5th Avenue and he seems to have a destination in mind. He rests his hand on my back and leads me into a turn on 55th Street. The fancy doorman at the St. Regis Hotel tips his hat as Max leads me into the elegant lobby.

"We're having tea here?" I ask, glad I'm wearing nice slacks and a tailored jacket.

"Yes, high tea. Would you prefer something else?"

"Oh, I love high tea, but I wouldn't imagine it's your style."

"See, one of the many things you don't know about me…I love high tea. I had high tea frequently with my mom, and this was her favorite place to go in New York."

My eyes grow wide. *He's taking me to his mom's favorite place for high tea? Why?*

The hostess leads us to a low silk-covered settee facing a linen-covered table set with elegant china and silver.

We must look like we're a couple, I think, noticing most of the other seating options have traditional tables and chairs.

We sink down into the loveseat with our thighs lightly touching. I open the tasseled menu to choose from a selection of over twenty teas, everything from English breakfast to exotic mango spice.

I pause to admire my surroundings and the frescoed ceiling with delicate painted cherubs floating in a cloud-filled sky, the layers of intricately carved moldings framing each scene.

I could get used to this.

"Does your mom still come here?" I ask, setting my menu down.

"No, she passed away." He looks down and shifts the fork on the table.

"Oh, I'm so sorry." *Good going, Ava. Ask about his dead mother. That would explain why he spoke in the past tense, idiot.*

"She's been gone for six years, breast cancer," he says calmly as the waiter approaches.

I'm glad for the distraction. The waiter takes our order, and after he moves away Max takes a deep breath and shifts to face me.

"So, I want to apologize for last night. I'm angry with myself for what I put you through."

Am I going to let him off the hook? I decide not to. "You're quite the party boy, Max, and that's okay I guess, if it's what you want. But I decided to get involved when you looked like a fool in front of Jonathan Alistair from *Art+trA*. It felt like a career disaster and I couldn't let that happen to you."

He grimaces. "I guess I deserve the party-boy line." He looks down. "But why did you help me, Ava? You don't even know me, not really."

Because you are the hottest man I've ever spent time with, and I want to be in your bed. I swallow and take a deep breath, glad my thoughts didn't escape my mouth.

"Well, I love working with artists. I seem to understand them. And I knew you needed help. It was my natural instinct," I answer thoughtfully.

"I knew it, Ava. I knew it from the moment we met that you would look out for me." He pauses. "Hey, I'd like to be completely frank with you. Is that okay?"

I nod, speechless.

"I'm in a bad place. I don't know why I'm so fucked up, but nothing…the fame, nor the success, seems to mean anything. So I screw around and party way too hard. It doesn't make me feel any better, but I do it because it numbs my brain and gets me out of my head for a while."

Whoa…this is way more information than I expected from the man who checked out last night the moment things got edgy. This isn't exactly high tea conversation, but in a way, I realize that I'd rather be discussing this here than in a bar. The civility of the tearoom presents a different weight to the conversation.

"Can I ask how much you drank or used last night?"

"Use?" He shakes his head. "I don't do the drug thing—left that behind at art school. I saw too many kids completely lose themselves.

But yeah, I had enough shots last night to forget how many." He runs his fingers through his hair.

The conversation halts as the waiter sets up a tiered set of plates full of tiny sandwiches, pastries and scones. He carefully pours out our tea, using silver tea strainers over our china cups.

"Anyway, the reason I had to talk to you today is because I laid awake all morning and thought about you. I was overwhelmed by the feeling that we were destined to meet right now, at this very point in time…and that somehow you would teach me how to do this right."

"Do what right?" I bite my bottom lip to prevent my mouth from gaping open.

"Find my way. You know, help me figure out how to be happy in my life," he stammers, as he taps his pen against the edge of the table and looks down where's he's doodled something abstract on the fancy menu.

"And what in the world makes you think I could figure that out for you?" I look at him incredulously. "I have issues myself I still haven't figured out."

"I know, Ava, I know…" He wrings his hands. "It sounds crazy, but I have this feeling about you and it's so strong, so damn strong."

"Let me get this straight…We were destined to meet so I could help you deal with your unhappiness with being rich and wildly successful?" I know I'm sounding snarky at this point, but what the hell? "How nice for me, Max? Isn't destiny more two-sided than that? What do I get out of this *Mother Teresa helping Max* thing?"

Max's expression falls. "I know, I know, what an asshole, right? I just haven't figured out that part yet, but I'm sure there's a way I can help you. Maybe help you get your writing career established. I know people in publishing."

I sit back, stunned. Why in the world does Max think I hold answers to his happiness in my hands? And even if I'm willing to be his supposed savior, how will it work?

"So, since you've had the morning to think about this, maybe you can explain how it'll work in practical terms," I say, nibbling on a little sandwich. I don't intend to play with him, but this gets more intriguing by the minute.

"Maybe you could work for me, help me manage my life?" he says, looking hopeful.

"I don't think so," I say, holding back a laugh. "First of all, I work for Adam and I'm very loyal to him. Secondly, what kind of career move would that be, professional babysitter and life coach for Maxfield Caswell?"

He frowns. "I suppose when you say it like that it does sound crazy. Promise me you'll think about it, and I will too. There's got to be some way we can help each other."

We polish off the tiny sandwiches and dig into the scones with the clotted cream. There's a pianist in the corner playing classical music. I wish I could take pictures of Max in this room to capture the incongruity of so much masculinity and intensity perched on a silk settee. If I had pictures, I could always remember our high tea and know it really happened and wasn't just a dream.

When we're done, Max insists on walking me back to my hotel, Le Parker Meridien, a couple of blocks away at 56th and 6th. I need to get up to my room to make the promised call to Jonathan and take care of other business before the car picks me up for the airport.

I smile brightly as I turn to him to say goodbye. "Thank you so much for high tea. It was really lovely."

"It was my pleasure."

Oh I love this gentlemanlike side of Max.

"Promise you'll think about we talked about?" he asks.

As I nod, he pulls me into a hug. As hugs go, this one's a standout. He holds me, really holds me. I feel so warm and protected, and he isn't letting go.

He tips his head down to my ear and whispers, "You know, I remember a few things about last night, Ava. I remember you took off my shoes and sweater and then tucked me in. You were so gentle with me. But most of all, I remember you stayed and ran your fingers through my hair to soothe me. I wish I could make you realize how that made me feel, how it was just what I needed at that very moment." And he pulls me even tighter for a moment and gently kisses my forehead before finally letting me go.

I pull back and look into his eyes, while trying to calm my pounding heart. I want to kiss him with every fiber of my being, but evidently he's determined that I'm destined to be his savior, not his lover. So instead, I walk to the hotel entrance and turn back one last time to smile and wave goodbye.

Chapter Five / Teetering between Euphoria and Terror

*The aim of art is to represent not the outward appearance
of things, but their inward significance.*
~Aristotle

Adam's in a particularly good mood on the flight back to L.A., probably because all but one of Jess's original paintings sold, along with a sizeable number of serigraph prints. He also got good responses to the three other artists he represented at the show, so it was a hit all the way around.

I'm happy for our success, but distracted as I think about Max and the way I felt in his arms as we said goodbye. To be that close and take in the scent of him, the hardness of his chest in contrast to the soft warmth of his hug, was a feeling I'll dwell on in the days to come.

In sharp contrast, I force myself to view an internal PowerPoint presentation on the dark and very real side of Max: Max entertaining the art groupies, Max insulting Jonathan, Max with the art slut on her knees grabbing his crotch, Max drunk and broken. Flashing red signs tell me to make a sharp U-turn and head quickly in the opposite direction of this man.

Despite my late flight, I'm happy to see that my roommate, Riley, is still up. She instantly lifts my mood. After I drag my luggage through the apartment, we curl up on the couch and I tell her about my trip and purposely leave out Max. I want to talk about him when I can think clearly and am not completely exhausted.

Riley frequently travels to New York for her design job, so once I tell her the restaurants, museums and galleries I visited, she can picture my time there vividly. One day, we will end up in New York at the same time and we'll paint the town red.

Before I finally head to my bedroom, Riley fills me in on the latest drama at her job overseeing the design of merchandise and packaging for the girl's accessory and costume lines. The irony of her position is that Riley develops a lot of their princess and fairy dress-up designs, which sounds like fun. Yet, the reality is that it's amazing how nasty people can get fighting over complications with tutu manufacturing and design issues with magic wands.

⚬—ᏋᎧᏋ—⚬

I sleep in late since Adam told me not to come in until after lunch. Wandering into the kitchen, I find Riley's note next to the coffee maker, asking me to join her for dinner. I put in a load of laundry before heading off to the gallery.

As we get ready for our meeting, Brian and Katherine give me big welcome-back hugs, but Sean stands silently to the side. I sigh in frustration. I'm not up for his moodiness today.

What have I done now? But just when I'm ready to confront him, Adam sweeps in, ready to hit the ground running.

He's clearly energized by the trip. We go over sales and the follow-up to accomplish in the following days, including a lot of printing. Adam asks me to finish out the week helping Sean.

Oh goody, I think sarcastically.

When we get to the print studio, I peruse the schedule Sean has posted and start preparing the inks for the first run. He's in the back burning the screens as I unwrap a new ream of archival paper. I love working in the print studio with the smell of the ink, the richness of the colors, and the handwork involved when so much of the world is mechanized.

Sean carries the first screen for the print run to the front of the shop. He holds it high over his head to protect the fragile surface as he walks past the equipment drying racks and pallets of paper. He wears a tight tank top and his formfitting faded jeans, accentuating his muscular build. Even when I'm steaming mad at him, I have to admit he has a beautiful body. He's classically defined like Michelangelo's *David*, and his movements have an elegance that make him addicting to watch. He notices I'm looking at him, and he smiles. He's a very proud man and undoubtedly likes to be appreciated. It's all part of our love-hate relationship.

As we step into position and start the run, he waits until we have a rhythm going before he addresses me.

"So was the trip good?" he asks with little inflection in his voice.

"Yeah," I reply with no intention of making this easy.

"Sounds like you sold a lot of art."

"Yup."

"Did you get out much after the show?" His tone sounds disinterested, but I know he thinks I'll share more if he doesn't come on too strong.

"We went out a bit." I see where this is leading.

"Jess tells me that Caswell was quite taken with you." He looks pissed as he says it. For a stoic, he's so transparent.

Bingo! The flashing lights go off in my head. Mr. Misogynist is out of his cage. He always thinks he knows better than I do what's good for me.

"Really? Jess has an active imagination, considering he was surrounded by art groupies the entire show." I stretch the truth a bit.

"Well, I saw a picture."

"Really?" I'm exasperated. "There were lots of pictures Sean. It was an *art show*. That's what they do, take lots of pictures." I point at him agitated. "Were you stalking me on the internet again?"

He backs down. "I worry about you, Ava. You don't realize what you do to guys, and I worry something's going to happen to you. That Caswell is an asshole, and I don't want him to take advantage of you."

You always assume everyone is going to take advantage of me, I think, frustrated. "You have to lay off, Sean. You aren't helping me when you get like this."

I can see that this agitates him. He turns away, his eyes hooded with anger, and I get a profile view of him with his high cheekbones and his smooth Hispanic caramel skin. Sean is good-looking in an exotic way, but when he's angry, he's hot. If we didn't work side-by-side daily in the studio, I would've slept with him a long time ago.

We work quietly the rest of the afternoon, only speaking when we have to give each other specific demands. The tension remains thick, and as soon as the last print is pulled off the press, I quickly hang up my apron and head out the door.

Riley and I do our monthly splurge and meet at Nobu for sushi, lucky to get the last table in the crowded restaurant. We check off a variety of rolls and specialties on the sushi order form and order large sakes to go with our meal. I'm finally ready to tell her about Max.

"Riley, there's this guy..." I start. Her eyes widen, since this isn't how I normally start our conversations.

I tell her all about him, the good and the bad, culminating in his nominating me to be his personal savior. As she hears my story she's amused, excited, confused and undecided, all rolled up into one.

"What are you going to do?" she asks, her big Tweety-bird eyes searching.

"I have no idea. But there may be nothing I *can* do. It's kind of up to him at this point. I'm certainly not going to contact him."

As we discuss various possibilities, I mention my makeover courtesy of Laura and Jess and how Max reacted to it. It's like giving the addict a hit. Riley chokes on her spicy tuna roll in excitement.

"She actually got you to dress sexy!" she says with delight. "Oh, and what I wouldn't have given to see the men around you dropping like flies!"

"Hardly," I scoff, pushing Max's heated reaction out of my mind.

"It's a new day, Ava!" she announces. It doesn't matter if you ever see Max again or not. It's time to own your fabulousness."

"Right!" I laugh, but Riley looks serious and announces a Saturday shopping trip to Agent Provocateur.

"Feeling sexy is the foundation to finding your inner goddess! And we'll get pedicures!"

Normally, I'd run for the hills with this agenda, but Riley's delighted...and maybe I do need to loosen up. So I nod with only a moderate amount of dread.

Riley then launches into a blow-by-blow description of a doomed blind date she went on while I was away, and we laugh hysterically while sharing a serving of green tea ice cream.

When we finally stand to leave, I sway.

Riley admonishes, "I knew you shouldn't have had that second sake. You look like you're going to fall over. You know you always have weird dreams when you drink sake."

"I'm just really tired," I whine, waving my arms.

As we tumble out the restaurant door and head back to the apartment, a wall of exhaustion hits me. My bed's never looked so good.

I'm not sure if it was indeed the sake or the emotional unloading, but Max takes center stage in my dream that night, and not in a PG kind of way.

It's dark, so dark, and I slowly crawl on the floor through the gallery. The rooms are deserted. I'm so low to the ground that even when I look up, I can't see the paintings clearly. I move to the back and see someone leaning against the wall but I can't tell who it is, and I'm very nervous.

As I get closer I realize it's Max. He hums but I can't distinguish the tune. I crawl closer until I'm under him and my fingers inch up his legs. He doesn't acknowledge me at all, just keeps humming. Even though I have a sense I'm dreaming, I can really feel the texture of his jeans.

My hands keep moving up, pressing on his thighs and feeling every tense muscle. Finally, I get to his crotch and my fingers press everywhere, but I can't find his cock. I panic, not understanding what has happened to it, but then he reaches down and strokes my face with one hand while unzipping his fly with the other. He pulls his cock out and it's substantial...how could

I have missed it? He lifts my chin and watches as I take him in my hand and rub him against my wet lips.

Suddenly, instead of the darkness, we're in a painting…something like a Jackson Pollock with paint splattered everywhere, and my mouth is moving over him as we float through the abstract landscape. I feel lost in his heat, the scent and feel of him. His humming gets louder and he starts thrusting. I'm jolted awake just as I feel his cum hit the back of my throat.

I pant, tangled up in my sheets, as I come down from the dream and slowly grasp that I'm in my bed alone. The dream comes back to me in pieces, my stomach churns as I realize that I'm the art slut in the dream. I swallow the bile edging up my throat. Even the idea of lowering myself to that level is enough reason to never see him again. It's four in the morning, and I curl in a ball and don't sleep another wink until my alarm goes off at six.

Wednesday afternoon Adam calls me in from the studio. I sit down in his office and he shares that Alistair has asked him if he's comfortable with me taking on a writing project for him.

I explain to Adam that Jonathan and I met at Max's show and he offered to review my work and look at samples.

"I thought he was just being polite. So I'm confused why he's wants to hire me for a project when he hasn't seen my work yet."

Although I need to find out what's going on, I'm happy to see Adam not only doesn't mind, but also encourages me to do the work. As long as I do it on my own time, I have his blessing.

He pulls off the Post-it, hands me Jonathan's number and tells me to use his office to call him. After he leaves for a meeting, I dial the number.

"Is Mr. Alistair available?" I ask his assistant, "Ava Jacobs calling."

There's a short pause.

"Ava!" He sounds happy to hear from me.

"I've had a good chat with Adam. Since we're colleagues, I felt compelled to speak to him before talking to you, and I'm happy to report he was encouraging about the idea of you working on a project for me."

"Yes, he just told me."

"Well, let's meet to discuss it. Are you free for drinks tomorrow evening?"

"Absolutely!"

"Meet me at the bar at the Chateau Marmont at six-thirty. Give them my name when you arrive."

"I'll be there. Thank you, Jonathan."

After I hang up, I clap my hands together excitedly. *My first professional writing job for a real client who isn't Adam!* Nothing against Adam, but it's like working for my dad. I happily float through the afternoon.

The following evening, I dodge a pack of paparazzi as I pull up to the valet at the Chateau Marmont. *It must suck to be a celebrity,* I think as the pack of animals with cameras strapped around their necks pace just beyond the entrance to the driveway.

I'm glad I put extra effort into my appearance. I have a silver silk shirt tucked into gray wool slacks. My hair's down and smoothed back, and I'm even wearing high-heeled sandals. I certainly look more sophisticated and elegant than I feel inside.

Jonathan greets me at the entrance to the bar.

Moments after we're seated, Jonathan's cell phone rings, and he looks at the screen then back at me apologetically.

"I'm so sorry, Ava. May I take this briefly?"

I nod, and he scoots his chair back from the table and turns away.

"Yes," he says quietly into the receiver.

"Yes, she's here…No, we haven't discussed it yet, we just got here." He sounds frustrated. "Yes, you've made that abundantly clear."

I realize I shouldn't be listening. I turn away and focus on the almost-empty bar, but it's early for this crowd. In the corner I notice a striking young couple huddled together. They're laughing, and he kisses her gently. It's like they're in their own bubble, and I feel a pang for that all-consuming love.

Jonathan pulls his chair forward. "I'll call you later, but right now I'm turning my phone off," he states firmly. As he shuts his phone down, he looks up and smiles.

"Now where were we?"

We go through the pleasantries of discussing the exposition, and he tells me some of his plans for an upcoming issue of *Art+trA*. We order martinis and, after they arrive, he brings up the project.

"So, Ava, do you remember our conversation at Max's opening in New York when I mentioned a plan for a coffee-table book about his work?"

"Yes." I feel apprehensive about where this is going.

"Well, after stalling, the project has been given the green light again, and Taylor and Tiden Press wants it out in time to correspond with Max's big show in Barcelona in early fall. The scans of the art were completed a while ago, and most of the layout is done, but the copy still needs to be written," he says with a smile. "And that's where you come in."

"Me? How would I be involved?" I'm confused, knowing this is a huge project.

He tilts his chin up and levels his penetrating gaze on me. "We want you to write it."

I fight to keep my mouth from falling open. He can't be serious. I struggle to get my bearings as a flush moves up my neck. "Don't get me wrong Mr. Alistair—"

"Oh, please call me Jonathan," he interrupts.

"Well, Jonathan, I'd love more than anything to work with you and write for Art+trA, or any other publication you see fit. But write the copy for a coffee-table book? That seems rather ambitious."

My mind's reeling. Part of me is getting excited, even though I know I shouldn't be. "I mean, you must understand—this is a huge opportunity. It'd be a dream come true."

He leans forward with his elbow on the table and rests his chin in his hand. The intensity of his look is unnerving.

"Can I ask one question?" I ask.

He raises his eyebrows and nods.

"Why me?"

"I have to be honest. I have my reservations as well. This is a big undertaking, and it's an important job; you were requested by the artist."

"Max." I take a sharp breath.

"Let me correct myself…He didn't request you—he insisted. He said it was the only way he would let the book be published."

"Why on earth would he do that?" I ask, baffled.

"That's exactly what I'd like to know. I hope you don't mind, but I have to ask…Are you intimately involved with Max?"

"No! We barely know each other."

Jonathan looks relieved, and I wonder if the look in his eyes could be about something other than Max. He leans back in his chair.

"That's good. I'm sure you can understand why. Max's very volatile, and what if you had a personal conflict in the middle of the project?"

"No worries there," I assure him.

"Good. I will say Max has always had a particular point of view about this book that makes his recommendation of you relevant and, possibly, very strategic. He knows a large portion of his collector-base is younger people, newer to the art market. Consequently, he wants his book to have a young, fresh point of view. As you must know, so many of the art books are written by longtime academics, who tend to pontificate to sound impressive."

I smile broadly. "Well, that's encouraging to hear. I'll definitely be young and fresh."

He nods. "I don't want you to worry. I'll make myself completely available as you work, and I'll assign you to a top-notch editor to help as well. It's of my utmost interest that you succeed spectacularly."

I study him for a moment and wonder how he really feels about this. I'm sure Adam spoke highly of me and Max may have his demands, but Jonathan must see something in me to go along and give me a career-defining opportunity. I'm so grateful and I feel a swell of affection. His eyes soften under my gaze.

"Thank you, Jonathan. I'm really honored and I won't let you down."

He smiles warmly. "Wonderful. Let's proceed then." He pulls out a card and hands it to me. "Here's the number for Max's agent, Dylan. You can call him about arranging a meeting to discuss the project. You should do this as soon as possible. I'm sure you realize the hardest part of this project will be managing the artist. And that's not easy with Max, not in any regard."

I nod, knowing he's absolutely right.

"Meanwhile our lawyer will contact you in the morning with an agreement. And my assistant will set up a time to for you to come by the office and go over technical issues, layouts, word count, fact-check-ing, etc."

This is all happening so fast. I'm teetering between euphoria and terror.

Jonathan signs the receipt and slips his wallet back in his jacket.

"If this goes well, Ava, this will open all kinds of opportunities for you."

He places his hand over mine and I'm immediately curious. What type of opportunity is he referring to?

We get up just as the bar is filling up and head out to the valet. Right before my car pulls up, he steps closer and runs his fingertips along my arm.

"You know, Ava, I really think you're something special. I'm looking forward to getting to know you better." He gives me an intense look before kissing me lightly on each cheek.

"Thank you for the drink, Jonathan, and thank you for the oppor-tunity." I smile, but I'm overwhelmed. Jonathan Alistair sees something special in me.

He's at the top of the art world hierarchy, and he's handsome and charming to boot. I also feel a thrill because it's feeling like some of his interest in me has nothing to do with publishing.

The next day, I step outside the studio three times with my phone before I finally get the nerve to call Max. Jonathan asked me to contact Dylan, but I need to get a sense of what's going on with Max before we meet. The only way to accomplish that is to talk to him directly.

He picks up the after two rings. "Hey, Ava. What's up?" I swear I can hear the smile in his voice.

Smooth, I think. *Let's all pretend his demands haven't changed the course of my career.*

"Hey, Max. I met with Jonathan last night and he asked me if I would write the copy for your art book. That's a pretty amazing offer for an inexperienced writer," I say, trying to sound as casual as possible.

"You haven't changed your mind, have you? Jonathan said you were a little nervous about it." He's the one sounding nervous now.

"No, I'm excited about it, and of course flattered, but I can't imagine why you think I'm the right person for this? I'm sure there are hundreds of writers in the art world far more qualified than me."

"But they won't be you, Ava. Remember all the things I said at tea, how I have a feeling about you…that we were destined to meet and help each other? And remember how I wanted us to work together? I haven't stopped thinking about that and then the book issue came up again. It was all so clear. This is our chance!"

I have to steel myself because the sheer joy in his voice, the conviction destiny has pushed us together is seductive in the most dangerous way.

Remember the dream, remember the dream, I chant to myself. The image of me on my knees in the darkened gallery is sobering. I try another tack.

"But Max, what if I screw it up? What if it sucks? I'm not even a published writer. You don't want to be embarrassed."

"Ava, I'd never let that happen. Surely you know how important this project is. I wouldn't want either of us to look bad."

"But—"

"Look, don't make up your mind now. Let's meet and talk about it. At least get your feet wet. Then if it isn't working, we'll move on."

"You promise? You promise if it's going badly and I suck, you'll let me walk away?"

"I promise," he says solemnly.

Somewhere inside, I don't completely believe he'll let me walk away that easily, especially if he knows my heart's holding me there.

We agree to meet for lunch at his home on Sunday, and he'll have Dylan join us. He assures me he'll talk to Dylan to update him on everything. I take down his landline number at his house and the address on Pacific Coast Highway in Malibu.

I'm a bit uncomfortable with the idea of two against one, and I ask if I can bring my roommate, Riley. I mention she's a designer and always has an interesting viewpoint.

He agrees and I find comfort in the idea. Riley can try to get a read on Max. Clearly, I've lost my objectivity with this man, and Riley will protect me if I'm stumbling down a murky road with no sense of how to get home again.

Chapter Six / Follow the Yellow Brick Road

If you ask me what I came to do in this world, I, an artist,
will answer you: I am here to live out loud
~Émile Zola

Bright and early Saturday morning, Riley wakes me up, excited about the day ahead. After coffee and bagels, we head to the salon for our pedicures. Riley gets polka dots painted on top of her polish, but I go for a solid burgundy. My pale white feet have never looked so exotic.

We hang out in the salon while our toenails dry, since Riley refuses to be seen in public, wearing flip-flops and little rubber strips between her toes. When it's finally safe, we put our sandals on and we head out to do a little window-shopping before going to lingerie nirvana. Agent Provocateur's presentation is minimal in a darker, kinkier and way more expensive way than Victoria's Secret. Once I've adjusted to the shock of hundred dollar panties, I'm able to appreciate the intricate detailing in the gorgeous lingerie. Riley convinces me that the real fun is trying things on. So we pick out a number of outfits and head to the dressing rooms.

I strip down to my plain panties, and I take the first bra off the hanger. It's an intricate design of satin with lace insets. When I put it on, it pushes my breasts up and out, making my cleavage look even fuller than it already is. I hold up the matching panties over my cotton ones as I look in the mirror. The lavender color is beautiful against my fair skin.

I wonder what a man would think of me in this outfit. It looks like something sophisticated Jonathan would appreciate.

I take a sharp breath, surprised I thought of Jonathan in such a provocative way, and remind myself where I am.

"Hey Riley, what's the point of spending so much money on lingerie? Anything that looks this good is going to instantly come off, if you know what I mean," I say over the dressing room wall.

"That isn't the point. The goal today is to get *you* to feel sexy and beautiful. When you wear the good stuff like this, you feel different. I swear it's true. And once you realize what a goddess you are, the men will naturally follow."

"Oh, okay." As I turn in the mirror and admire how the lavender lace accentuates the swell of my breasts, I admit I'm feeling pretty damn sexy.

Next I try on the black lace ensemble with the tiny, hot pink bows. It's so out of character for me that I giggle. This outfit has a garter belt, and I imagine how wicked I would look with black stockings and shoes with spike heels. The bra for this outfit is cut so low my nipples peek over the tops of the cups.

Max would appreciate this outfit. My breath hitches. *Surely it would inspire him.*

I close my eyes and imagine the feel of his hands all over me. Would he pull me against his hard body with a groan, slowly unhook the bra and slide the panties down? Suddenly investing in expensive lingerie makes perfect fiscal sense.

I've saved the virginal outfit for last. I fasten the top hook on the corset and look at my reflection. My skin's almost as light as the white satin. The overall effect is ethereal. I imagine I'm stretched out over fine linens on a canopy bed and surrounded by sheer white curtains with my hair fanned across the pillow.

I gaze at an imaginary bare-chested Max standing by the bed with a fierce look in his eyes as he unzips his jeans. I'm going to need a cold shower after this shopping trip.

"I'll meet you at the register," Riley says, as she leaves the dressing room, and I snap back to reality. There's no way I'm getting this white outfit—it's too wedding night-ish. I decide on the lavender bra and panties as I get dressed again.

A wave of buyer's remorse hits me as soon as I've signed the credit card slip. I've no business spending this kind of money on underwear, but I try to rationalize it by remembering the bonus Adam gave me from the art show. Besides, I'm usually careful with my money.

With our purchases complete, we get in the car and drive to the Kings Road Café to get a late lunch. We're about halfway through our salads when Jess and her posse stroll by.

"Hey Jess," I call. She grins and sweeps me in a big hug.

"Hey, Riley. What's shaking, ladies?"

"We're having a girlie day." I reply as I stick out my foot and wiggle my toes while holding up my Agent Provocateur bag.

"Cool," she says and turns to her friends. "Go on in and get a table. I'll be right there." She slides into the empty seat next to me.

"Lucy, you got some 'splainin' to do," she quips, giving me a stern look. "I heard from Adam that Jonathan from *Art+trA* hired you to write Max's book. Is that true?" She gives me the Jess-look of dubious judgment, and I can't hide my surprise that she heard the news already.

"Isn't it exciting!" Riley chimes in.

"Well, that depends on expectations," Jess replies.

"Can you elaborate?" I ask nervously.

"Look, Ava, we both know you can do this, and you'll do a great job while you're at it. But how much of this is about Jonathan and Max wanting to get into your pants?"

Riley groans. "Jess, this isn't helping her confidence with her writing."

I feel the sting as if I've been slapped.

"Well, Jess, even if that were true, and I don't think that's the case, I can handle myself. I'm not going to do anything I don't want to do."

Jess folds her arms over her chest.

"The project is a great opportunity and challenge. Should I really turn it down without seeing how it plays out?"

She purses her lips and nods. "Not a bad point. Okay, I'm going to go join my friends. But let me know if anyone steps out of line. I'll be happy to kick their ass," she says, as she playfully shakes her fist and smiles.

"Ciao, ladies. Give me a call next week and let's go out for a drink."

The next day, Riley and I decide to leave for Malibu by eleven-thirty to avoid traffic. Riley's wearing white capris and a halter top that shows off her tan shoulders, while I wear my new lavender lingerie under my sundress. I put the top down on my convertible, so we can soak in the glorious Southern California sun.

We get off the 101 at Malibu Canyon and wind our way through the hills. As we near the coastline, we see that spectacular view. It's a different world at the beach, and the clean air lifts my spirits. Following Max's directions, we pass Zuma Beach and turn into a driveway.

I pull up to a large gate and punch in the code Max gave me into the keypad. With a grand gesture, the tall emerald-green gates part.

Riley and I grin. It's as if we've been transported to Oz. We break into an enthusiastic round of "Follow the Yellow Brick Road," using munchkin voices as we drive through the soaring entry, and head down toward the ocean. Halfway down the hill, we stop singing.

Riley gasps. "Wow! He lives in paradise!"

I nod, quietly taking it all in. I shake my head with disbelief and realize I don't need another reason to be infatuated with this guy.

We reach the bottom of the hill where there are four houses in a row facing the ocean. Max's place is on the far left and set apart from the other homes.

My nervousness kicks in as we walk down a short path and through two large wooden gates. The portal opens to an incredible garden, complete with a koi pond and waterfall. A velvet green lawn is edged on all sides with clusters of lacy ferns and wild lavender. There are fig trees and rambling rose bushes and dozens of exotic plants I can't even identify. The entire garden is surrounded by a tall stone wall with fuchsia and apricot-colored bougainvillea crawling along its edge. There's no order or symmetry, just lushness, which only adds to its beauty.

"Wow," Riley says again. She looks as overwhelmed as I feel.

The front door is wide open, so we gingerly stick our heads in, looking for our host.

"Hello!" I call out, and after a few moments Max rounds the corner, drying his hands on a dishrag. He throws it over his shoulder as he approaches us. My breath catches in my throat at the delectable sight of him. He's gotten some color since returning from New York, and it's set off by his white linen shirt. His sleeves are rolled up, and he's wearing faded jeans and bare feet looking like Mr. California casual.

"Ava," he says, stepping forward and kissing me lightly on the cheek.

"And you must be Riley," he says, warmly shaking her hand. "Thanks for coming all the way out to the beach. I'm glad you're here."

Riley nods, star struck. I try to speak to Riley telepathically or at least with a look. *Close your mouth, girl, you're gawking.*

Max doesn't seem to notice.

"Come on in and say hi to Dylan. Hopefully he's off the phone by now."

After we join Dylan in the living room, Max heads back into the kitchen to finish preparing lunch. He insists he doesn't need any help.

And he cooks too…

I'm beside myself, so grateful for the distraction of Dylan. The one and only time I met Dylan was when I defended Max at the show. *I have some work to do to get on his good side.*

Luckily, he seems good-natured and doesn't appear to hold a grudge. He takes Riley and me out to the patio. There's a small steep hill at the edge of the property where the beach begins. The waves crash just beyond the narrow strip of sand, and the sound of the ocean can be heard inside the house.

The breeze whips my hair around my face, and it feels glorious. When I look to the horizon point where the water meets the sky, I can't believe the vast magnificence of the ocean. It must be incredible to live here, right on the edge of the earth.

Max beckons us inside, and we sit around a table facing the view. He carries plates of linguini with grilled salmon in a butter, lemon and caper sauce. There's a bowl with a mixed salad and a fresh loaf of French bread.

Dylan helps with the wine and pours everyone a glass of crisp Pinot Grigio.

There's music on the stereo, echoing through the large room.

Riley regains her bearings and entertains us with stories about product design gone bad and corporate shenanigans. Between the non-flammable PJs that burst into flames during product testing to her office-mate who was escorted out by security last week for spending hours 'researching' hard-core porn on the company computers during office hours, Riley has a way of making everything comical and much more entertaining than it probably is.

When we're done with lunch, Max explains the general idea and specs for the book. The work will be organized from the early years and influences to the initial notoriety, when Max became accepted as an important emerging artist and, finally, a commentary on where he is now and what the future might be. Obviously, the work is going to require a lot of research and interviews.

"So, Ava," Dylan asks, once Max is finished. "I'd love to read some of the books or articles you've written. What would you recommend first?"

I look up and a nervous knot forms in my stomach. "Um…I-I've never been officially published."

His blank stare shifts to confusion. "I don't understand. What do you mean, you've never been published?" He looks horrified.

"I haven't," I admit. It seems pointless to lie about it. He'd find out soon enough anyway.

He turns to Max. "You told me she was perfect for this. What the hell are you doing? Is this some type of joke?" He pushes his chair back angrily. "Don't you realize how important this is, not just for you, but for us and everything the gallery has worked for?"

Max is angry now too. "She *is* perfect for this, Dylan."

Not wanting to hear Dylan's response, I stand and walk down the hallway, hoping they didn't see the tears of frustration running down my face. By the time I get to the bathroom, I'm shaking with anger.

Why has Max done this to me? Why has he put me in a position to be ridiculed and questioned? He has to know this will only get worse.

I take deep breaths, willing myself to calm down before splashing cold water on my face. When I'm finally calm again, I gather up my nerve to go back to the table and tell them that my part in the project is over. Deep in my heart, I know that Dylan's right. They need a professional to write this story, not a neophyte with a full-time job.

When I open the door, Max is leaning on the wall of the hallway waiting for me. His somber eyes meet mine.

"Come on," he says and lightly touches my shoulder. "Let's take a walk."

I silently follow him out the side door, through the security gate and down the stone steps to the beach. We walk up to the shore and let the water wash over our feet. We stand there for a couple of minutes, not saying anything, just looking to the horizon.

I finally turn to Max. "You know what I'm going to say."

"No, Ava, you can't let Dylan get to you. He's so fucking wound up about the book that everything aggravates him."

"Max, I'm so flattered, really flattered, that you asked me to do this. But I let reason get away from me. It was a crazy idea. And as happy as I am to think it could work, I realize I'm in over my head. I think it's time to let it go, so you can find a real writer who'll do a brilliant job."

His face falls, and his reaction gets to me more than I would've anticipated.

"You can't give up, Ava. I need you. I need you to do this…for me," he says, looking like he's in pain.

I fight my natural inclination to soothe and take care of him, and instead focus on his words.

"What do you mean, *you need me, Max*?" You don't even know me." I say, shaking my head.

He turns to face me and he grabs my forearms. "I told you, Ava, it's just a sense I have. Nothing's ever felt more certain. You're going to help because you're good for me."

"Ahhhh," I groan in frustration, and I walk down the beach. He follows along beside me. "It's this *savior* thing again, Max. It's crazy. Can't you see I'm no one's savior? I'm just an ordinary girl…a completely ordinary girl."

"Ava, damn it," he grumbles, pulling on his hair with both hands, in frustration. "Why can't you see there's nothing ordinary about you?"

We walk another length of the beach until we reach a point where the jagged rock landscape prohibits us from walking further. A gust of wind off the ocean blows my skirt up. Max sees my lavender finery, but doesn't say anything, even though I'd like to know what he's thinking.

Embarrassed, I smooth my skirt down and we sit in the sand.

"It's such a beautiful day," I say softly, attempting to lighten the mood and change the subject.

He has a very serious expression and looks like he's not ready for small talk.

"How long have you lived here, anyway?" I ask.

He pauses for a moment and then looks back toward the ocean. "Full-time, about six years."

"Wow, what an incredible place to work and live." I smile. "But does it get lonely being so far away from the city?"

"Sometimes," he admits. "But most of the time I prefer solitude." He looks up at the house. "We better get back. They must be wondering what happened to us."

When we arrive at the house, Riley and Dylan are on the couch having an animated conversation and don't seem to notice we've returned.

I watch Riley with curiosity. *She's flirting with Dylan.* And it seems to be working. At least the day wasn't a total wash.

When it's time to leave, Max walks us to the car. He leans over my door. "Will you do something for me, Ava?" he asks with hopeful eyes.

"What's that?"

"Come with me to Hennessey and Ingalls next week."

"The art bookstore in Santa Monica?"

"Yes. Let's just look through some books on other artists, and talk some more before you make up your mind." He's giving me *the look*, that damn look. It's almost impossible to turn him down.

"It's only fair, Ava. At least see what Max wants to show you," Riley says, egging me on.

Thank you, dearest friend, for throwing me under the bus. I give her the evil eye.

He takes a step back and pushes his sleeves up his sculpted arms. My eyes wander up from his bare feet, over his worn jeans, his broad shoulders and handsome face. He's over six feet of masculine perfection and distracting in every way. A breeze from the ocean hits him, and he turns his face sideways. The sinking sun backlights his perfect silhouette.

This view of him engulfs me. I feel doused in flames and what I want at this very moment has nothing to do with writing. I'm burning for him. I desperately desire to be up on that deck wrapped around Max with the ocean breeze at my back. I don't want to be his savior nor his biographer, I just want to consume him, and I hate myself…knowing that doesn't make me any better than his art groupies.

"Okay, I'll go to the bookstore!" I say, exasperated.

Max smiles happily and offers a wave as he backs away from the car. He thinks he's won, but this game hasn't even begun.

Chapter Seven / Well, How Did I Get Here?

The job of the artist is always to deepen the mystery.
- Frances Bacon

"Ava!" Brian booms as soon as I step into the gallery Monday morning, and I laugh. Everything with Brian is big: his stature, his voice, his personality.

"You gotta see this." He waves me over to his laptop and points to the screen. "Look, I finally got it, my fifteen minutes of fame!" He laughs loudly.

On the screen is a photograph of Brian with his arms draped across the shoulders of artist Jeff Koons and a guy with silver hair I don't recognize.

"Was this at the Prada opening last night?"

"Yup! Everyone was there."

Brian travels in some pretty hip circles.

"And who's this?" I ask, pointing to the silver-haired guy he has his arm around.

Brian grins. "Thomas. He works for one of those entertainment shows."

"And…" I taunt him, smiling.

"Yeah, I'm seeing him tonight."

"Cool. Where are you guys going?"

"He has to cover a movie premier, but we're meeting afterward." He grins, looking very pleased with himself.

"Okay, I want to hear all about it tomorrow."

"You'll be the first to know."

It warms my heart to see Brian happy. He hasn't been himself since Christopher broke up with him and moved back to England late last year.

We discuss some business issues, including a schedule conflict with some installations. Two of our clients have tricky setups Thursday afternoon, and Brian asks if I can oversee the one in Bel Air while he takes care of the Weitz's in the Hollywood Hills. I note all the information, and he agrees to let the client know in case I need some type of security clearance.

By Wednesday, all of my experiences in New York and even my Sunday in Malibu feel like a million years ago. I'm surprised midmorning when I receive a text from Max.

"Still good to meet at the bookstore?"

So he hasn't forgotten our meeting, but his text feels businesslike. I respond likewise.

"Yes"

"6:30?"

"Okay"

"Hennessey & Ingalls, 214 Wilshire between 2nd & 3rd, I'll be in the back."

"Okay"

I slide my phone screen closed.

That's the shortest text I've ever sent and I feel disjointed. On the other hand, I'm not sure what I expected.

This is a business arrangement. That was a business text. I remind myself that a professional demeanor would probably be a smart way to approach him this evening. I got distracted by him and all his gorgeousness in Malibu, but I'm determined to regain my focus.

As I pass through the doors at Hennessey and Ingalls, a wave of delight pours over me. I could hang out here all day in the presence of so many wonderful art and design books. I note that I should do just that the next time I have a chunk of free time.

Max is in the back, as promised, surrounded by several piles of books. He's so completely engrossed in one, he doesn't even notice when I walk up to the table.

"Hey, Max," I say quietly.

He doesn't look up, but waves me to his side. "Look at this book about Gerhard Richter. Man, I'd love to hang out with him for a few days," he says with awe in his voice.

Max appears so comfortable that I get the impression he spends a lot of time here. I also remember seeing the piles of books in his house, so he must be a good customer as well.

He finally looks up, smiles and then pulls the chair out next to him and pats it. "Hey Ava, I pulled a bunch of books for you to look at."

I take the one off the top and examine the cover: Richard Prince. I open it and skim the pages.

Before moving to the next book, I look up and ask, "How long have you been here anyway?"

"I don't know, a few hours. I always lose track of time when I'm here."

We remain quiet for another twenty minutes, and I've almost gone through the first pile when Max stretches.

"I think this Francis Bacon book's good. I like the Jackson Pollock one too. Of course that guy was a lot more interesting and colorful than I'll ever be."

I laugh. "Well, let's hope so. He didn't have a very happy ending."

Max looks thoughtful. I wonder if the art groupies he hangs out with actually know anything about art.

"I guess it's up to you how you want to be perceived. It's your book after all. It's not my job to do a critical analysis of your work. My job is to tell your story."

"Hmm, *my* story." He gives me a big smile. "Hey let's get out of here. You want to grab something to eat?"

I grin. "Sure. Let me just pay for these two books."

He sweeps them out of my hands. "I'll get them. Shopping here is my retail therapy. Hmm, Kenny Scharf and Roy Lichtenstein, interesting choices."

"Yeah, well, I like the writing and the way the author presented the artist's life. I want to study them in more detail."

As he approaches the register, I know I have to make a decision about whether I'm going to continue working on his book. His behavior at the bookstore indicates that it's a given, but perhaps this is calculated to influence me.

My gaze travels across the displays of books, and I try to imagine a book I've written on a shelf here. This is such an unbelievable career opportunity. I would be a fool to walk away at this point. I can't deny the pull to spend more time with Max only makes my decision more resolute.

Outside, we wander toward the promenade and decide on a nearby Thai restaurant. We're seated next to the big picture window. After the waitress brings our bottles of Thai beer, we order *tom kha gai* soup, spring rolls and pad Thai noodles.

We talk about his experience four years ago when he was chosen for the Whitney Biennial at such a young age. His eyes light up when he talks about it. Clearly, it was a very exciting time in his life. I pull out my small notebook and take notes while we're talking, and he looks partly amused and somewhat impressed by my actions. I have specific questions I intend to get answers for.

"Why did you come back to Los Angeles when you were done with art school? Don't you think New York is the home base for any contemporary artist aspiring to the elite level in the art world?"

He tips his head to the side in thought. "Yes, I did think that way for a long time. I lived there my first few years after school but New York really overwhelmed me and I was always on edge. Then around that time, more and more cutting edge artists were setting up shop in L.A. I eventually came to see Los Angeles as the city of the future. Anything new is embraced here, and that was the spirit I wanted in my art. You can't fight new here. You're spurred on to go with it, to live it."

I scribble on my notebook furiously. *He's good at this stuff; it just rolls out of him.*

We're almost done with dinner when a couple strolling by the restaurant stop and point at Max in the picture window. The guy makes a silly face, and Max laughs and motions for them to come inside.

"You know them?"

"Yeah, it's Genna and Ari. They're old friends."

They approach our table and give Max a hug before asking what he's been up to, how his work's coming along and so forth. Judging from the smell of booze and the way they sway as they talk, they're ahead of us on the buzz patrol and have had a few drinks already.

The woman finally turns to Max and hits him on the shoulder. "Max, don't be rude—introduce us to your date."

Max looks at me as if he's just realized I'm still here. "Oh no," he says, a little loud for my taste. "Ava isn't my date. We're working together. She's helping me with my book."

My heart gets heavy with a weird sense of rejection, but I immediately recover, irritated with myself for even feeling that way. "Yes, I'd never date *him*," I say, playfully making a face as I reach out to shake their hands. Max looks at me with an expression I can't read. Maybe he isn't used to girls not fawning over him.

"Well I can't blame you," the woman agrees. "The way he cats around, I'd never know where his tail's been." She crinkles her nose in distaste. "That gets old pretty quickly."

"Speaking of which…" Ari turns to Max. "We ran into Sheila last night and she asked about you. She's back in town and looked hot."

Genna elbows Ari.

"Ow!" He grabs his side. "Babe, you remember the last time she was in LA."

Ari looks at me and grins. "Sheila and Max were in bed more than out of it."

Max looks down. Is he embarrassed? I hope so because I'm embarrassed for him.

Genna rolls her eyes. "From the way she goes on about you, I can only imagine."

How lovely. I try to cover my smirk by taking another sip of beer.

Max says. "Well, if you think of it, text me her number. I tried to call her recently, but it had been changed. Maybe we can all get together."

The wallflower thing no longer works for me, so I excuse myself to make a pretend phone call. I step outside and the cool air soothes my burning face. Waves of nausea roll through me. What the fuck is wrong with me? Am I really attracted to this player who will fuck anything in a skirt...except me?

Except me, and that's the crux of the matter.

Despite some flirting, he doesn't seem the slightest bit interested in actually taking me to bed. Considering his lack of discretion with women in general, it's starting to bruise my ego. A girl wants to be desired, even if she has no intention of following through.

When Max's friends prepare to leave, I press my phone back to my cheek and pretend to talk as they walk away from the restaurant. I feel like an idiot reciting "Twinkle, Twinkle, Little Star" into my phone, and then I notice Max observing me through the window.

Damn, he better not be a lip reader.

I say a pretend good-bye to my pretend friend on the phone and head inside. The waitress has just delivered two fresh beers.

"So, who's this Sheila?" I can't seem to help myself.

"Oh, just a girl I see once in a while. We met at one of Ari's parties a couple of years ago, but she lives up north, so I don't see her often." He takes a long swig of his beer.

"I've been wondering...how much of your girl action do you want me to put in the book?"

He looks surprised and then pissed. "Girl action?"

"You know, this parade of women you seem to have following you." I look down and draw some swirls on my pad.

"Just because I don't follow convention, pretending to date just to get laid, doesn't mean I'm a player. Anyone who's with me knows there are no strings attached, so it's not sleazy."

I want to argue with him, but I bite my tongue. In fairness, though, I have to wonder if I'm being judgmental because I'm fighting feelings for him.

He narrows his eyes as he watches me. "Well, what about you, Ava? Do you have a boyfriend or do you just sleep around?"

"How about neither?" I fold my arms over my chest.

"What?" He looks amused now. "Are you trying to tell me that you pitch for Jess's team, that you're an official member of the girl power posse?"

Such a man; of course he would go there. "No, I just prefer to be intimate with someone I'm really into, and I just haven't met anyone that has earned that distinction for a while."

Why am I even having this conversation with him?

"So…you want to be in love, hear the violins and get cupid's arrow up your ass."

"So romantic, really." I take several gulps of beer, which emboldens me. "A girl can dream, can't she?" I look into his eyes. "I hate that empty feeling after meaningless sex. Don't you?"

He stares at me for a moment and then looks away. He presses his fingers to the tabletop as he looks out the window. After a long moment, he looks at me again and shrugs.

"I guess I always feel kind of empty. I'm used to it. I'm not even sure I could feel anything else."

"Haven't you ever been in love?"

His eyes cloud and the memory plays out painfully across his face.

"Well, I thought I was in love once. It became my everything, and when it was gone, it completely fucked me up. No thanks. Never again." He shakes his head.

For the first time since I'd met Max, I feel sorry for him. Although, in many ways, I'm afraid to fall in love, it seems that he doesn't even know how to anymore, and that just feels worse.

He must've cast some magical spell, because my resistance to the book project has now completely waned. As we part that night, I agree to work up a preliminary outline by the end of next week.

I have the entire drive home to think, so when I get to the apartment I'm ready to spill.

"Hey Riley, what are you working on?" I ask, as I squint at her computer. She's moving around little jeweled crowns and flowers on the computer screen.

"I'm trying to finish this pattern for princess pajamas. We have a presentation tomorrow, and my designer—you remember Erin—she went home sick." She glances up. "How'd the thing go with Max?"

I flop down on the couch. "Okay, I guess. I found some good books to reference, and got some ideas while I looked through others."

"How did you guys get along? It's late. Did you go get dinner or something?"

I tell her about our conversation, including the story about Sheila, all topped off with his reveal about his inability to get emotionally close to anyone.

She shakes her head. "Well, it sounds like red flag time. And since you're going ahead with the book project, it's good you guys aren't dating."

"Yeah, good thing," I reply, not sounding entirely convincing.

"Focus on getting the work done. It'll give you guys a chance to get to know each other better. If it evolves later, then so be it. I'd just be really careful."

She sounds pretty wise for someone whose work life is all about princesses and fairylands.

"Dylan called me today." She watches me for my reaction.

"Really? And what, pray tell, does he want?"

"He needs to visit a gallery in Santa Barbara, so we're going to drive up there together on Saturday and make a day of it."

"You have a date with Dylan? How did this happen?" I ask incredulously.

She gives me a shy smile, as if she's about to share a secret. "We just hit it off at Max's. And then he called me Monday night and we talked on the phone for almost three hours. He's the greatest guy, and we like so many of the same things, it's eerie."

"That's cool, Riley, I'm so happy for you." I give her a big hug and we chat for another minute about Dylan before she gets back to work.

As glad as I am to see Riley find a potential love connection, there's the selfish part of me that wallows in the idea that I may never find love.

I carry the two new art books to my room and flip open my laptop on the bed. I open the Lichtenstein book and study some of the paintings before I turn to my computer and open Google search. My fingers twitch as I hesitate, then surrender: *Maxfield Caswell artist.*

The page fills up with entries. I read a number of articles and reviews about Max. Most of the analysis of his work is favorable. Things get dicey with his antics away from the studio.

One review from the previous year in the *New Yorker* succinctly summed up what others had tried to say.

Caswell's work is thoughtful and uniquely his, unlike many of his peers who try to seduce us with derivative work. Yet, at times, Caswell seems more interested in being notorious than developing himself as a serious artist. Only time will tell if he can rise to the opportunity his talent has bestowed upon him, or be consumed by the partying and narcissism that threatens to establish him as the pop star of the moment of the art world.

Ouch, I think, cringing.

I click on the image gallery. Most of the shots are from gallery openings and parties. In almost every shot, he has his arm around an attractive woman and seldom is the same one seen more than once. In one photograph, he's with a young actress I recognize. They both have drinks in their hands and are laughing as she leans into him. I enlarge the image and study his face, wishing I could step inside his head and understand what he really thinks of all this, why he has chosen to live his life this way.

Finally, I decide to look at the image gallery of his paintings to clear my mind. *Beyond the Sky* is the first work that comes up. It's completely abstract with waves of color that bleed from light to dark and back again. It's an emotional painting…dark, yet hopeful. This painting reminds me why I want to do this book: to put into words the intense feelings his work provokes in me.

Hours later, the emotion of *Beyond the Sky* is the last thing I think about in that brief moment between wake and sleep.

Chapter Eight / Move Along

Do not fear mistakes—there are none.

~Miles Davis

Adam calls me into his office after I arrive at work Thursday morning.

"So how are things going with Max's book?" He stands up behind his prized Mies van der Rohe desk, moves over toward a pair of black leather chairs, and motions for me to sit down.

"Honestly, I still feel overwhelmed about the whole thing and worry I'm in way over my head." I look down at my hands and then back up. "I figure all I can do at this point is try. I'm working on an out-line, and as I break it down into smaller parts, it becomes a little more manageable."

"Ava, I have complete confidence that you're not *just* going to be able to do this, but you'll do a great job. If I was a betting man, I'd bet on you." He beams.

I want to hug him. He's so dad-like, so good to me. "That means a lot, thank you."

"And Max? Is he behaving himself?" He's fishing and it makes me smile.

"Yes, he's a perfect gentleman—apparently not to the rest of the fe-male population, but with me, he's been very professional."

Adam nods. "Glad to hear it. Let me know if he acts up."

It's almost two in the afternoon when I drive my car up a winding driveway with Henry and Francisco following in the van. This installation shouldn't take long, but our clients appreciate it when we make a big production out of hanging the art. Of course, everything has to be handled with the utmost professionalism.

The clients, Stephan and Stella Matthews, are major collectors and philanthropists. Mr. Matthews is on the board at the Museum of Modern Art in New York where they've donated many works over the years. They prefer to bring the work of young artists into their home to keep their collection updated.

We walk up the grand entrance and a woman who introduces herself as Mrs. Matthews's assistant meets us at the door and leads us into the marble foyer. This particular house, designed by Paul Williams, is in the Hollywood regency style and has sweeping views of the city. To my right there's a Jeff Koons' large silver dog balloon sculpture and several feet behind it hangs a Jackson Pollack drip painting. I've never seen a Pollock anywhere but in a museum, and I'm stunned.

As Mrs. Matthews approaches us, I'm struck by her elegance. Tall and regal, her sleek silver hair is worn in an angular style, and she's dressed in a black cashmere sweater and charcoal narrow slacks. Her only accents are her massive diamond ring and her architectural earrings.

After introductions, she leads us to the game room, which is more casual than the rest of the house. The plan is to hang Jess's painting above the carved Italian fireplace. While Henry and Francisco get to work, Mrs. Matthews turns to me.

"So, Ava, what do you think of Jess's work? Do you get to deal with her directly in your job at the gallery?" she asks in a kind voice.

"Well, I have to admit, Jess is one of my best friends, so I'm extremely biased, but I'm a big fan of her work. To me, she's a modern day impressionist, but instead of painting ballet dancers and girls in the garden like Degas and Renoir, she captures the people in our daily landscape."

Mrs. Matthews nods.

"She's a great person too. We held a show for her in New York last week and a number of her friends from her years at Pratt were there. They all talked about her with great affection."

"Yes, that's right, she went to Pratt. Have any of her classmates done as well as she has?" she asks.

"I'm not exactly certain, but the only one that really stands out in terms of success is Maxfield Caswell. They're still friends."

"Yes, Caswell," she answers thoughtfully and pauses. "We bought one of his pieces a couple of years ago. I still love it, but my husband is over him, so I had it moved to my study."

"Really? Does your husband not care for his work any longer?"

"It's not his work; it's his attitude. My husband was standing near him at an opening a month ago and overheard him trashing MOMA in New York. It's really so unfortunate because Stephan's on the board and had been encouraging the curator to include Caswell's work in an upcoming show called *Urban Legend*. He would've only been one of two artists under thirty included. It could've been pivotal for his career. They're making the final decision in the morning, but I'm certain Stephan is against Caswell being in the show now and he has a tremendous influence."

"Oh no," I gasp, shaking my head.

"Do you know him personally?" she asks me, her curiosity piqued.

"Yes, we're friends," I say, stretching the truth a bit. "I'm actually writing the text for a Taylor and Tiden book about Max."

"Taylor and Tiden?"

Her eyes widen.

My stomach churns. I have the possibility to help Max in a very important way, but to do so will require more lies and well-executed manipulation than I'm capable of. Yet the next words come out of my mouth so smoothly, I surprise even myself.

"Actually, I spent time with Max in New York last week and we went to MOMA to see the *Bauhaus* exhibit. He told me it was his life's dream to have one of his paintings exhibited there."

I'm on a roll. I take a deep breath. "I believe Jess told me about that incident your husband overheard. Max had a crisis that day, along with a series of events that led to those comments that actually had nothing to do with MOMA, but he didn't know it at the time. I only wish there was a way for him to explain it to your husband."

She holds her focus on Jess's painting for several moments. "Well, you believe in Caswell. Am I correct?"

"Yes, I do, Mrs. Matthews. He's unbelievably talented, he lives for his art and he highly values his place in the art community."

"Well, let me talk to Stephan and see if he's willing to speak with Maxfield. If so, I'll text you with a time to call."

I thank her repeatedly as I write my number down. I desperately hope I've done the right thing.

On the way out the door, I tell Francisco and Henry that I'll meet them back at the gallery. From the side of the road, I dial Max's cell phone. When he doesn't pick up, I leave him a message.

"Hey Max, it's Ava. I have something important to talk with you about as soon as possible, so please call me back as soon as you can. Thanks."

I hang up, disappointed he didn't answer.

I have a lot to do when I return to the gallery, but when an hour passes without a call back from Max, I get nervous. I call again and leave another message.

A few minutes later, I receive a text message, and I slide my finger across my phone's screen.

> *Hello Ava, Stephan has agreed to talk to Max.*
> *We have a dinner event, so Max needs to call this number exactly at ten tonight.*
> *Best, Stella*

My heart nearly jumps out of my chest. I text back,

> *Mrs. Matthews, I will let him know. Thank you so much for your help.*
> *Regards, Ava*

After I hit send, I look through my phone contacts for Max's home number I entered before we drove out to Malibu. When I get his answering machine, I break out into a cold sweat. What if he's on a plane, or in a double feature movie with his phone turned off or somewhere else unreachable? It's already five.

I call Dylan and when he picks up, I pray my luck's changed.

"Hi, Dylan. It's Ava, Riley's friend."

"Hey, Ava. What can I do for you?"

"Well, I really need to get ahold of Max right away, but he's not answering his cell or home phone. Is he with you, by chance?" I cross my fingers and hold my breath.

"Nope, he's not with me. Is this something I can help you with?"

Even though Dylan is Max's manager and I should probably let him know about this situation, I'm not sure I can handle it if he gets mad at me for sticking my nose in their business. "No, but thanks. I really need to talk to him."

"Well, when I spoke with him this morning he said he planned to paint all day. When he works, he doesn't like to be disturbed, so he doesn't answer the phone. He'll take a break eventually and I'm sure he'll get your messages."

I thank him and hang up, not feeling very reassured. I decide to text Max using shouty caps.

MAX PLEASE CALL ME ASAP-VERY IMPORTANT!

By the time I pull out of the parking lot to head home, I'm a nervous wreck, and I almost run into a cyclist, despite the fact that he's wearing a neon yellow jersey. He yells at me, waving his fist and I sink down into my seat.

When I get home, I pace the living room for about fifteen minutes before I call him again. As the phone rings I chant in my head, *Answer, answer, answer, damn it! Why did I do this? If I'd just kept my damn mouth shut, I could be sitting on the patio right now enjoying a glass of Pinot Noir.*

I get his machine again.

Feeling out of options, I get back in my car and head to the free-way. It's going to be a long drive to Malibu, and God knows how Mr. "Doesn't Like to be Interrupted" will feel when I crash his work session.

Six-thirty on a Thursday night is a very bad time to drive to Mal-ibu—drive being a relative term. The 101 is a parking lot and I'm having fantasies of doing a *Thelma and Louise* and gunning it through the empty emergency lane. I turn on the stereo and crank it up to take my mind off things. "Move Along" by The All-American Rejects plays, and I sing at the top of my lungs, taking strength from the words.

Despite my singing, the apprehension lingers. It's eight when I fi-nally pull up to Max's house, and I'm tempted to turn around and leave. For a moment, I seriously consider the possibility. He doesn't know yet what the issue is with Mr. Matthews. Yes, I left a bunch of messages, but I could make something else up. He'd never know.

But what if this situation with MOMA ever got back to him? He'd never forgive me, knowing there was a chance to salvage his chance to be in that show. I slowly climb out of my car and face his house.

I notice a structure to the far left of the garden with large windows. The door's wide open, light streams out the windows and aggressive hard rock music blasts into the garden. I assume this to be his studio and move toward it, the dread of telling him about my interference testing my nerves.

I get to the open doorway and peer around the corner. The building has high ceilings with wooden beams crossing the room. The atmo-sphere is the complete opposite of Jess's clutter-filled fantasia studio. There's a calmness to the interior that belies the hard-edged music pounding against the white-washed walls.

I see movement out of the corner of my eye and spy Max working on a large canvas leaning on the wall opposite the door. He has his back to me and holds a brush in his right hand and a silver can with paint running down the sides in the other. But these are just extraneous details.

What I'm really fixated on is the man himself. He's a vision with messy hair and bare feet, while wearing faded jeans and a white T-shirt splattered with paint...and oozing the most intoxicating energy I've ever felt.

I freeze in place. His gestures as he works are wide and sweeping, the brush dipped in the can and then stroked across the canvas. He does it again and again, so sure of each movement, each stroke a decision that takes the art in a specific direction.

I'm not sure what I would've imagined, but it's captivating to watch this man at work in his creative element.

He's working with a brilliant orange, but he's already painted areas of verdant green, warm white and deep sienna. At one point, he drops the brush and uses his hands to move the paint around and make gestures on the canvas. When he's done stroking and blending, he wipes his hands on a rag.

I'm aroused watching him. I want to be the canvas his hands are moving over, stroking and blending—his work of art.

Finally I gather my nerve and call his name. But with the loud music, my voice is but a whisper and he shows no sign of having heard me. I try again, louder this time. Nothing. Finally, on my third try, I yell his name loud enough, and he turns around.

As soon as our eyes meet, I step forward, but his eyes instantly fill with rage and it terrifies me.

"Stop!" he yells.

I freeze with fear.

"What in the hell do you think you're doing?" he roars. He slams his hand on a remote and the music suddenly shuts off. The silence is deafening.

I step forward once more, "I'm sorry to interrupt you, Max, I just have some—"

"FUCKING STOP! NO ONE COMES IN MY STUDIO! NO ONE!"

I'm shocked; his anger is a wall of fire. I step back from the burn until I'm just outside the doorframe. "I came over t-to…i-if I could just expla—"

"Why did you need to come here? Couldn't you have just left me a message without interrupting my work? Fuck, Ava, what makes you think you can just drop by?" He shakes his head furiously.

"I've tried all afternoon to reach you, and you weren't answering your messages." I feel a combination of rage and tears building in me. I'm not sure which will explode out of me first. My chest heaves and my cheeks burn, and I arch back like a cat about to fight.

He shoves his hands in his hair and pulls hard as he groans loudly.

My fury wins over the tears.

"Do you think I fucking wanted to drive all the way to Malibu in rush hour traffic, Max? Do you think I would even consider interrupting you in your home unless I had an *extremely* good reason?"

I have hold of my anger now, and the release feels good. Hating him feels good too.

"But no…I fucking stepped foot in your studio. How dare I do that! Like I have any fucking ideas about your rules." I fold my arms across my chest angrily and wait until I know he's completely focused on my words.

"Here's the situation and listen carefully, because I'm only going to say it once." I take a deep breath and give him the evil eye.

"Today, I oversaw an installation at the Matthews home in Bel Air. You may've heard of them, they're major collectors. So Mrs. Matthews and I start talking about Jess, and your name happens to come up. She tells me they purchased a painting of yours a couple of years ago, but her husband made her take it down recently."

His breathing slows down and his eyes look less stormy as he folds his arms over his chest.

"So I ask her why. Apparently, her husband overheard you at a party totally trashing MOMA. And guess what, genius? Stephan Matthews is not only on the board of directors at MOMA, but he'd just convinced them to include some of your work in an upcoming exhibition." I watch the fury on Max's face turn to shock.

"So, you see where this is going, Max? While you were probably drunk and entertaining your art groupies with your big opinions, you were also brilliantly flame torching your chance to be in a career-defining exhibition and perhaps ever having your work in MOMA."

I drop my purse on the ground, bend down and rifle through the contents before pulling out a small pad, pen and my cell phone. I slide open my phone and scroll through my text messages. I can hear Max's heavy labored breathing, but otherwise we're cloaked in silence.

"Because I'm an idiot and thought we were friends, and I would do anything to help a friend, I lied for you, Max. I told Mrs. Matthews you had a crisis that day, you weren't in your right mind, and had made a series of comments that had nothing to do with MOMA. I also asked her if there was any way you could explain it to Mr. Matthews because it would mean the world to you."

His eyes have a faraway look. Maybe he's searching the recesses of his mind to remember what he may have slurred at that party.

"I told her how great you are, how much you love MOMA and about the Taylor and Tiden book we're working on. She finally agreed to talk to her husband on your behalf. She contacted me a few hours ago. You are one lucky bastard because he agreed to talk to you."

I copy the information from Stella's text onto the pad and tear out the paper.

"I don't know how you fix this, Max, what kind of dance you'll have to do, but the one thing I believed then—and I guess I still believe it now—is that you have to try. Here's the phone number. He's agreed to speak with you tonight at ten, *exactly* at ten. They're making the final decision tomorrow morning."

I look around for an exit strategy as I hold the paper in my hand. I finally take one more step back and set the note on the ground in front of me. "Since I'm not allowed to step foot in your studio, I'll leave this note here. I sure as hell hope you make this call, so I don't feel like a bigger fool than I already do."

With that, I pivot around, march across his yard and out the gate.

My hands are shaking as I buckle myself in my car. I keep glancing up to see if he's going to come after me. Taking a deep breath to calm down, I wait a few long moments before I start my car, slowly turn it around and head back up the driveway. I glance in my rearview mirror at his gate and note, for the last time, that it's still empty.

On the drive back home, I second-guess myself. I can't recall ever exploding like that. *Was I justified in being that angry?* But then I remember how he yelled at me and I get furious all over again.

Riley's waiting for me when I get home, and I tell her the story from start to finish. But exhaustion is now having its way with me, so I leave out some of my dramatic flourishes at the end.

By the time I'm done, she shakes her head. "If you wrote this drama in a story people would laugh and say it's too unbelievable!"

"Do you think I was wrong, Riley?" I ask, the corners of my mouth turned down. "Do you think I should've kept my mouth shut in the first place?"

Her gaze softens as she shakes her head. "No, you did the right thing. Dylan talks a lot about Max, and says Max lives and breathes art. Max is the real deal and has the potential to leave a lasting mark in the art world." She pauses, twisting her earring.

"I bet once Max gets over the shock of being surprised in his studio, he'll know how profound your help was, and he'll be very grateful."

I roll my eyes. "I highly doubt that, Riley. You should've seen him."

I put on my PJs and am too worn out to fix a real dinner, so I cut up an apple, put cheddar cheese slices on a plate and pour myself a big glass of wine. I put on *Blue*, my favorite Joni Mitchell album, and curl up on the couch and wallow.

Am I going to have to quit the book project? I have to consider it now that our friendship stepped on a land mine. *Ugh…just when it was all starting to come together.*

As the wine relaxes me, I start to drift off and wake up when my head snaps forward. I drag myself to my bedroom and glance at the clock. It's exactly ten o'clock. I feel a surge of panic, mixed with breathtaking curiosity. Will Max fix what's broken?

Despite all the hell I went through for him and what I may've given up with the effort, there's a part of me that sincerely hopes he can.

Chapter Nine / On Gossamer Wings

I dream of painting and then I paint my dream.
- Vincent Van Gogh

The line at Starbucks is precariously long, but I'm going to need a venti cappuccino to get through this morning. I glare at the chatty barista who's moving too slowly and glance at my watch to determine if I'm going to make it to work on time or not. There's nothing worse than rolling in late holding a cup of Starbucks, absolute evidence that you could have been on time if you hadn't fed your hard-earned dollar to the corporate coffee machine.

While I wait for my drink, I receive a text from Max. My heart thuds as a chill runs up my spine. I seriously wondered if I'd ever hear from him again. I slide open my phone's screen.

I need to talk to you.

I pause, unsure how to reply. As curious as I am about what happened with Mr. Matthews, I'm not sure I'm ready to talk to him. My phone prompts again.

I really need to talk to you. How long will you make me wait?

Completely irritated with his message I reply,

I, I, I…Definition: narcissist, egocentric, love of one's self

I hit send. My phone rings only seconds later. I don't answer, not trusting my snarky filter until I've had at least some coffee. I'm not even inspired to listen to the voice mail that chimes a minute later.

Luckily, Brian's in a great mood because of two nights in a row with the fabulous Thomas, so he graciously gives me mindless busywork after I stumble into the gallery. As I input the names of collectors into the new database, my phone rings again. It's Max. Now the ass knows how it feels not to be able to reach someone when you have something to say.

The rest of the afternoon, my phone remains quiet, and I descend into a very dark mood. I still haven't resolved if I'm going to quit working on Max's book, and I have to decide because Jonathan's office keeps calling to set up our meeting. I head home, not even happy it's the weekend and turn up my emo playlist while I change into my sweats. I flop on the couch and finally listen to Max's voice mail from this morning.

"Damn, Ava, I didn't mean for my text to sound like that. I just really need to talk to you. I didn't sleep at all last night thinking about what happened, what you did for me, and how mad you are.

I want to explain and make things better. Please, can't we have lunch or talk or something?

I'll wait to hear from you. Okay, call me please."

I listen to the message two more times, trying to figure out how it makes me feel. I'm so confused.

Suddenly, Riley bursts in the door, takes one look at me and stomps her foot down. "Oh no, missy…it's Friday friggin' night! I'm not allowing you to do this *goddess of angst* thing tonight. Now you go in there, take off those sweats and put on something sharp. We're going out."

I give her a blank wide-eyed stare. "Do I look like I want to go out, Riley?"

"That's the point. This isn't about want. It's need. You can't let *art boy* do this to you, then he wins."

She's starting to make sense. "So, where would we go if 'hypothetically' we went out?"

"You know my friend Calliope, the one I went to high school with? She's doing stand-up at the Comedy Store tonight, and she reserved tickets for me."

Comedy sounds good—it could be just what I need, so I get my ass off the couch and change. I put on my best jeans, black high-heeled boots and a fitted black top before we head out. Dylan's working an event but he'll join us later for drinks.

The show's a riot, and I tell Riley that Calliope was better than the guy she opened for. It felt great to laugh and forget about all the stresses in life outside the cocoon of the club.

We meet Dylan at the House of Blues. He's a member of their Foundation Room, so we sit in the private area surrounded by the most wonderful outsider art and the lush colors and lighting of the eclectic Moroccan theme. The walls are a dark cobalt blue, and there's a patchwork of worn Asian rugs on the floors. There are low leather couches with carved wooden tables. Intricately etched Moroccan lanterns hang at different heights from the ceilings.

Riley's so happy to see Dylan she practically sits on his lap, and he looks equally smitten.

"So, Ava," he says after kissing Riley's neck. "What'd you do to Max? He's been completely wacked out all day."

Riley jabs him in the arm.

"What did I do?" I raise my eyebrows in wonder. "It's more like what did he do. I was just trying to help him with something, and he went postal."

"Well, whatever you said or did really got to him. I've never seen him like this. When he heard I was joining you guys tonight, he insisted on coming, but I refused to tell him where we were going."

"Well, thanks. I'm not ready to talk to him yet."

He nods. "I just hope you work it out soon. He's got a lot to get done, and I hate seeing him like this."

"Well, if he hadn't been such an ass…" Riley says, but stops herself.

Dylan eyes her and then me. "Ava, I know Max can be an ass, but at the core, he's a really good guy. If I were in trouble, he's the first person I'd call. I know he'd take care of me. There's more depth to him than anyone else I know."

I'm doubtful of Dylan's words but study his face and note the sincerity of his tone. "Well, Max is lucky to have a friend like you."

"And I him," he replies.

It's late when Riley and I meander up the stairs to our apartment, and my breath catches when we get to the top. There's an extraordinary flower arrangement waiting for us. It's a celebration of color: hot and pale pinks, flaming oranges and soft peaches. The exotic flowers spill out of a tall glass cylinder vase lined with strips of bamboo tied together with sea grass. The whole effect is breathtaking. Riley moans, like it's for her. But when she opens the card and hands it to me, its message is simple.

> *Ava,*
> *Can I start by saying thank you?*
> *Max*

Riley gives me *the look*.

Feeling overwhelmed, I carry the flowers into our dining room. I can sense my rough edges softening with Max's efforts and the things Dylan told me earlier.

By morning, I'm tempted to call him, although I'm not quite ready yet. I decide to take a long walk on the beach and head out to Santa Monica. It's another glorious day; the sky is a vivid blue and the hot sun is tempered with a cool breeze. I take off my jogging shoes and wiggle my toes into the wet sand as I walk along the waterfront.

What do I want? I can call Max and we can easily make up and agree to be pleasant with each other and finish the book. But is that enough at this point?

What do I want when I lie awake in bed at night, imagining him on top of me? Max filling me up and whispering my name while his hands caress me, his lips burning a path from my breasts to my lips and back again.

And what do I want, knowing his history with the kind of women I look down on in disgust? They're women with little aspiration but to win him for a night. Ironically, I admire them for their unwavering confidence in the power of their sexuality. In contrast, I hate him for subscribing to their agenda.

By the time I head back to my apartment, I'm even more confused, and I decide to zone out and watch a movie. I make a sandwich and decide it's time for a Darcy fix. I pull out my well-worn copy of *Pride and Prejudice.*

Why, oh why can't I find my very own Darcy?

I never tire of this movie. I fast forward through the titles and eagerly await one of my favorite scenes—the community dance at a country hall. I pump my fist when Lizzy gives it to Darcy on how to promote affection, astutely getting revenge for insulting her earlier. After she delivers the line to the pompous ass, she confidently walks out, leaving him stunned. I rewind the scene and watch it over and over until my phone pings an incoming text from Max.

I have a delivery for you, are you home now?

I reply *yes*, and then feel guilty for not thanking him for the beautiful flowers. *What can he be sending me now?* I refocus on the movie, and right at the scene in the rain where Darcy first declares his love, the doorbell rings.

Damn. I pause the movie and looked through the peephole. The delivery person is holding a large wrapped package. I grab my wallet and take out enough for a tip before opening the door.

I am gripped with curiosity as I carry the package to the table and carefully unwrap it. I gasp when I see the edge of a very ornate frame. *Is this one of his paintings?* My heart pounds. *I can't believe this.* As I pull the main piece of wrapping away, I step back…shocked.

The painting is of an angel, an exquisite angel with flowing hair and gossamer wings, yet she's of Max's world of color and expression. As I look closely, I can see where he has put his hands on the painting. I can even see pencil markings bleeding through in spots where he first drew her and then markings he added once the paint was applied.

As much as I love the painting, as much as I'm overwhelmed to receive the most exceptional gift of my life, those feelings are superseded by the stunning recognition that the angel has my face. I'm Max's angel.

I take several breaths to calm myself. When on earth did he paint this? What depth of emotion would cause him to not only do the painting, but give it to me? Much less importantly but curiously, how did he get it to dry and then framed so quickly? The whole thing represents an extraordinary effort.

I see a note in the pile of wrapping, pick it up, and slowly open it.

> Dear Ava,
> I stayed up all night, painting this for you. Maybe now you'll understand.
> Max

I hold up the painting and shift it slowly in the light, trying to comprehend all that he could've meant with those words. Then it occurs to me to turn it over. Sure enough, he has written something on the back.

> Ava, I believe Edward Rochester said it best:
> I knew you would do me good in some way, at some time. I saw it in your eyes when I first beheld you; their expression and smile did not strike delight to my very inmost heart so for nothing.
> Thank you, Ava, my angel.
> Max

Okay, now I've melted.

I'm but a mere puddle on the floor. *Jane Eyre* is my all-time favorite story.

It occurs to me that Max is more like Rochester than my initial impression of Heathcliff. Either way, it's starting to feel as if my life has become a Brontë sisters' drama.

I carry the painting to the living room and carefully place it above the fireplace, leaning it against the wall. I stand back and gaze at it, my heart racing and tears brimming my eyes. It's almost too much to believe. I need to call him right away, but opt to cautiously text first.

> *Max, the painting, the flowers, I'm completely over-whelmed and unbelievably touched.*

He responds immediately:

> *Are you ready to talk?*

I dial his number.

"Wow, Max. You really know how to say thank you," I say when he answers.

"By completely overwhelmed, I hope you meant in a good way?"

"Yes, of course. I've never received such an extraordinary gift. I'm crying right now, if you must know."

"Don't cry, Ava." His tone is gentle and soothing. "I don't want to make you feel bad anymore. You scared me yesterday. I didn't think you had it in you to yell like that, to get that mad."

"Yeah, I surprised myself. I was so wound up when I couldn't reach you. And then I was terrified I'd done the wrong thing by convincing the Matthews to give you another chance. I had no right to involve myself like that." I take a long breath. "So when you freaked out, I just lost it."

"How could you have done the wrong thing, Ava? You're my angel," he states categorically.

I decide to shelve the weird angel talk for later. "Yes, well, angel or not, it wasn't my place…it just happened so fast, and I made a split second decision to help you."

"Thank God you did. I was able to convince Stephan that I appreciated his initial support of me and would do anything in my power to regain his respect. I was able to explain the events of that day and the evening of the disaster, and I gave him another perspective of my intentions. I feel good about it and hope the bridge has been mended."

"Oh, I'm glad for that, Max." I let out a sigh of relief.

"Today at noon, I got a call from Lisa Forrester, the curator at MOMA, and she told me they want to include me in their feature exhibit early next year."

I could hear the joy in his voice. If he'd been here, I would've grabbed and hugged him.

"I'm so happy for you! It's a dream come true, isn't it?"

"If you only knew what this means to me. Well…it's everything, and it would've never happened without you."

I'm quiet because I know it's true, and the satisfaction in knowing that is another gift I can hold in my heart.

He clears his throat. "I wish I could redo that whole scene in my studio. I feel horrible that I got so angry and yelled at you."

"You were pretty scary. Is it true no one comes into your studio?"

"Yes. Making art's such an intimate act that I hate anyone watching. I always struggled with it in my studio classes at school, but it's gotten worse over the years."

"Well, I did surprise you," I admit.

He laughs. "Yeah, I'm not good at surprises either."

"Noted. But I don't put up with yelling, understood?"

"Agreed. So, I want to do something to celebrate. I thought I'd get some friends together for dinner, maybe tomorrow if we can get it figured out. Will you come?"

"Okay, sure." I smile.

"So we're good? Still friends?"

"Yes, still friends, and thanks again."

"You bet. There are plenty of good times ahead for us."

I hope so, I think as I sit back on the couch to look at the painting. *My* painting.

Max succeeds in getting a small group together for Sunday night at The Ivy on Robertson. Riley and I take extra care getting dressed. She insists

I wear my Agent Provocateur lingerie under the Derek Lamb dress I splurged on at a Barney's warehouse sale. I'm feeling pretty damn good.

When we arrive at the restaurant, Max and Dylan are already there, and Max looks exuberant. He gives me a big hug and swings me around. When he puts me down, he steps back and holds me at arm's length. "Hey, angel. You're the honored guest tonight."

I smile from ear to ear, my cheeks flushed.

Jess, Laura and Joe arrive, and we're seated on the heated patio under the twinkling lights. Max orders several bottles of Veuve Clicquot champagne for the toast.

"As you guys have all heard, I found out Friday that I'm being included in a group show at MOMA. But what you may not have heard is…this never would've happened if not for Ava."

Jess, Laura and Joe look at me in perfect synchronization. I look down, embarrassed.

"Having my work in MOMA is a lifelong dream, so thank you, guys, for helping me celebrate this. And thank you, Ava my angel, for waving your magic wand and making my dreams come true." He picks up his champagne flute.

"To Ava!"

"To Ava!" Everyone repeats the toast.

The table's immediately buzzing in conversation as Jess, Laura and Joe listen to the story of the Matthews' installation and resulting phone call that changed Max's fate. Everyone's in a festive mood, and we're in a wonderful bubble when the food arrives.

In my mind, I take a step back and look at the group of us…laughing and joyful. A swirl of colors and warm light envelops us. I'll always remember the feeling of this moment. I'm truly happy.

"So, Max, how are you going to thank Mr. and Mrs. Matthews?" Riley asks.

"Yeah, did you promise them your first born or something?" Joe asks, laughing.

"No." Max laughs before his expression becomes serious again, making me think he's thought about what he can do to thank them.

"I'm giving them my best painting. I'm delivering it on Monday. I really want them to have it, and it'll mean something to all of us."

His declaration makes me smile when I realize how right that feels.

When the restaurant starts preparing to close, it's time to leave. As we wait for the valet to bring us our cars, Max and Dylan try to convince Riley and I to go for a ride. This idea is dubious at best, even if Dylan barely drank and seems to have his wits about him.

Yeah, let's drive up to Mulholland and watch Dylan and Riley make out in the car...

It's been a long eventful weekend, and I need to get home and sleep if I'm going to be worth anything tomorrow.

While having a final discussion with Jess, Max, who's fairly lit from a steady flow of champagne and martinis, stands behind me and affectionately wraps his arms around my shoulders. As they talk, he progressively pulls me closer to him and the heat from his body gets me thinking about things I shouldn't.

This time spent in close proximity to Max has thrown gasoline on the fire burning inside me. I take a very deep breath. My crazy thoughts imagine his hands sliding over my breasts while I grind my ass against him. Heat surges between my legs, and I fight an inner war to stop pressing back against him.

Oh God, I can't take much more of this. Is he so drunk he doesn't understand what holding me like this is doing to me?

When the valet brings Riley's car forward, Max pulls away, turns me around and gives me a hug. The good-byes are brief. Max and I agree to talk in the next day or so to plan our next book meeting.

My raging libido is still sparking, and I struggle to keep my focus straight.

Thank God Riley's driving.

When we stop at the first streetlight, Riley turns completely sideways and stares at me with wide eyes.

"What?"

"Oh, you know *what*, Miss Ava. The sexual energy between you and *art guy* was unbelievable. At the end, I thought he was going to throw you on the table and have his way in front of all of us," she says, provocatively.

"Oh, girlfriend, you're so kinky and have an overactive imagination to boot. If any vibe like that was going on, it was only because he was drunk and, in his stupor, confused me for one of his art groupies."

She rolls her eyes.

I didn't convince her. *Did I convince myself?*

"Really, the only wild passion I witnessed tonight was between you and Dylan. I saw those provocative looks he gave you all night. I promise you, Max isn't interested in me in that way, so stop trying to get rid of your roommate."

"Well, that's a relief, but it doesn't change what's as clear as day." Riley gets a faraway look in her eyes. "Mind my prediction, Ava, you'll be in Max's bed much sooner than you think."

Chapter Ten / Down Dog

If I could say it in words there would be no reason to paint.
~ Edward Hopper

Newly inspired, I wake up extra early to get some writing time in before work. I finish the outline for Max's book and write almost a page of text before I leave the apartment. On the way in, I call Jonathan' office and arrange to come by during my lunch break to go over the procedures and paperwork. Jonathan has generously offered to bring lunch in, since he knows my time is limited.

Art+trA's West Coast offices are on the twenty-fifth floor in a sleek glass tower on Wilshire Boulevard. While I wait in the reception area, I marvel at the views of the city below. I can't imagine what it must be like to work in a place like this every day.

Jonathan's assistant leads me down a long corridor to Jonathan's office suite. She motions to a leather couch on the far side of his office and tells me he'll be with me momentarily. I study the various black and white framed prints around his office: Vasily Kandinsky, Kiki Smith, Louise Bourgeois, Paul Klee and Kara Walker. There's also a beautiful Robert Graham nude bronze on a pedestal by the window. Although I'm pleased with myself for being able to identify all the artists, I'm fighting panic out of sheer intimidation. I'm not even a published writer; I'm just pretending to be one. I'm really out of my league.

Moments later, Jonathan sweeps in, looking polished in pressed jeans, a white button down shirt and navy wool blazer. His tortoise-shell glasses still make me swoon.

"Ava," he says smoothly. He moves toward me as I rise off the couch, and he lightly kisses me on the cheek. "I'm so glad you could come by today."

"Yes. I really appreciate your working me in on short notice."

"My pleasure." He places his hand on my lower back to guide me forward. "Let's move to the table so we can get started." I find his alpha presence appealing. He's so calm and sure of himself.

"So Ava, have you met with Max yet? I do hope he's cooperating since he was so insistent on bringing you on board for this project."

"Yes, we've met a couple of times, and we'll meet again this week to go over things. I've brought a copy of my outline, and I'm making progress with the text."

"Very good, I'll look at that in a minute. But first I want to make sure he's being a gentleman. I hope you don't mind my being frank with you, but I'm most concerned with that aspect of this collaboration. For some reason, you bring out the protective side of me."

As he studies me, I can almost feel his protectiveness like a shield around me. It's surprisingly comforting. This man, who appears to be in control of his career and his life, has taken a special interest in me. Affection swirls up in my emotions as I imagine what it would be like to be cared for by someone like Jonathan. He already makes me feel special and appreciated, and I'm happy I've earned such distinction by someone so notable.

"Well, I appreciate your looking out for me, Jonathan, but so far he's been a perfect gentleman." The scene where he held me tightly in front of the restaurant last night flashes in my mind, but I quickly refocus. "I don't think I'm his type anyway, if you know what I mean."

He laughs softly. "Yes, sadly Max has a propensity for women whose physical allure outweighs depth or intelligence. But don't sell your enormous attraction short, Ava. He just knows you're not an easy target. I wouldn't be surprised if he's planning his strategy while he lurks, and he'll pounce when you least expect it."

Okay, that was over the top.

"Well, I'm not interested." I hope I've convinced him. Do I hear a touch of competitiveness in his tone?

"Yes, and for a man like Max there's nothing more alluring than a beautiful woman who isn't interested. She's a desired prize to be won."

Convinced he's being overdramatic, I open my folder to refocus the conversation. After a longer stretch of work, I look at my watch. I'm going to have to leave to make it back to the gallery on time.

I assure Jonathan that I'll alert him if anything changes with Max and agree to meet him for drinks Thursday after work to go over the outline. As I ride the elevator down, I realize I'm already excited to see him again.

That afternoon, Everett's assistant delivers four new paintings, and I catalogue and price them. There are already several clients lined up to come in and see them.

Jess calls right before six to check in. She's on some type of health kick, so we're going to a yoga class. "Are you ready to go?"

"I just wrapped up, but I still have to change. I brought my stuff here so it'll just take a minute."

"Okay, but hurry. We have to get there early, baby. Those fierce yoga bitches will take you down if you're late and try to squeeze your mat in next to theirs."

I laugh. "Okay, okay! Be there in fifteen!"

I grab my yoga bag and slip into the bathroom, then quickly change into my yoga pants, tank top and flip-flops. When I step out, Brian and Sean are talking a few feet away in the hall. They both stop and check me out.

"What, you've never seen yoga gear before?" I challenge, blushing furiously.

Sean smiles. "Is that what that is? Nice."

"Yeah, those stretchy yoga pants make your ass look great," Brian adds.

"Gee thanks, guys. I'll remember that when my great looking ass is up in the air and I'm twisted like a pretzel." I charge out of the gallery, the fear of Jess's wrath fueling my fire.

I score a parking spot right in front of the Sun Moon Yoga Studio, dash inside, and find Jess. She's already rolled out her mat near the front of the large studio, and I flop my mat down next to hers.

Even though class hasn't started, she still whispers, "This class is a blend of restorative and hatha yoga, and it's taught by the studio's owner, Cheri. It's the most popular class they offer. I've seen the class so full they've had to turn people away, and let me tell you, it wasn't pretty." She shakes her head, remembering.

Anyway, it's supposed to be really good for de-stressing. I thought it'd be good for you right now."

"You got that right," I whisper with a smile.

The room has filled up with stressed-out women in stretchy clothes sitting on purple or blue foam mats. A beautiful, serene woman with long flowing dark hair glides to the front of the room and starts the class. As hypnotic Indian music plays, she talks in a sweet voice and guides us into different positions we hold and hold and hold. She encourages us to breathe into our tension and release it. She also walks around and helps people get into position.

When every pose makes me think of Max or Jonathan, and not in a *PG* kind of way, I realize how messed up I am. There's the down dog, where I image Max behind me—no further explanation needed there. All that holding and deep breathing gives me lots of time to imagine things.

We move into the dolphin pose with our asses all the way up in the air. Next comes the bridge and open plow poses, which give new meaning to flexibility while spreading ones legs. But the last straw for me is the bound angle pose, which just sounds nasty as the ethereal Cheri explains how it opens the groin and hips. At this point, I'm a quivering mess on my little sheet of foam. Jess looks over and rolls her eyes.

I finally calm myself down by trying to remember my grocery shopping list one item at a time. Cheri then puts us in the final pose, savasana, which is essentially laying down flat—my favorite kind of pose. She does a guided meditation that's so hypnotic the next thing I know Jess is waking me up because the class is over.

"You were snoring." She shakes her head as we walk out the door.

We stroll the two blocks down Melrose to the Urth Caffe, a nearby eatery that caters to all the beautiful health-conscious people this city is overrun with. I'm glad that it's warm enough to sit outside on the patio.

After ordering salads and organic green tea, we catch up with each other's lives. Jess tells me she and Laura are researching a wedding ceremony. I'm surprised they feel the need for the formality, but she explains they are thinking about having a child, and it would be nice for their kid to know they'd made the commitment. She promises to make me maid of honor if they go through with it.

Our salads arrive, and as I tell her about my meeting with Jonathan, Max pulls into a parking space across the street. He gets out and slowly walks around to the other side of the car. It's rather jarring to see my fantasy man in the flesh out of the usual context.

"Hey, look Jess, it's Max." I point him out right as he opens the passenger door and a blonde head pops out. Jess and I silently watch his passenger get out of the car while he puts money in the parking meter. She's undeniably pretty, tall and lean with notably large breasts.

"Who's that?" I ask, trying to keep my voice steady even though I feel as if I've just been kicked in the stomach.

Squinting, Jess says, "Oh man. It's that stupid bitch, Sheila. She must be visiting from up North. I can't imagine what he's doing with her again. I mean that chick is clueless, definitely one French fry short of a Happy Meal."

Neither one of us makes any move to say hello or get Max's attention. Instead we silently watch him lead her into the restaurant across the street.

I remember Max's friends talking about her and decide to find out what Jess knows. "Is she an old girlfriend or something?" I ask once they're inside.

"No, just another in the long string of bimbos he occupies himself with. He's seen her more than once, so I guess you have to give her some credit for that."

I can tell Jess is disgusted, and I take some satisfaction in that. As I tell Jess about my recent conversation with Max and his defensiveness against being called a womanizer, I silently wonder if seeing Max with sex goddess Sheila will finally push him out of my fantasy life.

"When was the last time you saw him in a real relationship?" I ask.

She takes a bite of her salad before answering. "There hasn't been anyone he's really cared about since Chloe. She was his girlfriend in art school, and he was wild about her."

"What happened?" I ask, remembering Max talking about the girl he was obsessed with. Perhaps it was this Chloe.

"Oh, that's a long sordid story. I'm not in the mood to tell it now. Another time, okay?"

"Sure," I agree and take a sip of my tea, my mind churning with curiosity.

When I awaken the next morning, my first thought is, *I'm seeing Max today*. When I'd asked him about his formative years, and he came up with the idea of giving me a tour of where he grew up. He'll pick me up at six at the gallery after work.

I'm interested about what I'll learn tonight. There's no question it'll help me gain a better understanding of him.

When he comes to pick me up, he's wearing his painting jeans and T-shirt with a worn leather jacket. The Ray-Bans complete the rebel look he has going. This is definitely going to be a distraction, since he's the essence of raw sexuality.

He gives me a warm smile as he opens the passenger car door. I'm reminded of the last time I saw him. He had his arms wrapped around me at the Ivy. If I don't push that image out of my mind, I'll never focus on what he's showing me tonight.

"Ready for the official Maxfield Caswell tour?" He winks.

"Can't wait!" I wink back.

I slide into his Porsche with my notepad and folder, attempting to exude a professional air. I glance at him as he fires up the engine. "Were you working today?"

"Yeah," he responds, looking down at his clothes. "Oh sorry, I'd lost track of time and didn't have time to change. I didn't want to be late."

"Oh, I don't mind. You look good actually." I blush, realizing how that sounded.

His driving is smooth and confident, as he turns on to Beverly Boulevard, heading east. We pass street after street of eclectic boutiques, cafes and coffee bars before he makes a right onto Alta Vista and pulls over in front of a house about eight houses down from the corner.

He gazes past me at a small Spanish home with hand-painted tile wrapped around the picture window and a tangle of palms, bird of paradise and flaming fuchsia bougainvillea in the yard. An old decorative wrought iron gate is open to the front patio. He has a soft look in his eyes.

He grips the steering wheel tightly and clears his throat. "This is where I grew up."

I smile. "It's beautiful. I love the style of the house. It has so much character."

"Yeah, my mom loved old Spanish homes, the hardwood floors, thick plaster walls and coved ceilings. The house is built around a wonderful tiled patio with a fountain. We used to eat outside a lot. I have a lot of good memories from the years I spent here with her." He opens the door of the car and gets out.

We stand on the sidewalk in front of the house, and he looks up and down the street, taking everything in. I wonder what he's thinking and how he's feeling.

"Do you come here often?"

"No, I never do. It's still too hard because it reminds me of my mom and how much I miss her."

"I understand." Sadly, I do…better than he may realize. "How long did you live here? This is where your mom raised you instead of Malibu, right?"

"Yes, Mom bought it after the divorce when I was four, and I lived here until I left for college." He tips his head, still gazing at the house. "I'm so glad to see they haven't changed it. I was worried they might have torn it down and built some big modern house in its place."

"What about the Malibu house? What's the story behind that."

"My parents actually bought that house before I was born, and my mom got it in the divorce. My dad took the Beverly Hills house. People thought she was nuts when she used up all her money to buy this. They assumed we'd live in Malibu, but she didn't want to raise me there. We'd only go for the occasional weekend and sometimes in the summer."

It's fascinating and so different from my childhood.

He shrugs. "My mom always felt the kids in Malibu were entitled and disconnected from the real world?"

I nod. "I bet she was right."

"She wanted to raise me in the city and send me to public school so I'd have a realistic understanding of things." He pulls back his shoulders and smiles. It makes me feel that he's proud of his mother for raising him the way she did.

"And your dad?" I wonder out loud. "Is he alive?"

His expression falls. "He's still alive, but we don't have a relationship. I haven't seen him since Mom died, and I barely saw him before that."

"I'm sorry, Max."

He looks at me and starts to say something, but he closes his eyes and takes a deep breath. "We can live our lives with regret or resentment for what we didn't have, but whatever our experiences were, they shaped who we are now. So I just have to believe this was the path I was supposed to have."

I study him, surprised to see some of the depth Dylan had talked about. After a moment, I decide to lighten things up.

"There are a number of houses on this street. Did you have a lot of kids in this neighborhood?"

He laughs, "Oh yeah. We would organize our own Olympic games in the summer. Those were good times. Oh, and kick the can. We would play until it was so dark we couldn't see any longer."

"We had this tent Mom would let me and my friend pitch in the back of the garden and we'd play survivalists in the wilderness."

"That must have been fun. I would've loved to have met you when you were a little boy."

"In retrospect, I was a nerd and really shy, always drawing and reading and lost in my own imagination. The bigger kids teased me, but my best friend Bobby lived next door, and he defended me. He also dragged me outside to play as often as he could."

I smile, happy to know he had a friend to look out for him.

"See that Mexican restaurant down on the corner called El Coyote?"

I nod as he points to a low white building with red awnings, a trio of payphones on the side, and an old metal sign on the roof. It's the type of place that looks like it's always been there.

"Mom and I would have enchiladas there every Sunday night. The waitresses wore these traditional Spanish dresses with big hoop skirts that were so big they couldn't walk down the aisles without their skirts tipping up. I always tried to sneak a peek under those skirts."

So he was always a ladies man. I laugh to myself.

"This must have been a fun area to live in."

"Sure, there was an art supply store just down Beverly that I practically lived at. The owner, Kirk, had to kick me out at night so he could close the store. Every Saturday I used to ride my bike to the museum. All the guards knew me and would sometimes bring me food from the cafeteria."

"So that's where you honed your power of persuasion."

He shrugs. "Maybe. Come on, I'll continue the tour. Let's drive by my high school and then go to Farmers Market and get something to eat."

We get back in the car and drive west about a mile until we get to a big public high school at the corner of Melrose and Fairfax. "Three years before I started high school, they established a fine art magnet here so I was lucky. It was like a small art school within the school. I had some great art teachers who encouraged me in my work. I probably would've never ended up at Pratt, hell I probably wouldn't be who I am today, if I hadn't had that experience."

After that, we head to an L.A. mainstay, Farmers Market, a collection of permanent stalls with every kind of prepared food, including stands with baskets of fresh fruit, bakeries, a doughnut shop and a place where you can watch them make candy. Metal tables and chairs from the 1940s are grouped together so people can pick up a sandwich or some coffee and hang out with friends. And since it's entirely outdoors, clusters of old-fashioned scalloped-edge umbrellas in different colors provide shade.

"I love this place," I say as we weave our way through the market.

He nods. "It's always mixed with an eclectic group of people, from L.A. hipsters, to old locals, to tourists from all over the world. My favorite group is the game show contestants who wander around, still wearing their name tags from CBS Studios next door."

I smile. "That's great—so LA."

"Bennett's Ice Cream!" Max calls out as we walk down an aisle. "That's where I had my first job. As a matter of fact, I had my first hand job in the storeroom. Emily Young...I wonder what ever happened to her?"

"The storeroom? How romantic. Why don't you Facebook her? You could become Facebook friends and have a repeat performance. I have several ex-boyfriends stalking me on Facebook."

"No thanks."

We wander around until we decide on Middle Eastern food for dinner, and we share a falafel plate and gyro sandwiches. About halfway through dinner, I realize I've never seen this side of Max—happy and relaxed. Maybe making peace with his past and present has been good for him.

We're both quiet on the drive back to the gallery. He parks next to my car and turns off the engine. There's a heaviness in the air, and I wait to see if he'll address it. Another minute passes in silence before he finally turns to me.

"You know, Ava, I've never shown anyone my past. It's too private and invasive. Yet it felt so right to share it with you. I mean, I know this is research for the book, but to me it felt like something more. I'm not sure what yet, but I want to find out."

His blue gray eyes search mine, full of emotion and maybe fear. I hold his gaze, unwavering and hoping my eyes will tell him how much it meant to share these memories with him. I'm too scared to speak and I'm angry with myself for my fierce attraction to this complicated man. I'm afraid this delicate web woven between us will dissolve from the sheer force of my confused thoughts.

He looks at my lips and parts his before he leans a bit closer to me. The air is charged with electricity.

All of my logic escapes me as my guard and reservations come crashing down as I desperately hope he wants to pull me in his arms and kiss me.

All I can do is close my eyes and wait, hoping his heart's desire will overcome the cautious inclination of his tangled mind.

Chapter Eleven / Free fall

I would rather die of passion than of boredom.
- Vincent van Gogh

The seconds pass and, with my eyes closed, I imagine his lips are almost on me. I prepare for my libido to spontaneously combust from the resulting heat and friction.

Max clears his throat. "Thanks again, Ava."

The snap of the door locks provide the final shattering of my sad delusion.

I open my eyes and I try to conceal the horror creeping up and re-shaping my face. I'm completely stunned. *How could I have misread his intentions so completely?* I can't get out of the car fast enough.

"Yeah okay, bye," I snap and jump out of the Porsche. I don't look back as I fumble with my keys to unlock my car and finally fall into my seat. The tears of frustration fall as I start the engine.

What is wrong with you? Fuck, fuck, fuck! Why do you do this? Are you an idiot? You're an idiot! Have you not paid attention to every signpost that man has held in front of you? You're such a fucking idiot. Why in the hell would you want that womanizer to kiss you anyway? Have you lost your mind? He probably thinks of you like a sister—worse than his sister, his idiot loser moron sister. He's probably on his way to pick up Sheila so he can fuck her brains out. Tomorrow you should quit this project and tell him you're just not interested in writing his stupid fucking book. You should fuck Jonathan. You should fuck those stupid ex-boyfriend Facebook friends. You are so fucked!

This thread of destructive thoughts churns through my head until I'm finally home and have ingested three shots of Grey Goose. I'm almost glad Riley isn't coming home tonight so I can spare her my epic tale that sinks my loser love life down to a whole new low.

In my drunken state, I stumble to my bedroom and board my bed—the ship to drift through a murky sea. I pray I'll reach shore by morning.

I blink a few times, trying to understand the source of the annoying bright light before I realize it's the morning sun pouring through my window. I sit up long enough to gulp an entire glass of water at my bedside and throw myself back on the bed with a groan. As I recall snippets of my late evening free-fall, I face the humbling realization I've hit bottom. Theoretically, things could be worse in the battle of the sexes, but it doesn't help my mood.

I allow myself to wallow for a few more minutes and then give myself a talking to…it's time to move onward and upward. And although I'd love to walk away from the project and never humiliate myself in front of Max again, I'm going to be adult and get the book done.

I get in the shower and plan my strategy for the day, remembering that Sean needs me to work in the printing studio.

I'm glad to work the press that day, the mindless repetitive motion, the beauty unfolding as we apply one color at a time on paper until the image forms. It's good to spend the day around Sean. Despite his occasional bossy moods, he's someone who makes me laugh and feel like I'm worth having around.

As I'm changing to meet Jonathan for dinner, I realize I didn't have all my wits about me this morning. If I had, I would've never brought this outfit. The black pants are too fitted, although I have to admit they make my ass look great, the lavender sweater's almost a second skin.

My Agent Provocateur bra prominently defines my cleavage, adding to the effect.

I suppose by most girls' standards, my outfit isn't a big deal, but for me it is. I should be serving drinks in Vegas, not having a serious business meeting.

But if Jonathan is surprised when I join him in the bar at Chaya Brasserie, he doesn't show it. He greets me warmly, kissing me on both cheeks.

"You look lovely in that color, Ava," he says with a smile.

We start the conversation talking about an event *Art+trA* is holding for the opening of a *Women in Photography* show at the L.A. County Museum of Art. Jonathan has a particular passion for fine art photography so he's very enthusiastic. As he talks, his expression's warm and lively. It prompts me to pay more attention to the details about him.

I appreciate his handsome face and the way his sandy blond hair sweeps back off his forehead in waves. He must be in his late forties, but he's obviously taken good care of himself. His body appears very fit with a flat stomach, strong arms and broad shoulders. But the detail that always delights me most is his tortoise-shell glasses. I love the cool retro style.

I feel a subtle shift while I study him, and I catch myself flirting more as we talk. When we go over the outline, he gives me specific directions for the interviews I've lined up. He seems pleased with how things are progressing. His compliment of my writing style is particularly gratifying.

He offers me dinner when he hears I didn't have a proper lunch. He even stands and pulls my chair out for me when I return from the powder room. After the ambivalent messages from Max, it's a boost to my ego to have a man of Jonathan's caliber showing interest in me.

After dinner, we have a couple of drinks and loosen up.

"Ava, you may not know this, but it's unusual for me to be so hands-on with a freelance writer on a project. Normally, this type of thing is handled by one of my associates."

"That thought's crossed my mind. I just assumed you were involved because you had a personal interest in the subject. I know using me wasn't your idea." I bite my lower lip and narrow my eyes. "Did you take a greater interest because you weren't sure what to do with me?"

I see a spark flicker in his eyes. "I know exactly what I want to do with you." He lightly runs his finger along the inside of my wrist. A thrill echoes through me. His bright blue eyes smolder as his professional demeanor falls like ancient Rome.

I'm surprised by the wave of desire that washes over me. It's not the all-consuming fire I have when I let my guard down around Max, but it's still exciting. *I wonder what he's like in bed.* I imagine this man knows how to take care of a woman.

My alcohol haze creeps in, and I decide to end the evening before I do something impulsive. But I'm still feeling frisky, so when we walk out of the restaurant, I step off to the side and turn to Jonathan.

I give him a coy look. "Mr. Alistair, my curiosity is getting the best of me. What exactly do you want to *do* with me?"

He looks at me and he tilts his head and lets out a long sigh. "Ah, Ava." His quiet smile and heated look get me all stirred up. He steps to my side and brushes his lips right up to my ear and begins to speak quietly, so only I can hear.

"First, I'd pull you into my arms," he whispers and slowly runs his fingertips down my side and grasps my hip. "I'd kiss you like you've never been kissed."

I'm too stunned to speak. *Did he really just say that to me?* I knew he liked me, but this is something else, and it's so unexpected and hot that I'm losing my power to resist.

"You'll like the way I'll make you feel, Ava. I promise you...you'll like it a lot."

My heart's pounding, and I'm still frozen in place as I blink and bite my lower lip. Desire is surging through my body.

He pulls me closer and I feel where he's hard pressed against me.

"You must know what you do to me."

Oh my God. I've never had a boyfriend talk to me like this, let alone someone I barely know. I can't decide if I should be completely freaked out or thrilled I can evoke such passion in a man like Jonathan. My cheeks feel hot as I teeter between dark desire and social restraint.

I snap out of my shock-induced stupor and look directly at him. His eyes are wild with lust, but it seems like he's completely in control. I find this unbelievably sexy. I sway and he places his hand in the center of my back to steady me before leaning closer.

"Tonight, Ava, when you're in bed I want you to think about all the ways I could please you. I promise you, I'll be thinking about that too."

In perfect contrast to the verbal foreplay he's just performed on me, he walks me to my car, takes my hand and kisses it. I'm undone, completely undone. I sit in my car for several minutes, calming myself before I'm able to drive.

I'm supercharged as I drive home. I can't believe I managed to rise from my bottomless pit this morning to experience a day that ended like this. Even if I never see Jonathan again, his seductive story restored my faith that I can be desirable to a dynamic man.

I feel like a phoenix just beginning to rise from the ashes until I reach the landing at the top of the stairs to my apartment. Something's horribly amiss. Our front door is open and it's dark inside.

My stomach takes a free fall and panic sweeps over me. Other than my pounding heart, I'm still as a mouse listening for any sounds of movement in the apartment. There's complete silence. I tentatively take two steps closer to the door and peer inside. From the cast of the streetlights and porch light, I can see that the TV is gone. With greater dread, I look at Riley's desk and see a gaping hole where her computer was.

Oh my God, we've been robbed!

I run downstairs to our neighbor's apartment, but she isn't home. I'm still on her porch when I call the police on my cell phone. After the dispatcher confirms with me that the robbers appear to be gone, she warns me they are extremely busy tonight and it may take a while for the cops to get there. She instructs me not to wait alone.

After I hang up, my mind races. *Whom should I call?* Not Riley. She's an hour away in Orange County at an executive meeting. She's going to flip out when I give her the bad news. I hope she backed her computer up before she left, since she has a lot of design work on it.

Jess and Laura are in Palm Springs. I call Sean, but his phone goes directly to voice mail. My hand tightens over the phone in frustration. Half the time Sean doesn't even turn his phone on.

With my hands shaking I start to call Brian, but I remember that he and Thomas were meeting Adam and Katherine for dinner at the Saddleback Lodge for Thomas' birthday. If I had Jonathan's cell phone number, I'd call him.

Damn! Tears of fear and frustration roll down my cheeks, and I do the thing I least want to do. I dial Max's number. The phone rings once, twice and after the third ring, I panic and hang up. It's eight-thirty, which means the Kesters are probably still at the restaurant, but I try Brian anyway because I'm getting desperate. An automated voice informs me the number I'm trying to call is in a zone with no service.

I dial Sean again, but again it goes directly to voice mail. I don't know when I've ever felt so alone.

I call Max again and let it ring until his voice mail comes on, and I start to leave a message, but right after I say his name, I panic again and hang up. At this point, I crumble into the chair next to my neighbor's door and start to cry.

A few minutes pass when my phone pings, and it's the best sound I've ever heard. I slide it open before checking to see who it is.

"Ava?"

"Yes," I sob into the phone.

"Are you okay? I just noticed you called twice, and it's so loud in here I didn't hear my phone." I can hear pounding music and a woman asking Max something in the background.

I'm too freaked out to even respond to his question, so I just cry into the phone.

"Ava! What's wrong?" The growing alarm in his voice is strangely comforting.

"We were robbed, and I'm too afraid to go into my apartment."

"Oh no. You were robbed? Damn! Where are you now?"

"Downstairs on my neighbor's porch, but she isn't home, and I can't get a hold of anyone to help me."

"Well, you did the right thing by calling me. I'm in West Hollywood now so I can be there within ten minutes. Hold on a sec."

The sound is muffled like he has his hand over his phone, but I can vaguely hear him speak to a woman. She doesn't sound happy, and he barks something back in response.

He speaks into the phone again. "Okay, I'm back. What I want you to do is get in your car and lock it and wait for me. Is your car out front?"

I sniffle. "Yes. You'll come?" I sound pathetic.

"Yes, Ava. Just get in the car and I'll be there in ten." The phone clicks off.

I get in my car, fold my arms across the steering wheel, bury my face in my arms and continue to cry. Part of me dreads seeing Max, and the other part is incredibly grateful he's coming. I'm going to need support to face my apartment. A moment later, there's a gentle knock on the window, and I look up. His face is etched with concern.

I unlock the door, he opens it, and gently pulls me out of the car and into his arms. My crying gets louder, and he rocks me slowly, running his hand over my head repeatedly until I calm down. He pulls away and looks at me.

"I'm going to go into the apartment and make sure no one's there and it's okay to go in. I want you to lock yourself back in the car while I do that."

"Can't I go with you?" I plead.

"No, just let me do it." He puts me back in the car and moves quickly up the stairs. The lights of the apartment snap on one at a time and then a few moments later he comes back out and down the stairs.

"I'm sorry, Ava." He shakes his head as I step out of the car. "It looks like they were pretty thorough."

A new wave of dread overcomes me. "Is your painting still there?" I'm not sure what I'll do if they took my angel painting.

His expression softens and he takes my hand and squeezes it. "Yes, it's still there."

I let out the breath I've been holding. "Thank God. Stupid robbers left the most valuable thing in the house."

He fights back a smile, but then looks serious again. "I've already called a locksmith. Have you called the police yet?"

"Yes, but they have no idea when they'll get here." He puts his arm around my shoulders and calls the police again while we slowly move back toward the apartment.

When the police come, Max holds my hand as we walk room to room and assess what's missing. Every drawer is open, many overturned. My mind is a jumble, so the realization comes in waves. I remember my camera full of recently-captured memories. I keep looking at the shelf where I always kept it, hoping it will magically reappear. My iPod's no longer on my bed stand where I left it this morning. Someone has my playlists and something about that and my photographs feels intimate and wrong. It's a violation. My mourning begins for things small and large.

My only gleeful moment is when I remember that my laptop is safely in my bag at work. I had hoped to steal some writing time instead of taking a lunch. On a normal day, I would've left it at home. I've been working so hard on his story that the relief that my words about Max haven't been stolen is palpable.

I share that with him, and he smiles sadly and rubs my shoulders.

As the police officer wraps up his report, he informs me it's highly unlikely we'll ever see our stuff again. We also have to be careful because it's not uncommon for them to return for a second round—even clothes. I feel myself sway as the blood drains from my face. *Come back?* The idea is more than I can take.

Max assures me we'll get the place secured. The locksmith he called is a childhood friend, and he's asked him install an alarm on the door and the window that faces the porch. His clear thinking under pressure is reassuring.

"Okay, let's pack your bag. You're staying at my place tonight."

As much as I know I can't stay in the apartment alone tonight, I have no idea how I will navigate being alone with Max in Malibu in this state of mind.

"Don't worry. I have a guestroom."

His locksmith friend shows up with his equipment, and Max assures me that he's completely trustworthy and we can leave while he does the work. We'll get the new keys, alarm code and instructions in the morning.

There's nothing good left to steal anyway, I think sadly.

Packed and numb, I follow Max to the door, but something suddenly occurs to me, along with a feeling of dread. My heart's pounding, fear overtaking me, and I pray that the one thing I can't be without, the thing that can't be replaced, is still here.

I stop and Max looks back concerned. I rush back to my bedroom with him on my heels. I look at my bottom desk drawer overturned on the floor, papers and folders scattered everywhere. I flip the drawer back over and desperately rifle through the worthless contents. It's not here. My heart sinks...*It's not here.*

I fall to my knees and crawl around the floor, frantically lifting up everything and throwing it back down again. I sift through the drawer again, and when I do it a third time, Max reaches down and puts his hand on my shoulder.

"Ava, you've got to stop. I'm so sorry," he whispers, having no idea what I've lost.

I jerk away from him and crawl around some more, my breath now heaving, a shrill shriek tearing out of my chest. "No, No, No!"

He reaches down again, takes me by the shoulders and pulls me to my feet. He holds me up and speaks firmly, "Ava, you've got to stop. It's gone, I'm sorry, but it's gone."

The sound that comes out of me next is unlike any I've ever heard, something between a sob and a cry of complete and utter despair. Nothing, not Max's strong arms, not the love I've received from the Kesters, nor the recognition from Jonathan can restore what's lost. I feel myself float away, and Max reaches out just a moment too late as I crumple to the floor.

Chapter Twelve / Stolen Memories

Just remember—when you think all is lost, the future remains.
~Robert H. Goddard

I have the vague sensation of Max picking me up and carrying me, followed by the muffled sound of his conversation with the locksmith while I press my face into his chest. I'm trembling and I can't find words to speak. Max and the other guy continue to talk while we're moving forward. It feels like we're going down some stairs, but I'm too afraid to open my eyes to be sure.

"Tommy, put her bag in the trunk. Thanks, man."

I hear a car door opening and then I'm being lowered into a seat. Behind me, I can hear the trunk popping open.

Why is he trying to let go of me? I don't want to fall down the rabbit hole! I cling to his shirt desperately.

"Ava, sweetheart," he murmurs gently. "You've got to let go so I can drive." He peels my hands off his shirt and as soon as the connection is broken, I start to sob again.

The drive to Malibu is endless without a word spoken between us. When I finally open my eyes, I see the pained look on Max's face. I'm sure this is a lot more than he bargained for. After he parks, he helps me out of the car, tucks me under his shoulder and walks me into the house.

Once he gets me settled on the couch, he takes a chenille throw and wraps it around me and quietly moves through the house, turning on low lights and starting the fireplace. He pours a glass of red wine from the bar. When he gives it to me, I take several large swallows in a row.

He finally joins me on the couch and sits close to me. "Do you want to talk about it?"

I nod, despite how weary I am. I feel ravaged inside, my spirit broken.

"What was it you couldn't find?"

I need him to understand that what I lost was a part of me.

"It was a box. I still can't believe it's gone."

He nods with great empathy. "I could tell it meant everything to you."

"My family, my past, all that was precious to me…the letters my dad wrote me from Iraq before he was killed…"

Max's expression is one of profound sadness. "How old were you when he died?"

"Fifteen."

"Oh, baby," he whispers.

"The poem my grandma wrote for me before she passed." I close my eyes and picture the poem and my eyes well up again. "Why didn't I make a copy of the poem? I just never thought…"

"Oh, Ava. How could you've known?" He rubs my shoulder to soothe me.

"My dad's class ring and gold watch. Grandma's pearl earrings. Oh…" I sink further, as if an invisible weight is pushing down on my shoulders. "The last thing I put in there was a letter from my mom."

He tips his head to the side with a curious expression. "Is she still alive?"

I let out a long sigh. "I have no idea."

I take another sip of my wine. I don't want to talk about my mom right now. Max waits patiently and I'm hoping he won't ask what I may not be ready to tell.

"There was so little to hold onto…and now it's been taken. It feels like my past has been stolen. None of my things will mean anything to the thieves. It's only cash to them. But I'd give anything to have it back."

More tears fall, but I'm calmer now that I've finished. It's cathartic to let it all out.

Max reaches over and pulls me close. He rubs my arm and runs his fingers through my hair. As we sit silently, his touch relaxes me and my eyelids grow heavy as the exhaustion of unleashing so much emotion hits me.

"You know Ava," he finally says, "I had no idea what you've been through." He shakes his head. "And I'm so sorry for what you've lost tonight."

Instinctively, I slide closer.

"But do you know what's most significant about what you've told me? Your memories of your family are what's important, not the stuff they left you. You're lucky because they loved you, and they had a chance to tell you. Losing the letters doesn't take any of that away. You'll always have the memory of what they said in those letters, and they'll always live in your heart. You don't need the stuff to know it's true."

And even though I don't want to hear that now, somewhere deep in my heart a tiny part of me knows he's right. We stay on the couch, and as Max quietly comforts me, my eyes finally close and I fall into a deep exhausted sleep.

When I wake, it's dark and I hear the sound of the ocean in the distance. I sit up, but don't recognize my surroundings. The T-shirt I'm wearing isn't mine, so I check a little more. At least the bra and panties are mine. *Where are my clothes?* The memory of Max holding me on the couch comes back. *Did he change me and put me to bed?* I'm horrified and I break out in a cold sweat. The feeling is unnerving and familiar, and my heart starts racing wildly. Recognizing the signs of a panic attack coming on, I take deep breaths to calm myself. I get out of bed to see if I can find Max.

I step into a hallway with a terra-cotta tiled floor, dimly lit with old wrought-iron light fixtures. There are large paintings on each wall. At the end of the hall are double doors made of intricately carved dark wood. They're just open enough for me to stick my head through and look inside.

A dim light in the corner allows me to take in the details of the room. French doors are wide open and its sheer curtains flutter in a cool breeze that carries the sound of the ocean inside. In the middle of the room is a large four-poster bed with heavy velvet drapes hanging on the sides. Despite the carvings on the bed frame and the velvet curtains, the decor is very masculine.

When I spy Max, I sigh. He's covered with sheets, but I can still see he sleeps with abandon. He's diagonal on the bed, his arms outstretched and his wild hair a halo against the pale pillow. I slowly walk to the edge of the bed. To see him like this—so peaceful, so beautiful, stirs something inside of me.

"Max…Max," I say, trying not to startle him awake, and wait a moment before I try again. After I've said his name a dozen times, he finally opens his eyes.

"Ava," he says groggily and looks at the clock. "Are you okay?"

"Sorry to wake you, but…I'm trying to fight off a panic attack. I'm so shook up from what happened."

"Of course you are," he says, rubbing his eyes. "Can I get you something? Do you want me to sit up with you?"

"No, but would it be okay if I stay in here while you sleep? Maybe I could lie on the other side of the bed?" I ask meekly.

"Sure…as long as you're comfortable with that. Why don't you try to get more sleep too?" He scoots over to the right side of the bed and lifts the sheets and blanket on the other side so I can get in. When I sink down into the bed, I marvel at how soft the sheets are. I sigh, immediately feeling so much better with him near.

He settles back down and I lie there, frozen by the tension floating between us.

"Are you okay?" he finally whispers.

"Yeah, I guess I'm still nervous. I'll be fine." I roll onto my side, facing the open French doors to let the ocean breeze soothe me.

"Come here," he says quietly. He curls his arm around my waist and pulls me to him until we're spooning. As he holds me, he caresses my head and whispers in my ear, "It's okay. I've got you. Everything's okay."

Being in his arms and feeling safe and cared for is heavenly. I settle into a deep, calm sleep.

When I wake up, I feel rested, despite the night I endured. The ocean air is healing and this bed's probably the best I've ever slept in. I amuse myself remembering Riley's prediction that I would be in Max's bed sooner than I thought. *I don't think this is what she had in mind though.*

I turn toward Max, but his spot is empty. I feel a little abandoned without him here, but then decide it makes the morning less awkward not to have to wake up in his arms and then try to compose myself. There's a note on his pillow.

> *Went for a run on the beach, be back soon.*
> *-M*

Peeling the sheets back and stepping out of bed, I take a long stretch. I decide to find the kitchen and see if he's made any coffee.

At the bottom of the stairs, I stand under the arch leading into an open room. Floor to ceiling shelves full of books line the walls, and there's a large fireplace on the left wall. French doors open to the front garden and provide a direct view of the koi pond and fountain. On one side of the room, an oversized antique wooden desk covered with piles of papers, books and an Apple laptop is angled to look out on the garden.

An old Asian rug frames the sitting area that has a pair of oversized worn leather chairs facing the fireplace. I almost swoon. This is my fantasy room. I can imagine sitting here for hours with a favorite book, the fire roaring and the French doors just parted so I can hear the water cascading into the pond. I wonder if Max realizes how lucky he is to live here.

I wander around a bit more until I find the kitchen, and note that everywhere I look there are piles of books, both art and literature. I have to wonder how the busy artist and party boy has time to read.

I'm rewarded with a pot of coffee already brewed. I help myself to a mug, and then wander out on the patio facing the beach. Leaning on the railing, I gaze at the ocean and watch a kayaker cut across the low horizon. Something catches my eye and I focus on the water in time to see two dolphins leap out of the water and dive in again. They repeat the motion three times with incredible grace until the water is quiet again.

Finally, I gaze along the shore, taking in the jagged, rocky coastline of Malibu. The beach is still quiet except for a lone jogger gracefully moving my direction as he runs along the water's edge. As he comes closer, I recognize him. Max is barefoot, wearing a pair of navy board shorts and apparently nothing else. I watch him run up to the beach in front of the house. He stops and stretches for a moment, and then I lose sight of him as he moves to the gate leading up to the houses.

He bounds into the kitchen and stops when he sees me leaning against the kitchen counter.

He smiles. "Hey sleepyhead. I see you found the coffee."

I'm desperately trying to regain my focus to answer him. It's one thing to see Max partially disrobed at a distance on the beach. But the sight of him so close with a thin glistening layer of sweat across his beautifully-defined body combined with the bright look in his eyes and color in his cheeks renders me speechless.

Finally, I manage to ask, "How was your run?"

His smile widens. "Great, it's a beautiful morning, perfect weather." He takes a mug from the cupboard and fills it with coffee. "How are you feeling this morning?" His expression softens as he studies my face.

I run my fingers through my bed hair. "Well, much better than last night. I'm really sorry I woke you up in the middle of the night, but I slept so much better. I hope you were able to go back to sleep."

"I slept like a baby."

I feel my cheeks turn red and he smiles.

He refills his water bottle at the sink. "I've already mixed up some pancake batter. Let me jump in the shower and then I'll make breakfast."

"Shower," I repeat, distracted with the idea of Max naked with water flowing over him.

"Care to join me?" he teases playfully.

I grin. "Join you? Oh my, Max."

He backs out of the room, his hands outstretched. "Last chance!" he teases and then he heads upstairs.

I sit down in the booth at the end of the kitchen facing the patio, drink my coffee and consider running upstairs to surprise Max in the shower, but then the darkness starts to settle in my mind, and I wonder how many of the art groupies have been in that shower with him. Suddenly, the idea loses all of its appeal. But I still allow myself the luxury of picturing him in the steam, rubbing soap all over his body before the water rushes over him.

Minutes later, he's back in the kitchen taking a griddle out of the cupboard and removing various ingredients from the fridge. He has a perfect command of the kitchen. As I look around, I note a big bowl of fruit and various well-used cooking appliances.

"Was your mom a good cook?"

"Yeah, she loved to cook and she always took me with her to the local farmers markets. She wanted me to know how to cook too. I guess she figured it would make me more desirable to the female population."

"Like you needed help in that area."

He smiles. "Well, I'll take that as a compliment."

After we finish stacks of pancakes with bacon and drink our orange juice, I ask him if he has a picture of his mom. I follow him into the living room and he takes a framed black and white print off the mantle.

"It's my favorite," he says softly as he hands me the picture. It's a photograph of Max and his mom on the beach. He looks to be about twelve or thirteen and she has her arm draped over his shoulder. What's most striking is the photographer caught them laughing as they look at each other, and you can feel how much they love each other. They're both good-looking, but they aren't posing like models. They're just happy and laughing, enjoying each other.

It takes my breath away to realize he had that, and now she's gone. From the various things he's said, she obviously adored him and made choices in her life for the benefit of Max. She was a beautiful woman, but what mattered was Max and being a good mom. My mom was like that once. We've both lost so much.

"She's beautiful, Max," I sigh, handing the photo back. "You can tell in this photo how much you two adore each other."

He nods silently and carefully sets it back on the mantle.

"Is it hard living here since this was her home once too?" I feel bold asking him this, but everything in this house tells me something about Max, and I want to learn more.

"You know, even though she decided to raise me in the city, she loved this house and put a lot of herself into it. As a matter of fact, this is where she primarily lived after I went to college.

In the beginning, the first couple of years after she died, I kept everything the same. I guess it was a shrine, and I couldn't bear to let anything go. But I realized it kept me in a state of mourning. It was time to move forward. I changed a lot of the interior and hung new art, both my friends' and mine. All the changes made it easier. But as for the house itself, I find comfort in the connection I have with her here. She loved this place...designed the garden and put so much love into this house. I feel it whenever I'm here."

I look into his eyes and offer him a tender smile. It hits me how much he's shared—deeply personal thoughts I imagine he's shared with very few people, if anyone. And although he's avoiding getting physically intimate with me, I take comfort in the thought that I'm be-coming an important friend. He certainly proved what kind of friend he could be last night.

I look down at my makeshift nightgown and decide it's time to get dressed.

"Where are my clothes?"

"They're in the top dresser drawer in the guestroom," he answers, revealing nothing.

"I'm so embarrassed that you had to change me and I didn't even wake up enough to know it." I look down.

He huffs. "You should be embarrassed. That outfit was pretty damn tight...I had a hard time getting it off. And that lingerie...where did you go last night dressed like that anyway?"

I turn red. "I met Jonathan for drinks to talk about the book."

"You wore that to meet Jonathan?" His eyebrows knit together and his hands tighten into fists.

It's like he's implying I did something wrong.

"What the fuck is wrong with his office anyway? You guys always go out for drinks. Is he hitting on you?"

I blush even more thinking about Jonathan and his seductive talk, but that's the last thing I'd tell Max. "We've only met three times, and once was in his office! Besides, why does it matter?"

"I don't like it and I don't trust him."

"That's rich coming from you."

"What the hell does that mean?"

"Look at you and your art groupies. What are your intentions with them? Should *you* be trusted?"

He glares at me silently.

"Seriously, tell me...who are you to pass judgment on Jonathan's intentions?" My anger builds and my mouth won't stop moving. "I know what this is. You have no interest in me, but you don't want any- one else to have me because then your *angel* won't be around to watch over you."

As soon as I say it, I feel really bad considering the guy just spent most of the last twenty-four hours taking care of me. I desperately wish I could take it back.

He looks like I've kicked his puppy and my stomach sinks with regret.

"I'm sorry, I didn't mean *that*, Max. I'm just so freaked out about things right now."

"Forget it," he mumbles.

Great. He's shut down.

"Look, I have work to do. So why don't you get ready and I'll drive you home. I already spoke with Dylan this morning and he's going to arrive at your apartment when Riley does. They're going to be there by

two. Jay dropped off the keys and temporary alarm code this morning."
He turns away.

We both remain silent as I head upstairs.

The silence continues as Max deftly maneuvers his Porsche through
the winding canyons above Malibu. By the time we're on the freeway
shooting toward L.A., I'm feeling even more like an ungrateful bitch. I
finally gather up my courage to speak.

"Max?"

Silence.

"I feel awful about what I said...I just don't understand why you
jumped all over me for my meeting with Jonathan. But I don't care
about that right now."

I look at him and he glances my way before turning back to the
road. At least he's listening.

"I can't or won't ever forget what you did for me last night. I was in
such a state and you dropped everything to help me."

Dropped. I smile inwardly at the picture I've painted of his date, the
assumed art groupies, being dropped—*hopefully from a high elevation.*
I can't seem to help feeling jealous when it comes to him. I look at Max
and refocus.

"You were kind, and took such good care of me. That says so much
about the kind of person you are, not the famous artist, but the person
you are inside."

His face relaxes and he takes a deep breath. I hope he's considering
what I've said.

I take a chance and touch his shoulder. "I'm sorry, Max. Please forgive me."

He clears his throat. "Just so you know, I think you're overstating
the womanizing thing."

"Okay. Maybe I assumed wrong about the girl you were with when
we talked on the phone last night."

He purses his lips and shakes his head. "You think you have me all
figured out, but I think you just don't understand me."

"You're right about that. I don't understand you. I guess I'm push-ing because there's something about you that makes me believe you're much more than who you present to the world. The party-boy artist with little regard for women…I don't think that's the man Elizabeth raised."

He's silent, but his fingers tighten over the stick shift as he focuses on the road.

I turn and watch the scenery blur by.

He clears his throat and says, "How about this—I think we should call a truce. I have to admit that, as guilty as I've felt about all that you've done for me since we met, maybe last night helped even up the score a little."

I nod. "I'll say, but don't be expecting any thank-you paintings. I don't have your talent so, unless unintentionally primitive art is your thing, I'll have to think of something else."

"Well, how about if you write something…something about me—like for an art book? That more than evens things out."

I smile. "Sounds like a plan."

When he pulls up to my apartment, he hands me the keys and alarm instructions.

"Will you be okay?" he asks tentatively.

"Yes, I think so. Thanks." I hug him, pressing my face into the curve of his neck. He softens a little as I hold him.

As I step out of the car, he says, "You know, Ava, I'm glad you called me last night…and that I could be there for you."

I turn back and, with a grateful smile, I gaze at my beautiful, hope-lessly complicated friend.

"Me too, Max. Me too."

Chapter Thirteen / Get a Clue

Those are my principles, and if you don't like them… well,
I have others.
  - Groucho Marx

Taking a deep breath, I enter my apartment. After the alarm shuts off without a problem, I survey the living room with the fresh perspective of a new day. It makes me feel better to focus on the beauty of the room, even with the bookshelves emptied on the floor and the furniture askew. I look up at Max's angel painting on the mantel and feel a wave of joy that his precious gift is still there.

As I put things away in the living room, I remember back when Riley and I painted three of the walls brown and one turquoise. Because of Riley's persistence, we spent several days stenciling a paisley pattern in a slightly lighter shade onto that turquoise wall. The effect was beautiful.

The turquoise and brown retro rug with large sixties-style flowers that Riley found set the tone for the room. She has such a great design eye. Eventually, we upgraded our furniture from hand-me-downs to low chenille couches and an eclectic group of lamps. We also framed several prints of art given to me by various artists. The overall ambience is very sophisticated.

I'm slightly calmer when I finish sliding the last piece of furniture back into place. At least one room is almost restored, sans a TV and computer.

As I start putting the kitchen back together, Riley and Dylan come in the front door. Riley still freaks out, even though Dylan has already broken the news to her and we had a conversation earlier on the phone.

I rush over and we hug tightly.

"Oh, Ava!" she wails, "I can't believe we were robbed. You must've been terrified to come home alone at night to this."

"Yeah, it was horrible. I couldn't reach anyone and started flipping out, but then I called Max and he came right over."

Riley's brows knit together with a worried look, and she reaches over and squeezes my hand.

"Riley, he was really great."

Dylan looks relieved. "Hey, Dylan. Thanks for being here for Riley."

He wraps his arms around her from behind. "Of course."

Riley surveys the living room.

I groan. "Your computer...I'm so sorry."

"I can't believe it...and I'd finally paid it off. At least I backed everything up on my laptop before I left. It would've sucked even more if I'd lost all that work. That's one relief at least."

Her somber expression doesn't make it easy when I remind her to check her bedroom and make a list of what's missing. She and Dylan head down the hallway. After we've finished our list of stolen goods, Dylan agrees to sleep over for a couple of nights until we feel settled again. He heads out to buy some beer and pick up dinner, while Riley and I do the last bit of work to get our bedrooms in order.

I keep hoping as I put each item back in its place that I'll discover my precious box, but with the last drawer replaced, I have to accept the loss once more.

It's no surprise that my attempt at sleep that night is dark and fitful. I fight my way through a dream where a sinister character shadows and haunts me. Every time I try to escape his grasp, his spindly fingers press me back beneath his black cloak.

Midday Sunday I check my emails that I haven't looked at since the robbery. There's an email from Jonathan sent Friday.

> *Ava,*
> *You've become a source of inspiration in so many ways. I look forward to sharing the dream I had about you last night. It was beyond exquisite.*
> *Jonathan*

My whole body flushes. Was he drinking when he wrote this? That's how I'd written off the scene in front of the restaurant. Maybe he's actually serious about pursuing me. I just don't get it—he's an older, sophisticated man. Why me? I hope this isn't a sport with me in the crosshairs. I squirm. I'd better send some type of answer right away.

> *Jonathan,*
> *Sorry for the delay in responding. As it turns out my apartment was robbed Friday night, and with all the frenzy, I haven't checked emails.*
> *It's nice to hear I'm inspiring dreams…I'm intrigued.*
> *Ava*

He responds immediately.

> *Ava,*
> *I'm so sorry to hear your news. Can I do anything to help?*
> *I leave for NY in the morning and am gone all week, but am completely reachable via phone or email.*
> *Remember, whatever you need…*
> *Jonathan*

The kindness of his words is comforting and there's a smile on my face while I respond.

Jonathan,
    I'm fine, but thank you. Let's talk when you return.
    Safe travels,
    Ava

I'm relieved to get a break from dealing with Jonathan in person. I'm overwhelmed and can't handle anything complicated right now.

Instead, I wonder what Max is doing. I should call him to thank him again for helping me Friday night.

When I call, a woman answers. She has one of those breathy voices. I fight the urge to hang up. "Is Max there?"

"He's working in the studio," breathy voice replies.

"Let me guess…he doesn't want to be disturbed."

"Uh-huh."

"Okay, will you tell him Ava called to thank him again for Friday night?" *Take* that, *art babe.*

As I hang up, I'm fairly certain Max will never get my message, but I hoped I ruffled art groupie's feathers enough that she'll give him a bad time anyway. *Damn him.*

Monday at the gallery, I immerse myself in my work to shake the lingering feeling of loss and violation from the robbery. Everyone's especially doting, which I appreciate, considering how raw I am. Jess calls and offers to take me out to dinner Wednesday night. It's times like this I'm grateful for my makeshift family. Even Sean takes me aside.

"Hey, my friends and I are going to a club tonight. Why don't you come?" He smiles sweetly.

"Who are you seeing?" I ask, not sure I'm in the mood to go out anyway.

"Wrecked at the Whiskey. My friend Charlie saw them in New York last week and said they were wicked." He grins broadly.

I smile. "Hmm, *wicked.* Well, let me see if I'm up for it later, okay? Thanks for thinking of me, Sean."

"Anytime," he says and it gives me comfort to know he means it.

I spend most of the afternoon working on a press release for Adam that involves some internet research. One of the sites we follow, *Art*

Happenings, has a write-up on the opening last Saturday night for the *30-Year Retrospective Show* at the Museum of Contemporary Art. My curiosity wins, and I scan the photos, hoping I don't find anything.

*Damn it, Max! This is my personal hell...*his gray blue eyes burn through the screen and right to my core, taunting me. His arms are thrown around two women in very short, low-cut dresses. I read the caption: Elise Dupre, Maxfield Caswell and Sarina Wolfe. I recognize the names of the women, both infamous art groupies. Sarina was married to a famous sculptor until he caught her having sex in his studio with his hunky assistant. Now she's determined to take full advantage of her freedom and reputation.

It's like he's throwing our conversation in the car back in my face, and I wonder which one was breathy voice on the home phone Sunday.

This picture was taken within twenty-four hours of when he'd pulled me into his arms to soothe me when I couldn't sleep, the same day he made me breakfast and told me about his mother. And our conversation about his womanizing? The sting is sharp, and I hold my breath and grab the edge of my desk. Will my Max torture know no bounds? I should reach into my chest and hand him my heart so he can slice it into tiny slivers and fan it out on a silver tray. Then he can wash his hands and be done with it.

The anger lights another fire under me, so when I get home from work I make a pot of coffee, skip dinner and plow into the book project. I want to be done with this job and get off this wonky roller coaster with Max. The tug and pull bulldozes my confidence and my pride.

At midnight, after I've wrapped up chapter four, I decide to email a particular section to him, as I'm uncertain about some of the facts.

> *Max,*
> *Please check this section for accuracy and get back to me*
> *with any changes.*

That's it, plain and simple. Read between the lines Caswell—*I'm done with our games. I'll never be one of your art groupies.*

He emails me back within minutes.

Are you mad at me? Why so abrupt? Are you okay?

I roll my eyes with a snarky flair. Now he's the rocket scientist of emotions. I email him right away.

> *This afternoon I stumbled upon another picture of you with your art babes from Saturday night. I guess it disappointed me after everything we'd talked about and the time we spent Friday and Saturday. I'm assuming the art groupie who answered your home phone on Sunday didn't give you the message I'd called either.*

The inbox chimes. Before I read his reply, I hesitate, imagining that he's pissed off. I can almost feel his anger singe my fingertips as I caress my keyboard. I open his message.

> *What do you want from me, Ava? Who are you expecting me to be? Because it sounds like I'm always letting you down, and that isn't good for either one of us.*

I can picture him running his hands through his hair, his eyes squinting and his jaw set. He makes me feel rash and impulsive, like speeding down the highway without headlights.

> *You're right, Max. It's not good for either one of us. Let's take a break, and we can try this friendship thing another time. I'll just work directly with Jonathan and you can do the same. Thanks in advance for your help in giving me the opportunity to work on this project.*

I hit send.

*Hmm, very dramatic and epically impulsive…*It feels satisfying for about five seconds, then I start wondering if I'm truly ready to let go of *art guy.*

Loud music starts howling from my cell phone. *Damn, I have to change that ring tone.* I grab the phone and slam it back down on the table without answering it. How pathetic that the worst thing I can do is not take his call? He definitely has the upper hand.

I watch my phone until the voice mail blinks and then listen to his message.

> *Come on, Ava. I don't want to* not *talk to you. I don't want to* not *be friends. Don't do this. Can you pick up the phone? I'm not going away that easily. Make me understand what it is you want. 'cause I sure as hell don't know what that is. Call me, Ava. Damn it. Call me.*

Fuck, fuck, fuck. There's nothing like drama at one in the morning on a workday. I reply via email and attach the photo of him with his art groupies.

> *Character, in the long run, is the decisive factor in the life of an individual.*
> *~ Theodore Roosevelt*

It's bitchy, but at this point, does it matter? I hit send.

I close my eyes and imagine his reaction. I've already soaked the bridge with gasoline and thrown a simmering match on it. I stare at my screen for at least ten minutes, hitting the receive messages button every ten seconds.

Nothing.

I don't think I've ever felt so tired.

"Hey, Ava, check this out!" Sean sounds so pleased.

I squint at his screen. "What does that say?" I study a snapshot of a plate glass window with hot pink writing scrawled across it.

"Get a clue…this ain't fucking mall art," he says, reading from the screen.

Lovely. I say to myself. "What's that from?"

Sean reads the description from the news report. *"Artist Maxfield Caswell took offense to the opinions of some of the collectors who attended Everett Callis' art opening last night. He used his companion's lipstick to make his feelings clear on the window of the gallery. He was escorted out by security."*

"Hey, Sean, can you send me a link to that story?" I ask calmly. My fingers itch to forward that gem, but it'll have to wait until I'm home. Once I'm in my apartment, I practically run to my laptop. I copy the photo and description from the article into a new email to *art boy*, and whip out my new quote.

> *You can out-distance that which is running after you, but not what is running inside you.*
> *~ Rwandan Proverb*

I'm halfway done heating up my Lean Cuisine meal when the email prompt dings.

> *What happened to my ally—the one who once stood up for me against the uninformed, uneducated dregs of the art-collecting community? Have you joined the other side?*

What a clever attempt at emotional manipulation. I dish it right back.

> *No Max,*
> *I applaud your sentiments and defense of Everett's work. I just think you didn't have to come off like a psycho sensationalist by scrawling (with lipstick) on the gallery window in a fit of fury. The photo of security dragging you off is not flattering. People will be expecting you to cut off your ear next.*

I congratulate myself on my crazy artist reference.

Well, at least I'd be in good company. And things worked out pretty good for Van Gogh in terms of his place in the art world.

So posthumous fame is what matters to Max? Should I be surprised?

Yeah, but long after he was dead. As I'm sure you know, he only sold one painting during his lifetime and shot himself at thirty-seven. He isn't exactly a role model.

I take my dinner out of the microwave to cool before checking to see if he responded to my last comment.

Oh Ava, I'm sure you know historians are now disputing that. But regardless, let's get to the crux of the matter. This is about the lipstick, isn't it? You're jealous of the girl.

The ass is right, but I'll never admit it.

Don't you wish.

I close my email and tear into the new chapter. At least these fits of anger help propel me through the writing. At this rate, I'll be done in a few weeks.

Later, I meet Jess at TBY's in West Hollywood for dinner.

"So, is Max making you nuts yet?" she asks as she licks some salt off the edge of her margarita.

I moan. "How did you know? We aren't even talking, just having an ongoing argument via email. Some days I hate his guts."

She looks concerned. "Those are pretty strong words, Missy. What's he done anyway?"

"I'm not even sure. He has the ability to get under my skin. He can be so sweet, like when he helped me after the robbery. But then he reverts back to his trashy side, which pisses me off, and we lose whatever ground we'd gained. During the good times, we're close and I get addicted. He's my own drug. The highs are so damn good."

"But then…"

"But then it all goes to hell. I just have to accept I can't be friends with him. Yet when I think of not talking to him or seeing him, I feel bad. What the hell's wrong with me, Jess?"

She shakes her head and groans. "This is what I was fucking worried about. I should've cut him off at the knees and stopped the book project. Damn it."

"What do you mean?"

"I warned him, but Max is so fucking stubborn. You're the perfect girl for him, Ava, and he knows it on some level, and it really freaks him out. He's acting out in all kinds of crazy ways. He's created a life where he never has to be dependent on a woman again. That's why he goes for the art sluts, because in a million years he'd never get involved with one."

"Perfect? Well, it's not like I'm looking for a boyfriend or pursuing him in that way." I cross my arms.

"I know that, and he knows it too. Look, how long have we been friends? In all that time I've watched you avoid getting involved with anyone. It's like a sport with you. You're almost as bad as he is."

"I don't think I'm that bad."

"Well, regardless, some people can't be together and they can't be friends either. Maybe that's how it is for you and Max. Or you can accept each other, flaws and all, and be friends."

I nod, trying to imagine my life without Max in it. What if we really can't be friends?

"I know the real Max, and that's why I'll always be there for him. But this bullshit he's going through lately is wearing on me. I hope he snaps out of it soon."

She's holding back something, but I don't press. Jess is the smartest woman I know, and I trust her.

Friday afternoon, Jess calls. Max has backed out of a group show for personal reasons. She is pissed. In her book, the only acceptable *personal reason* for such an action is being hit by a bus. Since she's pretty sure that isn't the case, she's heading over to his place now to conduct an intervention.

That evening, I find a fitting new quote to send after polishing off my takeout.

> *Have a very good reason for everything you do.*
> *~Laurence Olivier*

I wait for his reply, wishing I felt more satisfied. Then I second-guess myself. Maybe there's a good reason he backed out of the show. I should've talked to Jess first before sending another snarky email. Feeling a little unsettled, I grab a bottle of beer out of the fridge and look through my DVDs. I pick out *The Twilight Zone* Collection that had belonged to my dad, figuring it's just the right mood for how I'm feeling tonight. I pop the first disc in my laptop and kick my legs up on the couch.

About ten minutes into the second episode, the doorbell rings. It's nine-thirty. *What the hell? What if the robbers are back and testing to see if anyone is home?* A wave of fear runs through me. Why, oh why, did Riley have a date with Dylan tonight? I need reinforcements. The bell rings again, but three times in rapid succession. I look through the peephole.

Through the warped perspective of the peephole, I see a big distorted head as Max tries to peer through the peephole too. I jump back.

Shit! The emails! I'd better face the music, I decide and immediately regret the sweatpants and tight T-shirt I'd changed into when I got home.

I open the door. Max has dark purple circles under his eyes, and he looks wired and edgy, as if he's had too much coffee. He's slightly bobbing his head and twisting his hands together.

"Hey, Max. What are you doing here?" I ask as casually as possible.

At first he doesn't say a thing, just looks as if he's trying to figure me out.

"I have one question, Ava. Why are you fucking with me? Are you enjoying this? Your goddamned emails have me so agitated I can't sleep. I can't focus on anything. Do you hate me that much?"

He's hunched over and his hands curl into fists before he jams them into his pockets. I didn't think it was possible, but he looks pathetic.

"No, I don't hate you, Max. I don't know—I just couldn't help myself. But hey, you've been giving it back too," I say quietly.

"I've teased you, not assassinated your character repeatedly," he says, his voice getting loud.

I guess I was too heavy-handed, even for someone who seems impenetrable. Now I feel bad. "I'm sorry. I obviously didn't realize it would upset you."

He looks at me with disbelief as he folds his arms over his chest.

"Why the hell are you stalking me on the internet? Are you trying to make me feel worse than I already do about myself? Are you trying to destroy me? 'cause I have to tell you, I think it's working."

Destroy him? That's a little dramatic.

"Why does it even matter what I think about your behavior?"

He throws his head back with a frustrated groan. "Has it occurred to you that I care about what you think of me?"

"You do?"

"Isn't it obvious?"

"Do you mean because I'm writing your book?"

He slaps his open palms over his face and groans loudly. "You're killing me here, Ava."

This argument is getting us nowhere. "Do you want to come in? I have beer and great old black and white episodes of *The Twilight Zone*."

He rocks back and forth on his heels. "I don't want to watch *The Twilight Zone*. I'm living in the fucking twilight zone," he says as he walks into the apartment. He goes to the couch and crumples onto it, falling back against the cushions. He closes his eyes and lets out a low groan.

"Are you okay?" I ask tentatively.

He shakes his head. "No…I'm not."

Guilt bubbles up inside of me. I'll have to think twice before I send anyone a bunch of snarky emails again. "What can I do, Max? I feel terrible that I hurt you. What can I do to make things better?"

He opens his eyes slowly and gives me a sideways glance. "Look, I know I'm not easy, and I'm certainly no prince, but could you cut me some slack? Can we call a truce and try to get along before I lose it?"

I nod. "Sure." I certainly don't want him to *lose it* on my account.

He looks up tentatively. "Maybe we could even hang out for a while and forget all the stuff we're fighting about."

"Okay."

"You're sure?" He looks like he doesn't believe me.

I smile. "What do you want to do tonight?"

His eyes light up like he's just figured something out. "Go get some socks and a jacket."

What? Socks and a jacket? Art boy is kidnapping me? I'm beyond intrigued. I raise my eyebrows.

"I want to go bowling."

Chapter Fourteen / Strike!

There is nothing in the dark that isn't there when the lights are on.
   ~ Rod Serling`

*B*owling?

He stands up from the couch with a completely straight face and waits.

Has he lost his mind? Maybe he has and I don't want to agitate him further. I go to my bedroom for my hoodie and socks, and switch out my flip-flops for my Nikes.

When I rejoin him in my living room, he's pacing in front of the window.

I hesitate. "Max? Why are we going bowling?"

"Because it's fun, and mindless, and you get to drink beer while you play. Are you okay with that?"

"Sure. And I'll be nice. I promise."

He takes a deep breath and gives me the first smile since he showed up on my doorstep. "All right then, let's go."

I follow him downstairs and we get in his car. After we've driven several blocks, I ask, "So, where are we going bowling?"

"Burbank."

We're bowling in Burbank? Now it's getting even stranger. Despite being the home of Disney, Warner Brothers and NBC, Burbank is the closest you can get to Podunk in Los Angeles.

I watch him as he drives. He's totally focused on the road, but I'd pay money to know what's going on in his head. We pull up to the Pickwick Bowling Alley, a flat old brick building, where I expect everything to be aged and worn from the speckled linoleum floor to the 1950's style seating around each bowling lane. It's Mayberry from *The Andy Griffith Show,* and I half-expect Opie to walk by any moment. When we get inside, it's exactly as I'd pictured. It's kind of quaint, actually, and I'm glad it doesn't have the loud music and laser lighting of the newer bowling alleys.

We rent our stylish bowling shoes, which are an impossibly funky suede in wide stripes of burgundy, olive green and dirty taupe. *They must make them ugly so people don't take them home,* I think, as I finish tying the laces. We don't have any trouble getting a lane, considering the late hour. While I set up the overhead scorecard, Max buys a couple of beers.

Other than simple directions, like where I can pick out a ball and that I should go first, he really hasn't spoken much. I'm beginning to wonder if the whole evening will be like this. I still haven't discovered the secret to cheering him up, now that we're here in Burbank, dressed in funny shoes and sticking our fingers into different sized balls.

I bowl the first ball. Max watches me while he takes a hit of his beer. Unfortunately, my ball goes into the gutter halfway down the lane, but I'm too unnerved by this whole scenario to be embarrassed. On my next try, the ball rolls down the entire lane at an angle and, just before falling into the gutter, it takes out the corner pin. Max writes "one" with great flourish on the scorecard.

We trade places and he saunters over to his ball. I get a clue how the rest of the game will go when he snaps the ball up and aims, his body still as a statue. He unfurls and gracefully slinks forward like a tiger— if a tiger could hold a bowling ball. The ball spins as it makes contact with the wooden surface of the lane and shoots forward like a rocket.

The resulting explosion of pins is impressive. He's still in a dipped position, his shoulder and arm muscles beautifully defined. He springs up and turns to me.

I smile. "Hmm, looks like you could give me some pointers." *Closet bowler,* I surmise.

As the game progresses, I get a little better with each turn. After all, I haven't bowled in years, and it takes some getting used to. Max's improvement is in his attitude. He seems to lighten up with each play until he's smiling and joking about my unusual techniques. I over-play my goofiness, finally provoking him into giving me a mini-lesson, which involves touching as he moves my arm back to show the right motions. At one point, he even rests his hands on my hips to correct their position.

Every time he touches me, it feels as if his fingers are searing my skin. When he swivels my hips forward a second time, I flush and turn away. Who knew bowling could be erotic?

After several pointers, I have success. On the eighth frame, as soon as I release the ball, I have a good feeling, and I jump up and down and cheer as the ball slides along. When it meets the pins, there's no explosion. Instead, the pins seem to wobble and slowly surrender one by one. When the final pin falls, I let out a whoop, run to Max and jump up into his arms.

He throws his head back, laughs, and wraps his arms around me. I slide down his body until my feet meet the floor, and my victory hug becomes something more than buddy-like. The desire I have for this beautiful, flawed man is surging through me, and for a moment, I cling onto him feeling every definition of his body against mine.

I don't think I've ever wanted anyone this much, and I ache from it. The desire is so big, so overpowering, that I'd let him take me right here in the bowling alley if he wanted to.

I wonder if he can feel all this. I imagine it's obvious. He carefully pulls away, as if he's afraid I'll break.

"Yay, Ava! You did it…strike!" He smiles.

I step away and take a deep breath. "I guess the lesson paid off," I reply, trying to sound cheerful, as I struggle to regain my composure and push my desire out of my mind.

As we finish our game, Max announces that he's hungry, so we go get something to eat. Once again he takes the lead, and we pull up to Dupars, a coffee shop in Studio City that has watched many decades come and go. The place is empty except for a group of Goths in a booth in the back. Our waitress, Marge, wears a uniform that reminds me of an old-fashioned nurse's getup, complete with the little white cap. She has faded orange hair and tree stump legs and a cheerful disposition as she serves us stacks of pancakes and bacon.

We dig in with gusto. When Max finishes, he leans back and pats his stomach with a satisfied sigh.

"You look like a new man," I comment with a smile. "If I'd known it was this easy to make you happy, I would've taken you out for bowling and pancakes long ago."

He grins. "I know. This was just what I needed. We should do this again sometime."

"Sure, I had a great time—even though I thought you were nuts when you first showed up on my doorstep."

"Did you now? What if next time I show up in the middle of the night and take you swimming?"

"I'd insist the pool be heated."

He laughs. "You're pretty great, Ava. You're going to make some guy very lucky one day."

"Hmm, maybe."

He tips his head to the side as he regards me.

When we turn to my apartment, it's so late he insists on walking me to my door. Before we part, he gives me a big hug.

"Thanks, Ava." He sighs, and for a moment I can *feel* Max—his sadness, his emptiness, his need to just be okay and to go out bowling with a friend with no other agenda. Before he lets me go, I decide there will be no more nasty emails, no more fighting, and no snarky comments. It's time to figure out a way to be friends with Maxfield Caswell.

Sunday, I'm finishing the first draft on another chapter when my phone rings.

"What are you up to?" It's my new best friend and he sounds happy.

"Thinking about you…because I'm working on your book." I laugh.

"Oh, for a moment I got really excited, because I was thinking about you," he jokes.

"Were you?" I say with a flirty tone.

"Yes, will you play with me today?"

"Wow, two offers to play with you in the same weekend. And why do I get this honor?"

"Because you're more fun than anyone else."

I smile, loving how special he's making me feel. "Okay, so what are we doing today?"

"I'm going to drag you to thrift stores all over town."

"Ooo, hold me back! It's a dream come true! Now why on Earth would I want to do that?"

"'cause it'll make me happy and I want your company."

"I'm such a pushover."

"I'll be there in an hour."

"Okay, but I'm expecting a good meal out of this, at least."

"You bet."

After he hangs up, I feel an unexpected thrill, even though thrift-store shopping is probably the last thing I would choose to do on a Sunday.

Max arrives in an old flatbed truck. "It was my mom's. She used it for hauling stuff—like the plants she always bought from the nursery."

It makes a lot more sense to use this for our outing than his Porsche.

Max pulls out a printout of thrift stores and we pick the closest one to visit first. From there, we'll head toward downtown.

As we pull up to the Salvation Army, I ask him what we're shopping for.

"Paintings—and they must be hand-painted. No prints and they don't have to be good."

I'm not sure what I expected, but I definitely wasn't expecting that.

"Paintings of what?"

"It could be anything. I'll know it when I see it."

"Are you redecorating?" I tease him, knowing that anything we find in a thrift store won't be hanging in his home.

"Actually, I'm going to incorporate the paintings we find into a new series I'm developing. It's like when rappers sample parts of other musician's songs. That's why I have my camera," he gestures to the case on the center console. "The pictures I take may become part of the work, or at least part of the story."

I'm fascinated. The mind of an artist is bewildering to navigate.

When we step out of the truck, he takes a picture of the thrift shop's storefront. As we go inside, the sights and smells of a million disparate objects that have all once belonged to different people hit me. There are racks of clothes, stacks of dishes and shelves of books. Everything has a forlorn look, nothing matches and it makes me feel a little sad. It reminds me of those early days in L.A. when I frequented places like this for things I needed.

The efficient thing about looking for paintings is you can quickly scan through the store for anything to consider. This store disappoints because all we find is a framed Scooby-Doo poster and a needlepoint of a vase of flowers that's starting to unravel. Max takes a shot of their offering and we head out.

In the second store, we have better luck. Hanging crookedly on the wall are several prints and paintings. Max chooses a brown-hued landscape and a large, poorly executed painting of a ship at sea. He not only takes pictures of the store, but several of me paying for the painting with the cash he's handed me. He takes the receipt and carefully folds it into his wallet, explaining that it might end up in the art as well.

By the time we've snaked our way downtown, we have more than a dozen paintings crammed behind the seat of the truck. My personal favorite is the paint-by-number masterpiece of horses running across the plains, though I can't wait to see what he does with our finds.

He looks not just happy, but inspired. He keeps opening up a leather journal, making notes and drawling little thumbnail sketches. Being able to intimately watch his creative process develop is something I'll always remember.

"Okay, time to feed you!" He smiles as he pulls into a parking lot by the train station. There's a sign that says Phillippe, The Original French Dipped Sandwiches.

"Is this where we're going?" I ask.

"Yeah, I promised you good food and you're going to get it!"

If the long lines of people at the front counter waiting to place their order are any indication, then he's right about it being good.

Max shoos me away to find a table, and I score a little wooden booth near the vintage candy counter. There's sawdust on the floor and old-fashioned linoleum-topped tables with wooden stools. Vintage photos of the establishment over the years surround the sign on the wall that says Phillippe's has been open since 1908. The place hasn't changed much.

I smile, thinking about Max. He's happiest when he's focused on the creative process and relaxed enough to be himself. It must be a relief to spend a day with a friend without the spotlight of the art world focused on everything he does. This carefree, inspired side of him is a side of Max few people see.

He carries a plastic tray loaded with food—French dip sandwiches, little plates of macaroni salad, a slice of apple pie and two bottles of root beer.

"Just one piece of pie?"

"I thought we could share," he says, smiling.

After we unload the tray, I take a bite of the sandwich.

"Mmm!" I moan and roll my eyes with pleasure.

"I know, great huh?" He laughs, looking delighted. "Wait until you try the pie."

"You know all the good places, Max."

"Well, when I was in high school, I had friends from all over the city, so I learned where all the cool places were. I'll have to take you to Chinatown some day for dim sum."

"Sounds good to me."

"Hey, at your studio, do you guys print artists that aren't part of your gallery?"

"We do. Why? Are you thinking about making serigraph prints of your work?"

"Yeah, Dylan's talked about it for the Barcelona show." His eyes light up. "Hey, you said you've worked on the prints, right? Would you work on mine?"

"Oh, wouldn't that be great! I'll ask Adam if I can be involved."

"Well, I'll insist you're a part of it."

I give him a sly grin as I sip my soda. "I love it when you throw your weight around."

"Yeah, I'm unrelenting. And just think, I can help. How fun would that be?"

"Loads…but you need to know what you're getting into by helping. We screen the colors on one at a time, so it can take weeks before the final edition is printed. I'm not sure you'll be able to stand me for that long."

"I guess I'll suffer for my art." He winks.

When it's time to tackle the pie, he waves his fork happily before sinking it into the crust.

"So, one thing I can't figure out, Ava, is why you don't have a boy-friend," he says while fork fighting me for the next bite of apple pie.

"A boyfriend?" I tip my head, and arch my brows.

He gives me a sideways-glance and fights off a smile. "You know, a guy who's your only one—who you're involved with. The guy you're madly in love with."

"Oh, one of those," I reply coyly. "I don't know."

"I mean, you're a lot of fun when you're not sending bitchy emails, and like you said once when you were taunting me…the guys are lined up for you." He grins widely.

"Okay, let's forget those emails. I promise not to send them any-more." I look down and lick the apple goo off my fork. "I guess I'm emotionally stunted. I seem to have lost the ability to give my heart away."

He looks down and pushes the plate away. "Do you get lonely?"

I shrug. "Do I seem lonely? I have more than enough going on to keep me happily occupied."

"What about sex?" He looks into my eyes with an expression that is a little *too* curious.

"Ah, that's what you're digging at! You want to know if I have secret lovers at my beck and call."

He raises his eyebrows and waits.

"I'll never tell, Mr. Caswell. I'll never tell." I can't believe I'm being such a tease. But just because I know too much about my new BFF's sex life doesn't mean he has to know about mine. Besides, it's a lot less dynamic than his…unless you count Jonathan's flirting.

"What about you, Max?" I quickly turn the tables. "You told me you weren't into relationships. Do you think you'll ever change your mind, or are you going to continue down the swinging-single path?"

"I don't know. I guess time will tell," he answers cryptically.

As we get in the car to head home, I feel sad that our day together is coming to an end. When we're away from all the bullshit, Max and I really have fun together.

He's quiet as he drives, and I wonder if he's thinking the same thing.

I pick up his camera case from the floor, ask if I can check it out, and he nods. I zip it open, carefully remove it, and check out all the dials and modes. "This is a great camera," I say as I look through the lens. "Where'd you get it?"

"Samy's Camera. Why?"

"Oh, just missing my camera that was stolen in the robbery." I can't hide the sadness in my voice as I switch the camera to the view setting. "I'm trying to save up money to buy a new one. Do you mind if I look at what you shot today?"

He hesitates for a second and looks uncomfortable, and I almost retract the question, but then he quietly says, "Okay."

I start clicking through the images. He's shot a lot more than I would've guessed—not just the outside of the stores and the art we found, but candids of people shopping and close-ups of stacks of hats and toys.

"Do you always shoot this much?" I ask.

"Yeah, that's how I like to work. It's so easy to delete images after the fact, and I don't want to miss something in the moment."

As he's talking, I begin to realize something. There are pictures of me...not just the ones I am aware of like when I paid for the paintings, but all kinds of shots, close-ups and long shots that he must've taken when we were on our own looking for things.

As I flip back and forth through the images, my heart speeds up because there's something so intimate about what he's done here. In one close-up of my face, I'm looking up and biting my lip. The illumination from the window brushes across my face from light to shadow, and I look...pretty. Is this how he sees me?

Why did he shoot all these pictures of me? Does it mean anything or am I letting my imagination get the better of me? I shut the camera off and quietly put it back in the case.

"Will you give me an advance preview of your paintings from this series when they're done?"

He smiles and nods, watching me closely, but I don't give anything away.

When we pull up to my house there isn't any parking on the street, so he double parks while I unbuckle my seatbelt.

"Thanks, Max. I had a really great time." I lean over and hug him. We both hold the hug a little longer than is necessary...I suppose because we don't want the day to end. I pull away and open the door.

"Wait, Ava." He reaches down for his camera case, takes out the camera and removes the tiny flash card. After he puts the card in his shirt pocket and puts another flash card in the camera, he hands the case and camera to me.

My mouth drops open. "What, Max?"

He smiles at me warmly. "I want you to have it. I'll give you the manual and charging cord next time I see you."

"But, it's your camera," I say with a gasp.

"Now, it's yours. I want you to have it. Let's not fight about it."

I press my lips tightly together as I fight off my tears.

"Besides, I have to go to Samy's next week, so I'll just get another one then. I was already thinking about upgrading to the newer model, so it all works out."

"But, this is an expensive camera."

"Yeah, yeah, yeah. Here's the deal…how about next week you take me out to Huntington Gardens in Pasadena? It's great in the spring and I haven't been there in a long time. So, bring your camera, I'll bring my new camera and we'll take some shots. Deal?"

I sit for a moment, holding the camera case tucked into me like a running back holds a freshly-caught football. This is not a fair trade. It's almost too much, his being so nice to me. This side of him is too wonderful, and it takes my breath away. I fight back a wave of emotion.

I take a deep breath and calm myself. "Thank you, Max…thank you so much."

"You're welcome."

I open the door and, as I step out, I turn to him once more.

"You know, if you keep being this nice, it's going to be hard to get rid of me."

"I'm counting on that," he says quietly with a smile.

I sigh as I shut the door and watch him drive away until his truck is a tiny dot on the horizon.

Chapter Fifteen / Hello Kitty

Life is about using the whole box of crayons.
~ RuPaul

"Well, Ava, your influence knows no bounds." Adam announces at Monday morning's meeting.

"Influence?" I ask, startled.

"Yes. Dylan called me this morning about printing an edition for Max Caswell. It may be the first in a series."

More projects for the studio. "That's good news, right?"

"Absolutely! We want to develop a reputation of printing younger artists as well as the established artists we built our reputation on. This is very good news."

"So, what does this have to do with Ava?" Sean asks warily.

"Well, Caswell will do the project with us only if Ava's involved in the printing," Adam explains.

Sean looks irritated. He takes it as a personal affront.

"And…Caswell wants to be present during some of the printing. He may explore doing some remarques and manipulation on the prints," Adam adds.

"Oh, Ava! Looks like you have a not-so-secret admirer!" Brian exclaims.

I make a face at Brian and try to deflect the assumptions. "No, we were just talking about serigraphy the other day, and I spoke very highly of the studio. He may've just assumed I'd be involved with the printing. I can tell him it isn't necessary."

"When did you have this talk?" Sean asks.

Adam ignores him and addresses me. "No, I want you to be there with Sean. If it makes Max more comfortable having you there, it only makes sense to do that. You usually help Sean anyway on the more complicated print runs. I have the original in my office, and I estimate it's easily thirty colors."

Adam looks at Sean. "I told Dylan, with our schedule, it would take you at least a week to do the color separations, but that we'd probably start printing next week. So, give me an update after you've analyzed it."

Sean leans back defeated, but this won't be the last time I'll hear his opinion on this situation. I can only imagine his mood when we start the actual run with Max in the studio. *Fireworks, anyone?* I dread the idea of it, but hold onto the hope that it won't be as bad as I'm imagining.

When the meeting ends, I help Brian hang three of Jess's newest paintings. One of them is a huge canvas of Ba-roque Beat performing in Times Square, and it's a riot of hot colors: flaming oranges, sultry reds and electric yellows. I'm thrilled, for as I study the crowd in the background, I realize she's included all of us dancing that night in New York. We're now immortalized in Jess's painting.

I'm glad we gave her new work the prime spot in the gallery on the pristine white wall you face as soon as you step inside. I also like this location because, at night, the art is lit and visible through the floor-to-ceiling glass walls facing Robertson Blvd.

That afternoon, as I'm heading to Starbucks to refuel myself with caffeine, my cell phone rings.

"Hi, Jonathan. How was your trip?"

"Hello, Ava. It was good, thanks...very productive." He sounds happy. "Have you made progress on the book?"

"I've finished two more sections. Shall I email them to you?"

"Yes...Look, I have some news that you will undoubtedly find unsettling, but don't worry, we'll figure out a way to manage it."

My heart sinks. "Yes?"

"The museum in Barcelona called, and they want to move Max's show up to July. It seems that they had a dramatic confrontation with the artist from the originally-scheduled show for this time, and they banned him from the museum. Leave it to the Spaniards to be so dramatic."

My heart drops further. I am barely keeping up with the book demands as it is.

"This is completely unheard of in the museum world, but we can probably pull it off if we get the book to press in about four weeks. This will require putting your part of the project on an accelerated schedule. To accomplish this, I'm going to team you up with my best and brightest editor, Phoebe. She'll help you achieve what right now seems impossible."

I'm honestly too stunned to freak out. "So, you really think we can do this?" I ask, my voice steady and confident, betraying my significant degree of hesitancy.

"I know you can, Ava," he states firmly. Whether he actually means it, or is saying it to boost my confidence, the resulting message is clear—where there's a will, there's a way. We'll just have to get it done.

As I wait for his next directive, I hear someone speaking in the background. He pulls the phone away and replies, "Tell them I'll be right there. Sorry, Ava. Listen, I need to go, and I'm looking at my schedule for the next two weeks and it's completely crazy." He lowers his voice. "But I'd like to see you. There's an event at the Getty this Friday...if you're free, I thought you could join me."

"I'd like that," I reply, not exactly sure what I want, but he's caught me off guard. Attending an art opening at the Getty with Jonathan could be a tense situation. Because he's so well-known in the art world, I'll be under all kinds of scrutiny just being with him. It's the kind of attention I usually try to avoid. It's interesting that he doesn't seem worried.

"Good. Let's have dinner first and then head over. It's not formal or casual, but dressy works."

He's read my mind…since I am wondering what to wear. He's nothing if not thorough.

"Jacqueline, my assistant, will contact you about specifics. And Phoebe's flying back from Seattle as we speak, so she'll contact you first thing in the morning."

When we hang up, I push the new deadline out of my mind and distract myself, wondering if I'll finally hear about his dream on Friday.

Back at the gallery I hand Brian his blended mocha, and he reminds me that I'm coming with him to a charity event tonight. His boyfriend, Thomas, is one of the hosts for a fundraiser for the Pet Rescue Initiative.

"Damian's going to be there," he taunts me, unable to resist the impulse to set me up with the endless supply of metrosexuals he knows through his business dealings.

"I saw Damian at the nail salon getting a pedicure. Now I can't get the image out of my head. You're going to have to find someone a little more macho," I grumble.

Of course we're playing with each other. He gave up trying to set me up a long time ago.

"Okay, but I want sexy tonight—a short skirt and those Jimmy Choo heels I got you for your birthday."

"Ah, you'll make a diva out of me yet."

When he picks me up that evening, he lets out a low whistle as I playfully model for him. Riley's lent me her short black skirt with swirls of silver beading and it shows off my long legs. I matched it with a fitted black silk sweater and Brian's shoes. Well, the Jimmy Choo shoes Brian gave me. I suspect he'd secretly wear them if he could.

As we enter the charity event, I'm grinning from ear to ear. Sanrio's one of the major sponsors of the evening, and the party is a Hello Kitty wonderland. The first clue is the life-sized Hello Kitty as we walk through the entrance, and we stop to have our picture taken with her in all her furry glory. Inside, girls dressed in tiny tank dresses embellished with rhinestone Hello Kittys serve pink Kitty cosmo martinis.

We wander around taking it all in, and I'm immediately sorry I didn't bring Riley along.

Brian locates Thomas, and I'm thrilled to finally meet him. He's handsome and quite charming, and Brian glows as they stand together. We chat for a few minutes before Thomas graciously excuses himself for an interview, and I give Brian an enthusiastic "thumbs up."

We move into the next soundstage where there's a Japanese girl band playing. We walk to the far wall that's brightly lit and covered with different Hello Kitty paintings.

The mini-show is called *Hello Kitty the Muse: Twenty Artists Interpret the World's Most Famous Cat.* The artwork is fun and irreverent. One image of Hello Kitty as an angel is rendered entirely in glitter. Another that looks computer generated is of Hello Kitty in space, wearing an entire astronaut spacesuit complete with an oversized bubble helmet. My favorite is Hello Kitty the princess with her crown encrusted with real rhinestones and colored gems. I sorely wish I could buy it for Riley.

At the end of the evening, they hand us goody bags full of treats for humans and their little furry friends. There's a rhinestone Hello Kitty collar, a decorative tin of organic dog biscuits, and an adult-sized rhinestone T-shirt and embroidered coin purse. I save the T-shirt and coin purse for Riley and keep the box of gourmet chocolates shaped in kitty and puppy heads for myself.

Outside, we wait in a long line until the valet pulls up in Brian's Saab. He pushes a button and the sunroof opens, giving me a view of the silver crescent moon hanging in the sky.

"Wow, that was really something. I didn't expect the party to be so entertaining."

He nods. "Yeah, those charity events can be sooo boring, but Thomas really knows how to do things right."

"Well, he's impressive. You two look really happy." I smile warmly.

"You know, I thought I would never meet Mr. Right. When I'd finally given up on the idea and made peace with being alone, he fell right into my lap! I still can't believe it."

"You deserve someone terrific."

"What about you, Ava? You can't be single forever, even though you seem set on the idea. What about Maxfield Caswell? Do you have any interest in him?"

"Well, we're becoming good friends."

"Friends?" His smile turns down. "Does he have a girlfriend or something?"

"No, but he's not interested in me that way." Even I can hear how ridiculous that statement sounds. I decide to test Brian. If I can't figure out Max's platonic ways, maybe he can.

Brian's eyebrows shoot up. "Okay, let me get this straight…he's single, he's hot and he likes spending time with you, but he's not interested in you that way. I don't buy it. He must be into you, Ava."

"You're such a man. Things aren't always black or white. I know he likes me as a friend. I just don't think he wants me like that."

"Seriously? Oh please! Listen, Missy, must I remind you I have a bit more relationship experience than you? You're a dream girlfriend; you're gorgeous, sexy, smart, strong, fun and you have a huge heart. Those last two attributes are hard to find in this town in combination with the first five. Hell, if I were straight, I'd have you married and pregnant by now!"

I blush at his overstated compliments, and I giggle at the idea of Brian and me married. Now that would be a comedy.

"When was the last time Max was in a relationship?" he asks, as he turns onto Sunset Blvd.

"Evidently, years ago. I do know whatever happened messed him up."

"I see, and he knows you'd never be an art groupie, and you're serious about your work. He must respect you. And let's not forget… you're writing his book?"

"What about it?"

"It'd be risky to get involved in the middle of the project."

"Oh, you are full of excuses for Max. How about he doesn't feel the chemistry or the connection that I do? Maybe he's only attracted to art groupies. He's flirted, but I think that's all it is. He's never made the moves."

"Reason all you want, girlfriend, but I'm still not buying it. So Mr. Caswell may be taking his time…he may be working other things out, but take my word…he'll come around."

A cool breeze whips through the car and I shiver, so Brian flips on the heat.

"I overheard you mention to Katherine that you're going to the Getty opening Friday night. Are you going with Caswell?"

"No, actually I'm going with Jonathan Alistair," I reply casually.

"Alistair from *Art+trA*?"

"Yes, I've been working for him, writing the text for Max's book," I quickly add.

"Yeah…," he says with suspicion in his voice. "But that doesn't mean you go to fancy events like this together. Is he into you, Ava?"

I want to deny it, but it's hard to lie to Brian. "Well, let me just say he's attracted to me, so…yes, he's into me. I'm not sure how I feel about him, though. He's been so kind."

Brian lets out a low whistle. "Ah, what a tangled web you're weaving, darling. Isn't Jonathan a little old for you? Have you slept with him?"

"No." I look at Brian and consider what I want to say next. "But if I tell you something, will you promise to keep it a secret?"

"Sure."

"He's been rather suggestive." I swallow, hard. "And I mean in a very provocative way."

"Ohhhh, how hot!" Brian growls. "Did it turn you on? I mean are you at least attracted to him?"

"Well, he sure as hell surprised me, and I have to admit it turned me on. I don't know how to handle it, though, because as amazing as he's been, we're working together and he's my boss. Sleeping with him may not be a good idea." It's a relief to talk this through.

"Yeah, I can see how it complicates things. Of course this *is* L.A. and everyone sleeps with everyone. It's how business is done. Well, be careful, baby. Take your time until you know what's best for you."

As we pull up to my apartment, he says. "Too bad you can't combine Jonathan and his hot desire with Max, your friendship, and his stunning looks…then you'd really have the dream boyfriend."

"You've got that right," I say and sigh as I hug him good-night.

The next day is slower at the gallery, and I find myself thinking about Max too often for my own good. I wonder if he's purchased a new camera yet and if we're still going to Huntington Gardens this weekend. I'm curious if he's started working on the thrift shop paintings series. I can't wait to see what he does.

Will he be at the Getty event on Friday? If so, what'll he think when he sees me with Jonathan? And I keep wondering with dread, who he'll come with if he does go. My mind reels with the possibilities.

That evening, as I revise a section of the book, my computer tings with an email. It's from Max and titled *Ava Sunday*. I hold my breath as I double click on the message.

He's sent a high res image that slowly reveals itself starting at the top of my screen. *Is it my impatience, or is this taking forever?* I want to shake my laptop to get it to hurry it up.

It's a black and white photograph, and as it loads, the picture has a textured, hand painted look on the edge of the image. He must have manipulated the file. There are hints of color washed into the black and white. The top of a head starts to download and then a forehead with a wave of dark hair. I take a sharp breath…*it's me.*

Next come my eyes, large and bright, their corners crinkled happily. I didn't realize my lashes looked so full. Next comes my nose, but when I finally see my lips, I smile, remembering how my dad called me Rosebud when I pouted because of my lips. Max has caught me holding back a laugh as my hands delicately frame my face.

I can't remember why my hands are in this position, but I'm looking right at him, so this is a shot I must've been aware of. There's a flirty playfulness in my expression, and it reminds me how happy I felt.

When the bottom of the photo finally loads, there's something written underneath.

Beautiful Ava–A Perfect Sunday

I fall back on the couch, moaning. This guy's killing me. How can I stay friends without any benefits with a guy who does this? Surely he knows what he's doing. I email him.

> Subject: A Perfect Sunday
> Max,
> Thank you for my picture. You have such a talent for bringing out the best in me.
> Ava

He responds quickly.

> Yes, it was a perfect day.
> And without a doubt you bring out the best in me.
> I'm glad you like your picture. That's how I see you—beautiful, mysteriously textured and layered.
> Are we still on for Huntington Gardens on Saturday? Dylan wants to come and bring Riley. I'll pick you up at eleven. Don't forget to bring your camera.
> M

How should I respond to this unbelievably sweet email? I decide to be brief.

> I'll be ready.
> Until then,
> Ava

As I try to refocus on my work, I can't push this version of Max and the longing that he'd want to be my better half out of my mind. This Max is everything I want and, evidently, everything I can't have. The resulting agony has become part of me. It flavors the tone of my voice and sears the edge of each breath. I carry it close like a wounded animal I'm intent on saving.

Chapter Sixteen / Check Please

Man is not what he thinks he is, he is what he hides.
  ~André Malraux

My cell phone rings in the morning at eight sharp, and I study it warily, not recognizing the incoming number.

"Ava? Phoebe from *Art-trA*…Jonathan asked me to call," a woman says sharply.

"Yes, hi, Phoebe," I say as I stretch out my arms. "Jonathan explained the situation yesterday with the deadlines being moved up. He said you'd be working with me to get the project done."

"Yes, I've read what you've submitted so far, and we have a lot of work to do. Jonathan also said I need to work around your day job. I'm booked the next couple of nights. How about Saturday?"

*Uh oh…*I don't like her bitchy tone. "Ah, actually I'm busy Saturday, but I'm free Sunday."

She lets out an irritated huff. "Okay, Sunday. Why don't you come over here in the morning at ten, that way I can get in an early Pilates class before we meet. I'll email you the address."

"Okay, I look forward to it," I lie unabashedly.

Pilates early Sunday morning? Why would you do that when you could sleep in? She must be a case. This could be potentially hellish, but working with her is a means to an end, and I need to get this project done.

Laura is out of town for a film shoot and Jess is lonely, so I offer to bring dinner over and hang for a while. I stop at Chin Chins, Jess's favorite, and buy an assortment of Chinese food.

When I get there, she's working in her studio, so I step over to the burgundy velvet chaise not far from her easel. Like everything else in the studio, the chaise is splattered with paint, so I run my hand over it to make sure all the paint is dry before I stretch out.

I love the chaos of her studio. She has at least a hundred reference photographs haphazardly pinned up on the wall behind her desk and more than a dozen paintings at various stages of completion around the studio.

But that's just the beginning. To walk into Jess's studio is to enter a mad hatter's warehouse. There are numerous strands of paper lanterns crisscrossing the ceiling and a 1950s mannequin in the corner wearing an elaborate feather headdress and nothing else. There are garden gnomes, beach balls, empty birdcages and several pinball machines. A hammock hangs in the corner, suspended from the ceiling. In the opposite corner is a nine-foot-tall Bob's Big Boy statue someone must have kidnapped from the front of a restaurant. There's an antique rocking horse, a bobble-head collection, and strands of Mardi Gras beads draped on every surface.

For a long time, I was tempted to nominate Jess's studio for one of those home organization reality TV shows that clean out your house while publicly humiliating you. But eventually, I learned that the eclectic clutter inspires Jess, and far be it from me to slow down her prolific output. She did admit that Laura was a minimalist, and she'd break out in hives if she spent longer than a minute in Jess's studio.

I sit quietly and watch her work. She's adding detail to a small area of the canvas, and her focus is absolute.

Eventually, my attention wanders, and I notice new modular shelving on the far wall, already holding cans of brushes, jars of paints and a dizzying array of small props—everything from a human skull to a Peanuts metal lunchbox featuring Charlie Brown and Snoopy.

"Are those shelves new? I don't remember them."

"Uh-huh, Max helped me get those up today. They'd been lying in pieces on the floor for two weeks, and he's so good at that shit. Besides, he hates the crap all over my floor, so he had an agenda."

"Max?" I ask, amazed he would take the time to do that for Jess.

"He was being interviewed for a documentary at a studio on Melrose this morning, so we met for lunch and he came by and helped me."

"I'm surprised."

Jess laughs. "Oh, he's not always an asshole. Sometimes, he can be a real sweetheart. As a matter of fact, he was going to help me with some more stuff, but Dylan called and needed to meet with him right away about a new gallery show."

It occurs to me that Max is a lot busier than I even realized. "Does he always have a lot of meetings and interviews?"

"Frankly, I don't know how he has time to paint anymore. He's the "it" guy, so everyone wants a piece of him. He told me he ends up painting late into the night, so he hardly gets any sleep." She shakes her head and scowls. "That isn't good. It's really wearing him down. I was worried about him a couple of weeks ago. I thought he was losing it. But he seems better this week, so I don't know…maybe he's okay."

Jess stops painting, and as she cleans the brushes, I go inside to set out the food. Jess's kitchen is surprisingly streamlined, except for the backsplash above the counter, which she custom designed. It's a swirling mosaic of tiny pieces of broken tile and glass beads. It was Laura's trade-off for the pristine granite countertops. The entire house reflects a series of compromises between them, and they've made it all work.

As we dive into our vegetable fried rice with tofu, spring rolls, almond chicken and chow mein noodles, Jess excitedly tells me about their plans for a wedding. Max has generously offered the use of his house in Malibu, as long as they promise to keep the guest list under seventy-five. They plan to do the ceremony on the beach and the party at the house.

"Ava, I was serious before. Will you be my maid of honor?"

I give her a hug. "Of course! I'm so flattered you asked me."

"Well, you know you're the baby sister I always wanted. And you were supportive of Laura and me when our other friends didn't believe in us."

"And look at you now."

"I'm one lucky bitch. Oh…no prissy wedding showers! Okay?" She's beyond adamant. "A group of us can do a spa day or go drinking one night, but no idiotic shower."

"Understood." It's good to throw out tradition once in a while, and what better place than a lesbian wedding?

As I gather my things to head home, Jess asks me how it's going with Max's book.

"You know, he talked about you a lot at lunch today," she mentions casually.

"Hopefully nothing too awful."

"No, he seems to think you have a unique effect on him. He says he's happier when you're around. I don't know what that means exactly, but I'm glad to know he's spending time with someone who's a good influence, not those vapid women who suck the life out of him."

"Yeah, well, he still goes off on a tangent sometimes—saying I'm his savior or something—but for the most part, everything's easier between us now. Besides, I may not have a lot of free time to see him or anyone in the next few weeks. The book project's been moved up two months, and Sunday I'm working with Jonathan's prize editor to get things lined up. She's some bitchy broad named Phoebe. I don't think it's going to be fun."

"Phoebe…what's her last name?" Jess frowns.

"I don't know, but I think she's going to be tough to work with."

"Well, let me know after you meet. I used to know a whack job named Phoebe who worked in publishing, but she moved away."

The next night, my writers' group beats me up a little for not submitting a new story, but they ease up when they hear about my new deadline. Why do I still feel like a failure? Someday, I hope to learn how to give myself a break and not always be so critical of myself.

When I get home, I decide I need the comfort of my flannel PJs and a bowl of chocolate ice cream to lift my spirits before I get to work.

I've been staring at my laptop screen for at least ten minutes without a single thought or idea when my cell phone rings.

"Hey, Max."

"Ava, whatcha doing?"

"Thinking of you again." I pause for dramatic effect. "Seriously, I'm trying to work on your book, but I think I have writer's block."

"I'm that inspiring," he teases.

"Yes, surely this is your fault."

"Well, if it makes you feel any better, I'm going through the same thing tonight—artist's block. I've been looking at this canvas for over an hour and haven't felt inspired to commit brush to paint to canvas yet." He clears his throat. "I know, why don't you paint this canvas, and I'll write!"

I laugh. "That'd be rich. Stick figures are as good as my drawing skills get."

"Don't knock that idea. Remember Keith Haring's work? He was famous for painting those outlines of little men."

"And when you take over my writing project, what will you say about this artist I'm writing about? He's quite the handful, you know." I whistle softly.

"Oh, who is he?" he asks, feigning innocence.

"Maxfield Caswell."

"*The* Maxfield Caswell?" He says with a dramatic flourish.

"The one and only."

"Oh that's easy…he's so fucking brilliant. That's really all you need to say."

I giggle. "Max Caswell is so fucking brilliant. The end."

"That works."

"Wow, I should've talked to you earlier. I could've been done weeks ago. Instead, I have to spend my Sunday with some bitch editor who wants to slice and dice up my writing."

"Do you want me to call Jonathan and tell him to back off?" His tone gets darker and he sounds hot, offering to come to my defense.

"No!" I insist, despite his hotness. "Besides, now with this new deadline, I'm probably going to need her help."

"Okay, now that we've got your work figured out, do you have any ideas for my painting?"

"How about a portrait of Jess in her crazy studio?"

"No, I'm not painting Jess…it would make her big head swell even bigger. Hmm, I know…who was that artist that painted the naked girls and had them roll around on his raw canvas?"

I have a wicked smile, sensing what's coming. "Oh yeah, I can't remember his name either."

"Well, you could come over and we could do that."

"Watch it, buster." I'm playfully stern. "Besides, I'm not allowed in your studio, remember?"

"Oh, I'd make an exception for that," he says with a mock serious tone.

"Hey, wasn't this supposed to be *my* painting? I think you should be the one naked and rolling around on my—what did you call it—*raw* canvas?"

"We could do it together."

I almost choke. "Ahh, you're getting me all hot and bothered. I'm going to need a cold shower when you're done."

"Well, if you had a boyfriend, you wouldn't need a cold shower."

"Am I hearing correctly? Is Maxfield Caswell giving *me* relationship advice?" But before he can respond, I quickly change the subject. "By the way, I was at Jess's yesterday and saw the shelves you put up for her. That was very sweet of you. She also told me that you're letting her and Laura hold their wedding at your house."

"Yeah, well I'm not always an asshole."

"Funny, that's exactly what Jess said."

"Besides, I can't stand seeing that crazy crap all over her studio floor. I have no idea how she gets anything done in there."

"Yeah, it's crazy all right. Do you know she asked me to be her maid of honor for the wedding?"

"Is she going to make you wear one of those ugly synthetic bridesmaid dresses?" He knows Jess better than that, but he's being provocative.

"Hopefully hoop skirts will be involved."

We laugh together and, as the minutes pass, our conversation rambles. I close my laptop, turn down my lights and stretch out on my bed. My cell phone battery gives me a warning, and I look over at my clock. We've been talking for almost two hours. I yawn and burrow further into my pillows.

"Hey, sleepyhead, it sounds like it's your bedtime."

"I'll have you know that I got in bed over an hour ago. But I'm pretty tired…so I'll let you get back to your painting."

"Okay, Ava, sleep tight."

There's a long pause as if neither of us wants to hang up.

"Good-night, Max," I whisper, my eyes already half closed. "It was really fun talking to you tonight."

"Hmm," he hums. "Good-night, angel."

As my eyes fall shut, a contented feeling descends over me. I'm lured to a peaceful dreamland void of art groupies and bitchy editors…just Max, me, and all the warm feelings nestled between us.

The next morning, I wake up in a really good mood. The weather's great, unusually warm for April. It'll be nice for our outing to the Huntington Gardens tomorrow. I have to admit, my long conversation last night with Max left me uninspired about seeing Jonathan tonight, but while I take my morning shower, I still plan what I'm going to wear this evening.

That evening, when I pull up to Spago, Wolfgang Puck's flagship restaurant in Beverly Hills, the attendant drives Jonathan's car away. He waits as I finish up with the valet. I can tell he's appraising me, his gaze moving over me from head-to-toe as I approach. As I step up to him, he nods and his face lights up with a smile. I feel a flush work its way up from the top of my breasts, trailing along my neck and up to my cheeks.

"You look lovely, Ava," he murmurs. He rests his hand on my shoulder and kisses me on each cheek. When we move inside, the host immediately takes us to a table. There's a floor-to-ceiling glass wall where you can watch the executive chef and team perform their magic in the kitchen.

We make small talk, and after reviewing the menu, Jonathan orders a chilled bottle of Sauvignon Blanc. He orders salmon, while I choose scallops, and we agree to share an endive and apple salad to start. I have to admit, his confidence and command are very sexy.

He notices me watching him and peers over his tortoise-shell glasses. "A penny for your thoughts, Ms. Jacobs."

"Do you eat here frequently? I get the sense that everyone knows you."

"Yes, it's one of my favorites." He tucks some loose strands of my hair behind my ear and gently caresses my earlobe before resting his hand on the table.

A shiver runs down my back.

"I was really looking forward to seeing you again," he says quietly, his eyes a darker blue in the candlelight. "Perhaps, after dinner, I'll tell you about my dream."

The Sauvignon Blanc flows freely, and I drink, nervous for what the rest of the evening holds. I think I'm especially unsettled because I'm not sure what my boundaries are with Jonathan. I'm working with him on an important project, and this ongoing flirtation leaves me confused.

Being attracted to someone who holds such possibilities for my career is complicated. What if I sleep with him? Is that wrong? Will it be contrary to everything I've believed about how relationships play out while being an independent woman?

The way I feel about Max in contrast to Jonathan only confuses me more. Max just wants to be my bestie, my BFF, despite his flirtatious joking, and that only leaves me wanting him more.

Jonathan brings up Max's book, mentioning that he's pleased with the opinions section I just finished.

I admit that it was challenging to put together what twenty different artists, critics, curators and collectors wrote about Max and his work, but it was worth the effort. Each voice is different and intriguing and adds a lot to the weight of the book.

Over the course of the dinner, Jonathan progressively loosens up until he's more relaxed than I've ever seen him. He even orders a ginger crème brûlée for dessert, which I can safely assume isn't part of his normal regimen.

As we wait for our coffee, he slides his arm over my shoulder and pulls me closer. "Have you thought about me since our last meeting?"

I blush as I finger the stem of my wine glass and give him a shy smile.

"Because, believe me, Ava, I've thought about you." His smile is a mix of satisfaction and promise of what's to come.

"Good thoughts?"

"Very good. The kind that keep me up at night."

I feel my heart speed up when I note the fire in his eyes.

"What do you think? Remember what we talked about outside Chaya's? Do you still want to hear about my dream?"

In my wine-soaked haze, I nod, smiling. I *think* I want to hear it.

There's a long pause as he swirls the wine in his glass and takes a long sip. "So, picture my office." He looks at my bottom lip as I bite it and takes a deep breath before looking into my eyes.

I nod.

"In my dream, it's evening. I approach my office and the room is dimly lit. When I step inside, I see you sitting back on the leather couch, waiting."

"Waiting?"

He nods. "For me." He narrows his eyes as he drags his tongue across his lips. "Your legs are slightly parted, and you have a short skirt on which shows off your tantalizing legs, and I can't wait to run my hands up and down the soft skin of your thighs. I sit across from you, and you spread your legs very slowly until they're open for me.

I blink several times, trying to keep my mouth from falling open. It's apparent this dream's definitely not PG rated.

"You have no panties on and it takes every bit of restraint not to rush things. I imagine getting up, slowly stepping up to where you sit, then sinking to my knees and pushing your skirt up."

Whoa. I shift in the booth, trying to relieve the lust pulsing through me. My face is on fire from his graphic description, and I can only imagine what's coming next.

"As I approach you, you look at me with a sultry gaze and then tip your head back. Your nipples strain against your sheer blouse as you take several long slow breaths."

"Oh, Jonathan," I whisper, as an image of him sinking to his knees before me floods my imagination.

"So tell me, Ava, would you have let me pleasure you?"

I'm stunned, my heart pounding.

He looks so pleased when I nod.

"You and me on my couch for hours on end with the city lights before us, and everyone else gone. Think of the possibilities."

A faint moan escapes my trembling lips.

"Shall I go on?"

I nod, while pressing my thighs together, desperately craving any form of friction.

And to my great shock, he takes my hand and places it on the front of his slacks. I feel his cock swelling under my fingers. I nervously look around the restaurant but the heavy tablecloth covers everything, and the way our booth's situated, there's no way anyone can see what we're doing unless they perched under our table.

"Oh, yes. I like your hand on me," he whispers, gasping as he thrusts his hips a little forward.

He's fully erect now, and when I cup my fingers around him, his cock throbs in my grip.

He swallows hard and clears his throat. "Oh, the things I want to do to you, Ava." He reaches under the table, places his hand on my bare knee and ever so slowly traces his fingertips up my inner thighs, edging up the skirt of my dress as his hand slides higher.

"*Ahh*...your skin is so soft," he says quietly. The tips of his fingers skim across the silk of my panties and I can't help but shift my hips towards his touch. His features are remarkably calm, despite the build-ing sexual tension. I press my fingers over the length of him again, teasing and taunting.

Oh my God! We're in freaking Spago…his hand is between my legs and I'm grabbing his cock.

I down the rest of my Sauvignon in two gulps while he moves my hand slowly down his shaft. At this point, I'm feeling like a femme fatale. Waiters slide by and busboys remove extra plates from nearby tables while my hand grips his impressive erection.

"So, Ava." He leans back further into the booth. "Are you pleased to know how much you excite me?"

"Yes," I whisper, as with each stroke of his fingers, I fight the urge to spread my legs even further open.

Oh, Jesus, his cock is even harder now, and my thighs are quivering for the want of his body on top of mine…the need to feel him inside of me. I scan the dining room. *Surely someone in this friggin' restaurant knows what's going on. People can't be so distracted by their foie gras and New York steak that they don't notice a man a mere zipper away from a hand job under the Spago tablecloth?*

I look over and see the color rising across his cheeks, but otherwise he looks remarkably composed while his cock bucks and pulses in my grip. He finally presses his face into my hair and whispers hotly in my ear, "I desperately want to make love to you right now, Ava."

The wait staff removes the dessert dishes and startles us out of our bubble. Despite my embarrassment, I try ridiculously to main-tain enough composure to make up for Jonathan, who's increasingly distracted.

I slowly let go of him and slide my hand back to my lap. He finally pulls his face away from my hair and reaches over for his water glass, downing half of it in several swallows. I feel his hand move off my thigh onto his, and hear the rustling under the table as he adjusts him-self and takes a deep breath.

I'm sure Wolfgang would be pleased to know we found the evening so exciting, I think with wide eyes.

I wish the wine buzz wasn't fading because I feel awkward right about now. But when I glance over, he looks completely happy and gives me a big sexy smile.

He runs his fingers lightly over my hand resting on the table and summons the waiter.

"Check, please."

Chapter Seventeen / My Shiny Penny

The real lover is the man who can thrill you by kissing your forehead.
    ~Marilyn Monroe

Okey dokey, I think as I compose myself in the restroom. I'm amazed and a little shaken from so much sexual buildup without release. For such a sophisticated guy, Jonathan is rather shocking, and I'm unnerved that his dream got me so worked up.

When the valets bring our cars forward, Jonathan instructs me to follow him, even though I know my way to the Getty. By the time we pull up to the museum, there's already a good crowd gathering at the entrance. Not surprisingly, it's a sophisticated group in elegant attire… at least by L.A.'s standards. Before we reach the entrance, Jonathan pulls me aside.

"I want you to know, Ava, that I'm not a selfish man."

I look up, startled. What's he suggesting?

"During the entire drive here, I kept thinking about how you indulge me with your charm and beauty."

I give him a shy smile. "You're too flattering."

"I don't think so. You affect me like no other." He strokes my cheek. "You're so generous with me, and I want to make you feel wonderful in all the ways you deserve."

I'm overwhelmed and confused by my attraction for him and the expression in his eyes flusters me. The intensity's unnerving, especially since he understands how to get to me.

His hands slide along my hips, and I look down and wonder if I should talk to him about slowing things down. But as a large group bustles past, I decide to wait for a moment when I can think clearly without distractions.

Tonight's the Spring Event fundraiser for the Getty Museum and the party's set up in the Sculpture Garden where the latest acquisition, a large Alexander Calder, is featured. The primary-colored shapes of the Calder defy their actual weight as they shift and rotate in the breeze.

Everywhere we turn, Jonathan knows someone, and he keeps me by his side, introducing me before engaging in various conversations. I like watching him in this setting. He's so comfortable in his skin, and people respect him, which says a lot in this business. The crowd is on the older side, but I suppose that makes sense; it's an expensive fund-raiser to attend.

There's an open bar, but I opt for a glass of mineral water, figuring I should take a little break from the drinking. I want a clear head when surrounded by all these art world intellects. Jonathan introduces me to the Sturridges, who are longtime major patrons of the museum, and they have an animated conversation about the recent *Renaissance Masters* show.

After a few minutes, my attention wanes, and I start watching other people's interactions. To my right is a striking, petite Italian woman with very short salt-and-pepper hair, talking with a tall, older man in a suit. She's very expressive as she talks and, judging from the grin on his face, he's delighted by whatever she's saying.

Another man joins them and hands each of them a glass of wine. As he turns sideways, I realize it's Max and my heart jumps. He's so serious as he speaks. He doesn't smile, and he uses his hands to gesture in a more careful manner than he usually does.

At one point, he pulls a piece of paper out of his pocket and shows it to the woman. She takes out a stylish pair of glasses and reads what he's pointing to. She smiles at Max, shakes her head, and puts her glasses in her bag.

As they continue to talk, another couple joins them, shifting the position of their group. Max is facing in my direction and a bit of panic sweeps over me. Do I want him to see me right now? But as soon as the question enters my head, his eyes lock with mine, and it feels like we're the only two people on this vast terrace of the Sculpture Garden.

A second later, Jonathan puts his arm around my waist and pulls me closer, and I'm temporarily distracted. When I look back, Max is staring at Jonathan. Even at a distance, I can see his jaw tense and the dark brooding in his eyes. He looks angry as his gaze travels between Jonathan and me before refocusing on his conversation with the group.

I have a sinking feeling, although there's no reason for Max to have an issue with my being here with Jonathan. He might not like it, but he hasn't given me a good reason not to be with Jonathan. Max and I are nothing more than friends, after all. Regardless, I have an overwhelming desire to clear my head, so I lean into Jonathan and excuse myself.

I weave my way through the crowd and away from Max and his group. As I come to the edge of the gathering, I head for a stone bench facing the railing with a view of the gardens below. I sit and let out a sigh, grateful for the solitude. I take a deep breath. The air's finally cooled and feels refreshing as it fills my lungs.

Since it's evening, the garden is artificially lit and the effect is eerie. It feels unnatural to see a garden lit up at night. I reflect on how different my life has been since the New York trip. A month ago, I didn't even know Max or Jonathan; I wouldn't have been writing an important book soon-to-be published or attending such an upscale prestigious party.

This month's been exhilarating, yet I also feel completely out of control.

Jonathan dazzles me, and I'm not acting or thinking clearly. Max has stolen my heart and left me with a deeply-rooted longing for something that may never be within my reach.

So, at a time when I should be enjoying the new excitement in my life, I'm as splintered and fragmented as a cubist painting.

I recall, with a new sober clarity, the scene in the restaurant, and shock hits me once more. Who was that woman lustily feeling up a man she works for in one of L.A.'s most prestigious restaurants?

What in the hell is wrong with me? I double over and cradle my face in my hands, while resting my elbows on my knees, and let the disbelief wash over me. I'm so overcome with the feeling that I don't even look up when I hear footsteps behind me.

A moment later, someone settles next to me on the bench. I part my fingers and turn my head to peek.

Max.

He's studying the garden.

I resume my original position for a moment, but then take a deep breath and bravely sit back up.

"Hey," I say quietly.

"Hey, Ava," he responds, still watching the view.

We both sit silently for at least a minute.

"So, did you come with Jonathan tonight?"

"Well, we drove separately…but yeah, I guess you could say I came with him."

"I see." He nods.

But what does he see, I wonder? "Who did you come with?"

"No one. The Matthews invited me, but the only reason I came is because I knew Lisa Forrester from MOMA was going to be here, and it was a good chance to talk to her again. She's the curator for the show you got me into."

I smile.

"Jonathan seems quite taken with you."

"You sound surprised."

"No, I'm not surprised that he's attracted to you…I'm surprised you're responding to it."

I remain quiet, intently looking at the garden.

"I'm going to leave soon," he says, more to himself than to me. "This isn't really my crowd."

I wonder who his crowd is these days.

"Hey, let's go get something to eat."

Surprised that he's willing to leave already, I glance at him. "I've already had dinner."

"Where'd Jonathan take you?"

"Spago."

"Of course he did. Well, you could keep me company. I'd really like that. Hey, have you ever been to The Apple Pan?"

I shake my head.

"It's the anti-Spago—best burgers in town. You have to stand behind people as they're eating and grab their stool as soon as they get up to leave."

I give him a wide-eyed stare. "As fun as that sounds, I can't just leave, Max. Jonathan doesn't even know where I am right now."

"I'll take care of that. Come on." He takes my hand and pulls me toward the party, only letting go when I finally start following willingly. We pass a couple of women in party dresses heading toward the bar. As we get closer, he whispers conspiratorially, "Tell him you don't feel well or something that he can't argue with. Girls are good at that."

"You're trying to get me in trouble," I chide him.

"Of course I am. I know…tell him you have bad cramps." He snickers, clearly pleased with himself. "That always freaks guys out. Besides, you know you'll have more fun with me than these rich art snobs."

I shake my head. I can't believe I'm even considering this. It's so rude to do that to Jonathan, even if he's busy working the event.

"Look, let me introduce you to Lisa. I'll say hello to Jonathan and then you can drop the cramps bomb and make your escape. Then I'll sneak out after you."

"You've got this all figured out. What if I want to stay? Maybe I'm having a great time and don't want to leave."

"Yeah, that's why you were sitting on that bench with your face in your hands."

I glare, and as we weave among the groups of people, I struggle to figure out what I really want to do. I'm annoyed that Max can persuade me so easily, but in my heart of hearts, I'd much rather have another L.A. adventure with him. I'm an anxious little moth drawn to his flame.

We're almost back to where I left Jonathan when Mrs. Matthews and her husband catch my eye. We stop and Stella smiles at Max and then at me.

"Ava, how lovely to see you here. Let me introduce you to my husband, Stephan."

I extend my hand and smile. "Mr. Matthews, it's such a pleasure to meet you."

"Ava, please call me Stephan. I'm sure Max told you the good news about being included in the MOMA show." Mr. Matthews is an older gentleman with a sturdy build, and he pulls off that handsome bald look.

"Oh, he did, and I couldn't be happier. Thank you so much to both of you for supporting Max's work."

"Yes," Max says, sliding his arm around my waist. "And thank you, Ava, for being my advocate."

"That she certainly is!" Stella nods with a warm smile.

We excuse ourselves and join Jonathan.

"Ava, I was starting to worry about you," he says as he raises his eyebrows and sums up Max. He looks extremely aggravated.

I decide to alter the details about my conversation with Max, hoping to defuse a conflict.

"Sorry, I ran into Max and we started talking about the book."

"Well, don't worry, Max. It's coming along just fine," Jonathan comments dryly. "I'm really enjoying working with Ava on it."

"As am I," Max quips. "As a matter of fact, we're spending the day together tomorrow, but you know what, Ava? Let's just make it a fun day and not do any work at all."

I give him a dirty look. Why's he trying to provoke Jonathan? Am I just the door prize for some stupid pissing match?

"I don't know, Max…I'm really not feeling well right now. I may have to cancel tomorrow."

Max gives me a stern look. I guess our playacting isn't going the way he planned.

Jonathan moves closer. "You aren't well?"

"No, I'm sorry to say, but I'm having really bad cramps. You know... it's a girl thing. I may have to leave in a minute," I whisper.

His color drains as he nods, accepting my ailment without question. It's rather ironic that he looks extremely squeamish over my "female problems." Max called that right.

Jonathan suddenly takes my elbow. "Okay, but before you go there's someone very important here I'd like you to meet. Excuse us, Max." A couple moves toward us and smiles at Jonathan.

Max turns, and instead of walking away, he smiles at the woman and her companion as well. Jonathan tenses and looks really pissed.

"Lisa," Jonathan steps forward and kisses her on both cheeks. "You're a long way from home."

"Jonathan!" They embrace.

Jonathan shakes her companion's hand. "Lewis, so good to see you."

Jonathan turns to me. "Ava, please let me introduce you to my good friends, Lisa Forrester, who's a curator at MOMA, and noted artist, Lewis Sierra."

They both shake my hand warmly.

Lisa turns to Max. "Max, this must be the Ava you told me about earlier."

He nods and looks delighted.

What exactly did he tell them about me?

Jonathan's eyes narrow and his lips press tightly together. He's really steaming now. I would actually enjoy this if I weren't the tennis ball in this grudge match.

"To what do we owe this honor? Did you come out just for the show?" Jonathan asks, trying to gain control again.

"My best friend from college is celebrating a big birthday, so we came out for that and decided to come to this party too," Lisa says.

"Business and pleasure," Lewis says with a smile. His voice is a deep baritone.

We continue to talk for several minutes, until I finally decide to excuse myself and say my good-byes to everyone. Jonathan looks concerned and asks if he can at least walk me to my car, but I insist he stay with Lisa and Lewis. He reluctantly agrees.

Max watches me walk away, a devilish smile on his face.

I'm almost to my car when Max runs up behind me. "I'm just over here." He points to his Porsche parked nearby. "So, follow me out. It's about ten minutes from here."

After we park behind The Apple Pan, Max holds open the swinging screen door and we step into a single room with beadboard wainscoting topped with plaid wallpaper and grumpy old waiters wearing white wedge paper hats and standing behind a U-shaped counter. Luckily, there are several empty stools due to the late hour, and Max and I sit right down and order. Our sodas are served in cups that are really white paper cones perched in red plastic holders. This place is several steps back in time and I love it.

Max looks so happy as he eats his burger and I smile. The hickory sauce drips all over his chin as he laughs and tells me sordid stories about some of the patrons from the party. He shares some of his fries with me and I let him eat most of my apple pie. I swing my legs under the stool and feel the most carefree I've felt in days. We're in our own bubble, unaware of anyone else around us.

When we're done, Max pays and then walks me to my car. "Thanks for coming, Ava. Maybe you should be thanking me. I *did* save you from a boring evening with that old man."

I narrow my eyes at him. "I wouldn't say he's boring." *If he only knew,* I think. "But I did have fun with you tonight."

"Oh, admit it, girl," he teases as he grabs the lapels of my jacket. "I'm much more fun than he could ever be. You're just trying to make me wild with jealousy."

"Really?" I push him back as he pulls me forward laughing. "And is it working?"

"Mmm." He pulls me into a tight hug and groans. The feeling of his arms wrapped around me is almost too good and leaves me wanting more.

"And it's just a matter of hours until you see me again," I say as we pull apart.

"Yes, our Huntington Gardens outing." He smiles as he tucks me into my car. "Until then, Ava."

I start out of the parking lot, and when I glance back in my rear view mirror, he's watching me with a smile on his face.

The next morning I try to sleep in, but Riley is up early, singing and bopping around the house as she prepares for our outing.

She offered to pack a picnic, and when I go into the kitchen for coffee, I shudder. Our kitchen looks like a warzone with condiments, open packages of bread, cut up fruit and vegetables all over the counters.

"Riley, this is enough food to feed a small army. Besides, I thought you said that they don't let you picnic at Huntington Gardens."

"I know, but there's a park nearby. I figured we'd do the picnic there when we're done seeing Huntington." She slips a bottle of wine and corkscrew into the basket, along with plastic cups.

After I help her pull things together, I get ready. I pay special attention to rubbing lemon body butter all over my skin before slipping on a flowing skirt, fitted top and sandals. I pull out the camera Max gave me and put it in my bag.

Right before Dylan arrives, Max calls to tell us he will be a little late. They've shut down part of Pacific Coast Highway due to a rockslide, and the traffic's backed up. Natural disasters and the resulting traffic delays are one of the trade-offs for living in the paradise of Malibu.

When Max finally arrives, we get the food together, pile in the car and head toward Pasadena. It's already past noon, and Dylan announces that he's starving.

"Change in plans, kids. We need to feed my man…picnic first!" Riley announces.

Max carries the large blanket and Dylan the basket while we wander through the park until we find a secluded spot under a huge old oak tree. After Riley serves up the food, Max inconspicuously opens the wine and pours us all full glasses. Alcohol isn't allowed in public parks so we have to be careful, but it's not like we're a bunch of rowdy teenagers getting drunk at midnight.

At first it's a little awkward with each of us perched on the blanket holding our paper plates, but as the wine relaxes us and the jokes start flowing, it becomes an idyllic day in the country, similar to a scene from my beloved Jane Austen novels.

At one point, Riley leans back against the tree and Dylan rests his head in her lap. She gently runs her fingers through his hair, and they look like a picture-postcard of love. I pull out my camera and start taking shots.

Max smiles and pulls out his new camera and starts taking pictures of me. Then I take pictures of him taking pictures of me until we start laughing and fall down on the blanket.

We finally gather up our stuff and head over to Huntington. We're still a little giddy from the wine, so Riley skips through the Desert Garden with Dylan stalking her while Max and I take close up shots of the cacti and uniquely-shaped succulents.

We wind our way around the paths, past the lily ponds and jungle pavilion, until we end up in the Japanese Garden with its perfectly groomed gravel beds and bonsai trees. While Max and I sit for a minute to review some of the pictures we've taken, Dylan and Riley wander off. When I finally look up, I spot them in the distance, kissing under a canopy of wisteria.

Max follows my gaze and shakes his head. "Dylan's got it bad and that ain't good."

It catches me off guard. "What's not good about it? They're crazy about each other."

"I've known Dylan a long time. He has a history of falling hard and fast."

"How did you meet him?"

"We actually met in high school when we both took art classes on Saturdays at Art Center in Pasadena."

"Dylan wanted to be an artist?" I ask, surprised.

"Yes, he did. He was quite good too. But his parents always felt that the life of an artist wasn't good enough for their son. They wore him down until he finally gave up the idea. They funded his galleries to make him a businessman when he refused to go to law school. I think he gave up too easily, but maybe his passion for it wasn't great enough."

I shake my head. "That's too bad. I don't think there is anything more honorable than being an artist. What do his parents do, anyway? Riley said they're wealthy."

"Yeah, his dad is a partner in the oldest law firm in Pasadena. The family is old San Marino blue blood. His grandfather owned a lot of property there."

"Well, that explains why Riley was so nervous to meet them."

"Yes, I'm sure they assume she's after his money. Dylan's last relationship ended over a year ago, and he's been lonely. I've had a feeling that, the next girlfriend he meets, he'll marry." He shakes his head.

"What? You don't approve of Riley? Do *you* think she's after his money?"

He shrugs and doesn't reply.

"You know she has a great job and a high salary. It's not like her family is poor or anything—I think they'd be considered upper middle-class." My temper flares.

He frowns. "I don't know, maybe. I've a hard time trusting anyone when it comes to relationships. It seems like there's always an agenda."

I stare at him, trying to contain my surprise and disappointment.

He continues, "I've tried to talk him into slowing down, not moving so fast with Riley, but he clearly isn't listening. I just hope that she's genuine."

I've heard enough. My blood boils.

"Wait just a minute. How can you question if she's genuine? Riley's a good person. She's stood by me through thick and thin without ever wavering. Furthermore, she's crazy about Dylan. If she knew that you didn't believe in their relationship...she'd be devastated."

He leans back, seemingly shocked by my passionate defense of Riley.

"Well, sorry I offended you. I'm just telling you how I feel."

"Please tell me you aren't going to pull a Darcy and try to convince Dylan not to be with her. It'd kill her." I feel like hitting him.

"Pull a Darcy?"

"Yes, you know, Jane Austen…*Pride and Prejudice*? Darcy doesn't trust Jane's affections for his best friend Bingley, and he breaks them up. It isn't until the end of the story that he realizes he's made a huge mistake, and he encourages them to reunite and they get married."

He looks at me like I've lost my mind. "You've been reading too many of those girly stories. They're messing with your head."

"I'm serious, Max…don't interfere. You may not believe in love, but I do. And I think they have a chance to share something wonderful together. Don't ruin it for them."

He tips his head to the side and looks at me with wide eyes. It's almost like I'm a stranger, and he's seeing me for the first time. "Okay, I'll leave them alone…I promise." And then he breaks out in a wide grin. "I never would've guessed that sassy-girl Ava is a hopeless romantic."

I shove him playfully and make a face. "Yes, I am, you big cynic. So my Mr. Right is going to have to pour on the hearts and flowers if he expects to win my heart."

"So, fair Ava, how does one win the heart of a girl like you?"

"You know, stand under my balcony and serenade me, write me love poems…stuff like that."

"I'll remember that." He laughs as we head to the car.

We haven't been on the freeway long when traffic comes to a complete stop. As we inch ahead, my laziness overcomes me, and I start falling asleep sitting up. But every time I drift off, my head lolls forward and my neck snaps, waking me back up. After a few rounds of this, Max sighs, slides his arm over my shoulders and pulls me against him.

Heaven. All I remember from that is complete contentment. As the minutes pass, he instinctively pulls me in even closer, and I fall into a deep slumber.

"Dylan, look, they're so sweet," Riley's voice says somewhere in the edges of my mind.

What is she talking about?

"Should we leave them here or wake them up?"

"Leave them here? I don't think so. Wake them up."

A hand on my knee pulls me toward the waking world.

"Ava," she whispers, shaking my knee a little.

I open my eyes slowly and blink, realizing that I'm burrowed into Max.

Riley smiles, and I try to gently pull away, but realize he's asleep with his head tipped back against the headrest. It hits me that, not only is his left arm wrapped tightly around me, but he's holding my free hand against his chest, right over his heart.

For a moment, I want to close my eyes and settle back into him, but since Riley and now Dylan are watching me…

"Max," I say softly as I slowly wiggle my hand out of his grasp. "Max."

He stirs and lifts his head just as I pull away. He looks disoriented at first and blinks as he takes in all of our faces.

"We're home," I murmur and then catch my mistake. "I mean, we're at my place."

He presses his palms into his cheeks. "Okay," he responds, his voice sleepy and full of gravel. We slowly pull ourselves together and step out of the car.

As we turn to face each other, I can tell he's embarrassed and I try to set him at ease. "Do you want some coffee or something?" I gesture upstairs.

"No, I've really got to go. But thanks."

He looks at me and there's a thought shadowed in his eyes, as if he wants to tell me something, but can't or won't. The impression of this overwhelms me. I want to shake it out of him, like a shiny penny cascading out of an overturned piggy bank. But in my sleepy state, my courage fails me, and he turns away once again.

Chapter Eighteen / Ancient Pasts, Uncertain Futures

Everything has its beauty, but not everyone sees it.
~Andy Warhol

In my opinion, Sunday morning just before ten is a ridiculous time to be driving up Wilshire to work. Phoebe lives in a high-rise condo in Westwood and when I pull in the driveway, a valet leaps forward to take my car. I steel myself for what's to come as I glide up the elevator to the fifteenth floor. The front desk has already announced me, so Phoebe opens her door as soon as I ring the doorbell.

She's still in her Pilates outfit, and she's lean and fit with long, jet-black hair and an attractive face. She looks to be in her mid-thirties.

I step forward and offer my hand. "Hi, Phoebe, I'm Ava."

She shakes it firmly and leads me inside to the living room. The space isn't large, but the floor-to-ceiling windows give it an expansive feeling.

"Would you like some tea?" she asks politely. She's indicated that I can set my things down on the table in the corner.

"That'd be great. I'll have whatever you're having."

As she heads to the kitchen, I move to the window to take a closer look at the view. The building is set at an angle, so from her window you can see a distance down Wilshire Boulevard.

She returns with two steaming mugs.

"Yerba mate," she says as she sets them down in front of us. I lift my mug and smell. It has the aroma of burnt hay and tastes even worse.

Phoebe then scoots up her chair and gets right to the point. She explains that she's already spent a number of hours on what I've submitted, and she took it upon herself to do the edits and rewrites where necessary. This was the only way, considering the amount to be done within such a short period.

This is exactly what I was afraid would happen, and I work to push down the swell of emotion inside of me. Why the formality of a meeting if she's already changed everything? Perhaps she wants to look good for Jonathan.

I decide to start our discussion with something that doesn't have my handprints all over it—the Twenty Voices on Caswell chapter, a compilation of other people's writing about Max's work.

"Yes, this wasn't awful. Some of the things people wrote were actually thought-provoking, but the way you put it together was clumsy." She has each section in a separate folder, so she finds that chapter and pulls it open.

"What I did was move Lisa Forrester's quote first, then Edward Runyon's, and so on. Here, you can see what I've done."

I silently flip through her list.

"Okay. Can I take this home? I'd like to study what you've changed."

She nods abruptly. "Of course. I've made you a complete set of copies to take." She pushes a neat pile of folders toward me.

I pick up the top folder off the pile titled *The Early Years*. I open it slowly and haven't read much before the feeling of alarm sets in. I skim through several other pages, barely recognizing the writing.

"You've left out so much," I say, almost as a question.

"Too sentimental," she snaps.

"I see." I close the folder and place it back on the pile. "Well, I think what makes the most sense now is to take this home and read it thoroughly. Then we can meet, if needed, for a follow-up conversation."

"If it's necessary," she says, sounding like she definitely doesn't think we'll need to talk again.

"Can I get one of your cards?"

As she retrieves a business card from her Filofax organizer, she pauses and then looks up. "How much time did you spend with Caswell researching this?"

"I'm not sure—we've had a number of meetings," I answer, wondering where she's going with this.

"Was he agreeable?"

"I would say so. He's very excited about this book."

"Well, he should be." Her eyes narrow and her lips purse together.

The undertone to her words makes me pause, but the last thing I want to do is to explore this idea with the charming Phoebe. At this point, I'm counting the seconds until I can escape.

I stand, hugging the folders to my chest. "Well, I'll be going. Thank you for your time, Phoebe."

She silently walks me to the door.

"Oh, and thank you for the tea," I say with a friendly voice.

She shuts the door abruptly, thereby missing the scowl that crosses my face and stays there the entire way to the elevator.

I'm numb as I drive toward my apartment, thinking about Phoebe's changes. I pull into the drive-through at Starbucks to get a venti vanilla latte to get that foul tea taste out of my mouth.

Luckily, Riley's spent the night at Dylan's, so our place is quiet. I curl up on the couch and open the top folder, intent on working through the pile.

Once the shock of her dramatic edits wears off, I get a grip on my emotions. I have to read most section three times before I fully grasp the changes. In some cases, she's sharpened and focused the ideas I'm trying to convey. In other places, it just felt as if she took a hatchet to my carefully-constructed words. I flag the sections that upset me the most…figuring, at the very least, I can discuss them with Jonathan.

But as I read, another theme becomes apparent. The overall tone is very sharp, often bordering on unflattering. Max and I had already discussed mentioning his notoriety in the social world, but now it has a much harsher tone. And the digs aren't just about his public persona;

they hint that his work is derivative and that he borrows some of his more important ideas.

When I finally close the last folder, I realize if I were Mr. Joe Public and had read these words, I'd conclude that Caswell was a real asshole with questionable talent. I wonder if Phoebe has an agenda, and I even consider that Jonathan might too. Is this really what Taylor and Tiden wants?

An unsettling feeling creeps up my spine, and my mind scrambles for my next move. I turn on the stereo and make lunch before I do anything else. As music fills the silent apartment, I make a quesadilla and steam some veggies.

It feels good to avoid thinking about this mess, so I do a couple of chores to occupy myself until I accept that the issue with Phoebe's butcher job can wait no longer. I do the first thing that comes to mind...call Jess. Luckily, I catch her at home.

"Hey, babe, what's up?" She sounds happy and relaxed.

"I had a meeting with that Phoebe this morning, and it didn't go well. Now I don't know what to do." I can't hide the panic in my voice.

"Did you ever get her last name?" she asks calmly.

"No—oh, I got her card. Wait a sec." I grab it from my purse. "Phoebe Carter."

Jess gasps. "FUCK! I'll be right over."

This isn't good. I pace my living room until Jess bangs on the front door.

"Let me see that bitch's card," she growls.

I hand it to her, and it bows as her hand tightens over it.

"Damn, I had a feeling." Her face is tight with anxiety.

"What is it?" The curiosity is killing me.

"Several years ago, Max went out with this whack job a few times. As I recall, she was into some really kinky stuff, and Max lost interest quickly and cut it off." Jess shakes her head. "Well, she went ballistic... like they were engaged and he'd left her at the altar. She stalked him for months. He had to get a restraining order. A helluva lot of good that did, though; she still managed to cause all kinds of trouble. That bitch had an unholy obsession. Finally, she got in trouble at work, and they relocated her to the home office where they could watch her."

"Well, that explains the way she asked me about him. It was creepy." I chew on my fingernail. "But the worst part is, she reworked all my writing so he sounds like a complete asshole—not just a bit of an asshole like he actually is."

She smiles at my attempt to lighten the mood, but her face falls again. "Can you show me some of what you're talking about?"

We settle into the couch and I show her the sections I've marked.

She hisses as she reads. "This will kill Max. You can't let this be published."

"What should I do?" I search her face for answers. I don't think I've ever been so grateful for her friendship and guidance.

"You have to talk to Jonathan first thing tomorrow. Tell Adam you have a doctor's appointment or something. I wouldn't wait until lunch."

Memories of Friday evening resurface. "Ugh. Max and Jonathan had a tug-of-war Friday night at the Getty event, and I was the rope. Jonathan wasn't too pleased with Max by the end of the evening."

"Great, fucking great. What's wrong with Max anyway? He always makes thing difficult for himself."

"You can say that again," I add, remembering my intervention with the Matthews over the MOMA comments.

She looks at her watch and jumps up. "I was supposed to meet Sam ten minutes ago. Call me as soon as you're done with Jonathan and let me know what happened. Meanwhile, I'll think about how to break this to Max."

I give her a big hug. "Thanks so much, Jess. I'm so grateful for your help with this nightmare."

She pats my shoulder. "Sure thing, babe. Tomorrow…" She says before she hurries downstairs.

Luckily, Jonathan agrees to meet me at nine thirty.

Attempting to look as professional as possible, I dress in my black sweater, gray slacks and a jacket. He greets me warmly, and we move to the table by the window so that we can sit side by side as we go over the changes.

Before we begin, Jonathan takes a moment to address the editing process with me. Perhaps he's hoping to head me off at the pass. "Surely you understood when you took this on that your work would be stringently edited," he states firmly, not as a question.

"Yes, I understand that, Jonathan." I fight to keep my expression neutral. "But this is more than editing. Phoebe has changed the tone of everything I've written. When you read it, you'll see what I'm talking about."

"Ava, you must be exaggerating."

I don't like his suggestion and I frown as I consider how to reply.

"I hope you realize that Phoebe has far more experience editing than you do writing. I've always trusted her judgment implicitly."

"Really?" My anger bubbles up. "Well, do you know she has a personal vendetta against Max?"

"What are you talking about?" His eyes narrow as his mouth tightens into a straight line.

"Yes, they dated at one time, and when it ended, she didn't take it well. He had to get a restraining order against her."

Jonathan's face turns bright red, and the vein on his forehead looks like it's about to burst.

A loud commotion on the other side of the wall interrupts our conversation. Jonathan's office door bursts open with Jacqueline trying to physically hold Max back.

It's no surprise Max overpowers her as he storms into the office.

"Jonathan, what's this about Phoebe Carter rewriting my book?"

He's on fire—his voice is booming, and his expression is so fierce it's frightening.

Jonathan takes off his glasses and presses his fingers to his temples as he closes his eyes. "Max, can't you see I'm in the middle of a meeting? How dare you storm into my office?"

"How dare I? When this meeting is about me…about something that affects my entire life!"

"Very dramatic, Max," Jonathan says with a scoff.

"But it's true," I add.

Max glances at me with a glimmer of gratitude in his eyes.

Jonathan stands up and moves behind his desk. "As it is, Ava, was just explaining how inappropriate it is for Phoebe to be your editor. Obviously, I wouldn't have assigned her to this project if I'd known your sordid history with her. Once again, Max, your miscalculations in your personal dealings never cease to amaze me."

Max's rage is barely under control. Every muscle in his neck and arms tense, as if he's a panther ready for the kill.

For a moment, I wonder about Jonathan being judgmental with Max, considering his willingness to seduce me even though we work together. It's easy for things to go wrong professionally when lines cross personally.

Jonathan folds his arms over his chest. "Now, you're clearly not in any state to discuss this. Furthermore, you're interrupting my meeting with my writer. I'll call security to have you removed if you don't leave this office immediately."

Max stands still as a statue while Jonathan heads to his phone and begins to dial.

"Okay, I'll leave so you can finish with Ava. But I want to talk to you today, Alistair, and hear what the resolution is…or I'm going to demand that Taylor and Tiden drop the project." Max turns and storms back out, slamming the door behind him.

I'm shaken. Even Jonathan looks unfocused as he taps his fingers on the edge of his desk. He slowly returns to our worktable as I try to compose myself. I wonder about Max and what I'll say when we next speak. For all I know, he's holding me responsible for this mess too.

After glancing over the documents for a minute, Jonathan decides that he wants to take the time to go over Phoebe's changes and then he'll call me to arrange a meeting. He calls Jacqueline in and hands her the folder, instructing her to make copies immediately.

"It may be wise for you to talk to Adam and arrange a personal day tomorrow so we can spend the day sorting this to make the Friday deadline."

I nod and get up to leave, but as I turn from the table, he takes my hand. "Ava, I'm sorry for all this drama. I don't want you to worry. We'll get it sorted out."

I offer him a small reassuring smile, even if I don't feel it in my heart.

"Are you feeling better from what ailed you the other night?" he asks running his hand down my arm. "I'm so sorry we didn't get to finish our lovely evening Saturday."

"I'm feeling okay, thank you. How was the rest of the party?"

"Fine, but the remainder of the evening would've been a lot more engaging with you there."

Just as he moves in closer, Jacqueline pops into the office to return my folder and the copies.

I look at my watch. "I have to get back to the gallery. We'll talk later?"

"Yes, of course." He kisses me lightly on the cheek, and I head out the door.

When I get to the parking garage, I turn the corner near my car and stop in my tracks. Max is leaning against my car.

I pull out my keys and step forward. "Hey, Max."

His expression is extremely disconcerting.

"Ava, why didn't you call me?" He looks like he's in pain.

"I was hoping to resolve it with Jonathan so you wouldn't have to deal with it. Besides, Jess wanted to be the one to talk to you," I explain, although it sounds rather unconvincing as I listen to myself. Maybe I should've called him first thing. I scrutinize him. "You have to know, Max, I would never have accepted what she did to your story without going to battle over it...even if it meant war."

His whole body sags with my words. "Come here." He pulls me into a tight hug and doesn't let go. I feel him rest his chin on top of my head.

"I know, Ava, I know." He sighs. "It just freaked me out when I learned Phoebe was messing with my life again. I thought she was ancient history, and now she's back.

He suddenly sounds panicked. "She didn't do anything to you, did she?" As he asks, he holds me at arm's length and inspects me as if he expects to find evidence of a physical attack. When he seems satisfied that I'm unmarked, he pulls me back into his arms.

"I know you'd go to battle for me," he states with conviction. "You're my angel, right?"

As much as I don't understand his lingering fixation on my being his angel, I nod, press closer to him and try to offer what comfort I can.

"Yes, I promise; I'll always fight for you."

"You're too damn good for me. I don't deserve you, and it kills me that I keep dragging you through my garbage. I'm trying to get my life on track, but every time I feel like I've made a step forward, this kind of crap forces me two steps back. I keep wondering when you'll reach your limit and decide that I'm just not worth the effort."

Something about the tone of his voice and the feeling of despair seeping out of him makes my heart hurt. I want to shield him from the demons nipping at his heels. But what can I do when I'm not ever sure who or what the demons are? So I hold him for another long moment, trying to warm his spirit, despite being swallowed up by the gray in this cold cement parking garage.

When I try to pull away, he's hesitant to release me from the hug, but when I explain I'm already late for work, he lets me go. I assure him that I'll call as soon as I know more, and he promises to do the same. My heart is heavy as I finally head to the gallery.

Jacqueline calls me that afternoon to tell me that Jonathan would like to meet at nine the following morning and to plan on being there most of the day.

Luckily, Adam approves my request.

By the time I get off work, I'm completely drained, so I stop at the market and buy a pre-made salad and a bottle of wine, only to get home and find Riley especially cheerful.

"You're in a good mood," I say, feeling envious.

"Dylan just called me. He's taking me out tomorrow. He's such a sweetheart, always thinking of special things for us to do. Remember, Franco? He thought a movie and Applebee's was a special date."

I laugh, remembering Franco. He may have been tall and handsome, but in terms of boyfriend material, he definitely was a dud.

"Dylan treats you really well, and it's great to see you so happy." For a moment my mind drifts to Max's idea that Riley isn't genuine about Dylan. If only Max could see that underneath all the fashion and social talk, she has a good heart and truly cares about Dylan.

Talking to Riley reminds me that things have a way of working out. And although her Pollyanna tendencies can exhaust me, the sweet affection between her and Dylan is refreshing to witness.

In contrast, I have an up and down friendship with Max that's wearing me out. And as much as I don't fully understand his intentions, I do know my being his friend has come to mean a lot to him. I wonder if his partying and constant stream of art sluts has slowed down. I'm also starting to believe the chemical reaction I have when I'm around him isn't purely one-sided.

I shake my head, trying to jolt that idea out of it. It certainly doesn't serve my interests to hope that one day he'll sweep me up in his arms. He may never be capable of the kind of emotional intimacy I crave.

Then, to further complicate my life, there's Jonathan and his obvious admiration of me. Doesn't every young woman at one point have a handsome teacher or boss she fantasizes about? And if they show her special attention, the allure can be hard to resist.

Two hours into our work, Jonathan and I are already through more than half the folders. I'm impressed with his ability to cut to the quick of the issue and make snap, decisive judgments. The exercise showcases his brilliance as a publisher and I'm in awe, happy just to keep up.

He makes notes on the border of one of the pages. "See, Ava, just taking out this phrase pulls it together in a much more cohesive way."

He peers over the tops of his glasses. "Did I lose you, Ms. Jacobs?"

"Actually, would you mind if I got some more coffee?"

"No, go ahead. I need to make a phone call anyway."

When I return to the office, he's on the phone, speaking Italian. From what I can tell, he's fluent. The conversation goes on for another minute before he ends the call.

"You speak Italian beautifully. Have you lived in Italy?"

"Yes, Florence. I attended a special graduate program there. And I often take vacations in Tuscany, so it comes in handy to speak the language."

As he checks his watch, I marvel at his sophistication and accomplishments. He's a man of the world, someone to admire and learn from. I'm flattered he feels I'm worth his time and attention. He seems to see something special in me and it makes me want to prove myself that much more.

He gives me a warm smile. "Shall we?" He motions to our work.

As he reviews the next page, he shakes his head. "Apparently, Phoebe isn't a fan of Caswell in any regard. You were right. This *is* unflattering in a gratuitous way."

I'm inwardly relieved. "I'm glad you agree. Whatever one can say about his personal life, Max's work is powerful and uniquely his. She made him sound a few steps away from a theme park portrait artist."

Jonathan chuckles quietly. "Well, he definitely isn't that. Besides, I think you handled your portrayal of his public persona well. Brevity is key. No reason to reveal too much, yes?" He taps his pen on the folder. "We've both seen Max at his best and his very worst, but that doesn't mean the public needs to."

As the day wears on, Jonathan has a Japanese lunch brought in with sushi and sashimi, and we continue to work while we eat. This stage of the project has taken a huge amount of his valuable time, and I feel guilty. But he's focused and determined to get it done.

I enter the changes as we make them to the actual document on my laptop. But I'm not used to editing for so many hours at once, and I gradually lose my focus.

I study him. His shirtsleeves are rolled up, revealing his powerful forearms. The sexy tortoise-shell glasses are pushed back on his head, and his jaw is tight as he goes over a passage. I lose what's left of my concentration, and I fixate on the shape of his lips, the sharp edge of his cheekbones and the weathered crinkles around his eyes that narrow when he reads. How it would feel to be kissed by this man?

Jonathan looks up and notices that I'm watching him. My cheeks redden and I grab the last folder. He smiles with a knowing look in his eyes.

"Am I that interesting to watch, Ava?"

"Very interesting," I reply quietly.

"Good. Because you're fascinating." His gaze lingers on mine before he winks at me.

I shake my head and refocus on the page. There's nothing more seductive than a man who makes it clear that he wants you. As much as the feminist in me hates to admit it, his admiration is confidence boosting.

Minutes later, Jonathan closes the last folder with a flourish. "Okay, Ava, here's what I need you to do. Go through and input all the changes I've noted in the document. Triple-check everything and email it to Jacqueline. She'll forward it per my instructions to Sebastian Stone to proofread. Jacqueline will then forward it to us for another round of reviews."

He stops to consider something.

"I'm going to be in San Francisco for the next three days. As a matter of fact, I'm going to have to leave for the airport soon, but why don't we plan to meet Thursday evening when you get off work? Hopefully, it'll all be tied up and we can celebrate. If not, I'm afraid we'll have to roll up our sleeves again."

I feel a brief moment of excitement to realize how close we are to completing this project that's been the source of so much anxiety and drama. What will I do with my free time now? Will the completion of this job mean the end of my relationships with Jonathan and Max? I close down my laptop and slip it into my messenger bag, while trying to get a handle on my emotions.

Jonathan puts his things in his laptop bag, unrolls his shirtsleeves and slips on his jacket.

I approach the front of his desk. "Jonathan, you told me you normally don't get so hands-on with projects...Well, that was before this drama. You've had to give up an entire day and put up with undo stress." I clear my throat and my voice wavers. "I just want you to know how much I appreciate everything you've done. You've been amazing and I won't ever forget it."

He looks almost surprised and then gives me a warm smile, brimming with affection.

"Believe me, Ava, I'd only do this for you. But you have to know… you're absolutely worth it."

Jacqueline buzzes his phone and announces that his car's waiting, so he slings his bag over his shoulder and walks around the desk. He looks me in the eyes with a blinding intensity and cups my chin.

"Until Thursday." He kisses me softly on both cheeks, lingering on the second cheek with his lips barely grazing my skin. If he kissed me now, I'm certain I'd kiss him back.

There's a soft knock on the door.

"Yes, I'm coming," he says, before pulling back. He looks down at my lips, sighs, and strides out of the office.

Before I gather up the folders, I pause for a moment and admire his spectacular view of the city. I try on his words again to see if they fit.

You're absolutely worth it.

The idea he's presented becomes a question, a challenge…a signpost marking my path of ambition and muddled intentions.

Do I believe him? Have those feelings shaped my experiences, not just with Jonathan, but with Max too?

I say it to myself, "I'm absolutely worth it."

I gaze one more time at the view and remind myself what my grandma Oly used to tell me—the world's full of wonderful experiences if our hearts and minds are open. With all the possibilities my future holds, I excitedly wrap that thought around me and into my heart as I head out the door.

Chapter Nineteen / Fireworks and Earthquakes

I shut my eyes in order to see.
~Paul Gauguin

When I walk into the gallery in the morning, Adam pulls me aside and suggests a walk down to Starbucks. I'm immediately suspicious, but put on a good face.

The entire way there, he tells me about the plans Katherine and he are making to vacation in Greece, but soon enough we're in line, waiting to place our order.

"So, Sean keeps asking everyone if you're involved with Max."

"Why doesn't he ask me? Not that it's any of his business. What difference does it make?"

"You know Sean. When it comes to the choices his friends make, he always thinks he knows best. When it comes to Max, maybe he's justified."

"You can tell him not to worry. I'm not *involved* with Max like that."

The irony does not escape me as we talk that Adam is interested in my complicated relationship with Max too, with no idea that the only *real* action I've had is with Jonathan, who isn't even on his radar screen.

We get up to the front of the line and place our orders.

"Anyway, I want to talk about how things are going to go today."

"Well, barring floods, earthquakes, typhoons or some other natural disaster…I think it'll be fine." I laugh a little uncomfortably.

"Ava, I'm serious. It's important that things go smoothly today. Dylan thinks Max is volatile."

"What do you mean 'volatile'?"

He motions to a table and we sit. "Dylan's concerned that Max is a little, well, for lack of a better word…obsessed with you." Adam's face is somber as he takes a sip of his coffee.

"Obsessed…with me? Oh, I don't think so. He's just one super-intense guy. Granted, we've spent a lot of time together over the last few weeks because of the book, but that'll be coming to an end in a week or two. Things will level off after that."

My heart races. *Obsessed with me?* That idea could mean a lot of different things.

Adam raises his eyebrows.

"Did Dylan say what he meant by obsessed?"

"He told me that Max's been very distracted with his work, which is unheard of for him. He was supposed to have three more paintings ready for the shipment to Barcelona, but he still hasn't finished them. They're now going to have to pay to expedite them."

"Why would he assume it's because of me? Maybe he has artist's block?"

"He told me this has never been a problem for him in the past. But he said every time he talks to Max, you come up constantly in the conversation."

Really? I'm surprised to hear that. "It's probably about the book." But as I say it, I wonder just a little bit.

Adam opens his mouth and then closes it.

"What?" I ask.

"Well, I probably shouldn't tell you this, but the other day Dylan saw Max's sketchbook open, and he's almost certain he saw a drawing of you."

"But—"

"Ava, I know it's flattering to have someone admire you, even more so when it's someone as dynamic and good-looking as Max. I'm certainly not surprised to learn Max is intrigued with you. You're beautiful, smart and so kind…any man would be lucky to have you."

I'm embarrassed by this overstated flattery, and I cast my gaze downward.

"Katherine and I want what's best for you. At one point, we were, for all intents and purposes, your guardians. No one understands the psyche of an artist better than I do. Let's face it, Ava, Max always seems to me to be fighting some inner demon. He has more fame than he could've hoped to achieve, but he's more unsettled than ever. He's searching for something or someone to fix him."

I inwardly shudder. Max's words about angels echo in my head.

"Then you fall into his life. And you're so giving and kind, unlike the women he's often with."

"You make the whole thing sound predictable. Like there's a formulaic reason he would be taken with me."

"No, it's not that. I want you to be careful. I don't want you to get sucked into his darkness. I've always had a theory about why so many established artists get involved with young women and shuffle through them like a deck of cards. Artists need constant visual and emotional stimulation. They seem to crave the pursuit with all its passion and drama, thrive on the infatuation, and when the passion cools, as it usually does in any relationship, they move on to their next muse. I've never seen Max act in a way that would make me believe he's different from this stereotype."

I consider what he's said as I rest my chin in my hand and lean forward.

"I've been around Max now in every type of circumstance, including observing him with women that he was, for lack of a better word, entertaining. We've laughed and fought, helped each other out, and worked closely together. With as aggressively as he goes after what he wants, don't you think he would've made a pass at me already if that was the kind of relationship he wanted?"

Adam swirls the coffee in his cup as he listens.

"He's had many chances to make a play for me, and he never did. There's a reason for that. We're friends and that works for him."

Although Adam relaxes, I have no idea if he's convinced. As we head back to the gallery, we talk business until we step through the door.

"Okay, Ava, I'm counting on you…no fireworks today."

"I'll do my best." I smile, secretly hoping it's true.

Max is scheduled to come at three, so Sean and I set up after lunch. Our intent is to get the run started and work out any technical glitches before Max arrives. We want to be full-on printing when he walks in the door.

Luckily, Sean brought his tunes to work, so there should be plenty of good music to listen to.

As it gets closer to three, I realize I'm nervous to see Max after mulling over Adam's words. But I do my best to push it out of my head and focus on the job.

Sean and I have a natural rhythm when we work, which helps move things along even when I'm distracted. Sean spent the last week doing the digital work—analyzing the color paths in Max's original painting and dissecting them to create files for each color. We use these files to burn the screens we print with, one color at a time.

This painting of Max's has dozens of colors, and we're creating 120 prints—so we'll spend a lot of time on the press. Max will only get a taste of the printing experience this afternoon.

Just after three, Max walks into the studio and sets down his bag on the counter under the window. I can tell as he turns around that he's excited—there's a bounce in his step and his eyes are lit up. This is the first time he's attended a serigraph printing of his work.

Trying to maintain a professional air, I smile from my position at the press. He tips his head to the side, and I wonder what he's thinking. I'm not glamorous today with my hair pulled back and my old ink-stained jeans and tank top. But he still smiles warmly.

Sean introduces himself, projecting a definite alpha vibe, and he shakes Max's hand. I almost laugh out loud because Max is completely nonplussed by it. As they talk, Sean offers to show Max his computer system in the back studio where he does the color analysis. Max follows him, and I decide to stay up front and continue working.

I'm back in my rhythm when one of my favorite songs comes on the iPod dock, and I start singing and swaying as I print.

After sliding a new sheet of paper under the frame, I pull the scarlet ink across the screen with the squeegee. Some strands of hair fall into my eyes, and I push them away, smearing a bit of ink on my forehead.

Humming, I carefully lift the screen and pull out the thick textured paper. I hold it up to admire the perfect impression of ink on paper. As I lay the paper on the wire rack, I stroke the corner and sing softly.

The memories tie us,
They bind us it's true
Yet despite how I've fought it,
It's always been you

I slip in a new sheet, close my eyes, gently sway my hips to the music and sing the next lines a bit louder.

My heart's always known
It may break right in two
But there's no way denying
It's always been you

I take the wooden stick coated with vermillion and drag it along the screen, watching the soft puddle of color spread. I slide the squeegee up to the top of the screen, then stretch up and pull it back, my arms smoothly gliding as I stroke down, the color moving toward me.

At that very moment, I feel a shift in the room and look up. Sean and Max are in the doorway, silently watching me. And although the expression on each of their faces is completely different, I feel like there's an intimacy in what they've observed. The fire in their eyes takes my breath away.

Finally, Sean breaks the silence. "Hey, nice moves, Ava! Thanks for keeping the run going."

"No problem," I practically whisper as a flush of embarrassment fires up my cheeks. I glance at Max, but he's still standing in the doorway, watching me. I search his eyes and expression as Adam's words ring in my ears. He's unreadable to me.

Sean decides to take over the screen work for a while as I unload the finished prints from the press and then slide fresh sheets in. Max has a lot of questions while we work. He wants to know what other artists we've printed, the average number of colors used and how the edition size is determined. It's interesting to observe his natural curiosity at work.

Luckily, Sean slowly warms up to Max, and he even asks about progress on the book.

Max and I give each other wary looks.

"What?" Sean asks.

"Well, first the deadline got pushed up by almost two months, and if that wasn't bad enough, one of Max's ex-girlfriends tried to sabotage it."

"She wasn't a girlfriend," Max grumbles.

"Sabotage, how?" Sean's interest is piqued.

"Do you remember me telling you about Jonathan? He's the publisher of *Art+trA,* and they're publishing this book in a joint venture with Taylor and Tiden Press."

"Yeah, I've heard Adam talk about him. He's the one you keep meeting with."

Max gives me a stern look.

"What?" I purse my lips together while giving him a pretend stern look. "So anyway, Max's ex-whatever is an editor that works for Jonathan, and she was assigned to help me finish this project, now that the deadline is impossible. Unbeknownst to me, she and Max didn't have a happily ever after, so she tried to take him down in literary flames."

Max makes a face.

"Shit, that really sucks, dude," says Sean.

"In more ways than one," Max agrees.

I hold my hands up toward Max. "She's attractive and smart, so I get why you went out with her, but simmering under all that, she's full of surprises."

"And not the good kind," Sean adds.

"Yeah, well, I found out the hard way, and it was a long time ago," he states with a tense expression. I'm guessing he's fed up with being the focus of ridicule.

"So, what did Jonathan do? Did he defend the ex?" Sean asks with a crooked smile.

Perhaps Sean enjoys the fact that *art guy* doesn't have the easiest time with women either.

"No, Jonathan isn't like that. When I explained the circumstances, he immediately pulled her off the project. As a matter of fact, instead of assigning the primary rewrite to another editor, he's working directly with me."

"Really?" asks Sean as he waves the squeegee—reminding me to keep feeding the paper while I'm talking. We have a lot to print.

"What do you mean working directly with you? I thought he already was?" asks Max.

"I was working with him directly, but only from a broad perspective. Yesterday, we went through the text line by line."

"How long did that take?" Sean asks and then mumbles to himself, "That's why you took yesterday off."

"We started at nine and worked straight through until the late afternoon when he had to catch a plane. We'll go through it again tomorrow night."

"What do you mean tomorrow fucking night?" Max hisses.

I give him a dirty look and refuse to acknowledge his question.

"What, man?" Sean asks Max.

Are they're buddies now?

"I'm pretty damn sure Jonathan wants Ava for more than just her writing," Max snaps.

"Damn it!" Sean yells and jerks his arm mid-pass over the screen. He lifts it up for examination and presses his lips into a hard line when he spots a tear.

He lowers the screen and turns to me. "Is this true, Ava? Is he horn-dogging you? I'll kick his ass!"

I give Sean a hard look and do the same to Max. "No comment," I finally say and fold my arms across my chest.

"Isn't that fucker old enough to be your dad? What the hell!"

Since when is Sean on Team Max?

"Jonathan would never talk to or treat me the way you two are right now. So put that in your pipe and smoke it. This discussion is over."

I turn around and pick out a song I like on the iPod dock. The tension is thick in the uncomfortable quiet of the studio.

When I turn around, Sean gives me puppy dog eyes. "Sorry, Ava."

"Me too. I'm sorry. This whole situation has really stressed me out," Max adds.

"I know it has." I smile sympathetically and remember Adam's mandate. It's time to play nice. "All's forgiven. Now let's talk about something happier, okay?"

Sean groans. "Damn. I don't know about happier...but I have to burn a new screen to finish this color, and I put everything away. This is going to take me a while."

"Well, I can start with the second color on the dry prints if you set up the screen."

"Okay, that's good. Max, want to help?"

"Sure," he agrees.

As Sean leaves to retrieve the screen for the second color, Max steps closer to me. "So do you have dinner plans? We could grab something when we're done."

"I'd like that," I say with a smile, glad things have lightened up. "Ready to work?"

He nods with a huge grin.

Sean returns and hooks up the screen before heading to the back with a groan.

I'd be irritated too, since it's a long process to remake the damaged one.

I prepare the next ink, a vivid shade of violet.

Max moves closer and observes what I'm doing. His eyes have a pensive look, as if he's hypnotized by my movements and the swirl of color.

I roll the first drying rack over and show him how to align the prints that already have vermillion printed under the second color screen.

"Are you going to be able to keep up with me?" I tease.

He arches his eyebrow and gives me a smug smile. "I'll do my best."

I nod to the reproduction and original work in the viewing booth. "What's the name of this painting?"

"*Tropic of My Imagination.*"

"Mmm, I like that." I smile.

We begin the new run and remain quiet while we quickly establish our rhythm. We finish about a dozen prints before I realize he's not moving. I look up and catch the hooded dark look in his eyes. Color immediately burns across his face.

"What?" I ask tipping my head to the side.

"You," he whispers just loud enough to hear.

I stop printing and set the squeegee down.

"You're working on my art—you're part of it. I didn't know...I didn't realize how this would affect me."

He's breathing hard and his eyes are wide; it stirs me up. I want to reassure him that I understand that this experience makes me feel even more connected to his art.

"Ava," he says with urgency and holds onto the press as if he's trying to tether his emotions to something solid.

I'm moved by his show of emotion. "I know, Max. It means a lot to me to be working with you, too."

"But it's more than that." He takes a deep breath. "It's hard to describe..."

I wait for him to find the right words or simply surrender to what he wants to say.

He runs his fingers across his chin and down his throat as he gazes at me. "It's unbelievably erotic."

Now it's my turn to blush and my heart starts to pound. *Did I hear him right?* Is my entire world suddenly upside down, every straight line now jagged?

There's a long silent pause as his stare burns with intensity.

I feel like he's seeing me for the first time.

"I've really tried, Ava. God only knows how hard I've tried. But I can't fight it anymore."

I grip the screen's frame. "What are you talking about?"

"I can't deny how I feel another day...I can't stay away from you anymore."

Stay away from me?

My mind tumbles, trying to consider what those loaded words mean. The opposite of staying away is everything, an open sky that holds us together above our fears. I instinctively respond with an unrestrained heart.

"Then come closer."

He takes a sharp breath and closes his eyes as the softest smile works its way across his face. Is this an agreement, the ticket to ride with him on a speeding train?

"Will you show me how you do this, Ava?" He waves to the press. "I want us to experience it together."

I nod and gesture him toward me. "Come here—I'll show you."

He walks to my side of the press, and I can feel the energy surging off of him. As a result, every emotion's passing through me, and I worry that my knees are going to give out.

"Okay, take this and stand here," I say as my trembling fingers try to hand him the squeegee and step to the side.

"No." He shakes his head. "I want to do it *with you.*"

Oh my God…I'm going to combust. How can I do this? The rules have suddenly changed. How can I work so close to this gorgeous man and not lose all control?

"Okay," I say unsteadily. "We start with the ink." I take his right hand and place it over mine, take the stick and gently stir the paint in the can. The violet swirls, and I lift the wet stick and drip it across the screen.

I try to focus but his touch and the heat from his body permeate my senses.

Next, I pick up the squeegee, and we complete the motion, but it's awkward with his hand on only one side of the squeegee. As I lift the screen, he steps around and removes the print and reloads silently.

When he returns, he steps directly behind me, and since he's taller and larger than me, he curls around me and reaches everything easily. He slides both of his hands on top of mine.

I can hardly breathe I'm so electrified. Swirl, lift, stroke…His breath is hot against my neck.

We grip the squeegee, slide, pause, drag back with more force, lift. I close my eyes so I can focus on his scent and the feeling of his arms wrapped around me.

He pauses before he steps away to switch the paper.

When he returns, he steps even closer so that when we extend ourselves across the print, he presses against me.

I gasp. All I can focus on is his arousal pressing against me. I've never wanted anyone this much.

By the third pass, I'm trembling, and when he presses against me, I press my ass back into him, imagining him inside of me.

"Ava," he moans.

As much as I want to turn around and face him, I don't want to stop. I don't want this moment to end.

"Again," he groans.

This time, as I slide the squeegee up, he lets go, slides his hands up my arms and trails them down my sides. All the while, his lower body is firmly pressed against me. I could cry it feels so good to have him touch me in ways I never thought he would. I slowly grind my ass against him. His hands move down to my hips, and his fingers grasp my curves, pulling me closer.

I'm surprised he has the focus to change the paper, but he doesn't reach around to help me with the screen this time. Instead, his hands return to my hips as our bodies press together, and he run his hands down the sides of my thighs and back up. He slips his hands under my tank, moving up my sides, across my ribs, and just skimming the edge of my bra. My nipples harden, aching for his touch, and my breaths are quick and short.

I drop my head and moan, "Max."

"I know, baby, I know," he whispers, pressing his lips in my hair at the nape of my neck. He steps away again and replaces the paper quickly.

"Again, Ava, for me." He brushes his cheek softly above my ear and presses into me a little harder.

I try to concentrate on the trail of violet left from my stroke, but as I push up, his hands part. One slides down over my jeans, between my legs, and presses firmly against my sex. I drop the squeegee and grab the edge of the table, just as his other hand snakes under my shirt and pulls my bra down to cup my naked breast.

My breath catches in my throat as I revel in every sensation.

His fingers gently tease my nipple, and he kisses the side of my neck up to my ear.

I moan as the room spins, and I try to make sense of what's happening as I come undone. The room is hazy with the softest highlights and shadows. I wonder if this is a dream. There's only one way to know for sure. I take a deep breath, take a step to the side, straighten my shirt and slowly turn to face him.

Dozens of emotions cross his face—everything from vulnerability to command, with passion the most pronounced. He hesitates and then extends his hand.

"Ava?"

"I'm scared," I whisper, my heart still wildly pounding. Admitting my fear leaves me raw and vulnerable, and I pray he treads carefully.

He gazes at me tenderly. "I'm scared too," he whispers as he moves his hands slowly up my arms. "Ava, you don't know how dark things are in my mind. What I am inside…what I can be like. I wanted to protect you from all of that."

"You've been protecting me?" My mind can't make sense of the very thought of it.

He nods, his jaw twitching as he watches me intently.

Needing some space, I take several steps back until I'm under the arch to the hallway. I put my hands up to my face and back up until I'm against the wall. The coolness of the stucco is startling against my burning body.

I'm confused and under his spell. In the shadow of the hallway, the darkness becomes the sheerest veil between us, and I've lost all sense of what I should do.

Across the open space between us, my body and my heart call out to him. Max watches me for several counts before he approaches, and I realize he doesn't have it in him to stop either.

I close my eyes and wait until I can feel his presence in front of me. When I open my eyes, he has an arm positioned on either side of me, jammed against the wall and caging me. He lowers his head and presses his forehead against mine.

"Ava, I can't fight this anymore," he whispers, his stormy blue eyes a swirl of want. "I've got to have you." His moan is raw with desire.

I didn't know time could move that slowly…that I could live my entire life between the single frames that flash as his head tilts and his lips part. He moves lower and lower until there's just a sliver of light between us.

When our lips meet, seeming to spark as they press together, my world opens and time speeds up so fast that I have to hold on to him to keep from being pulled into the upper atmosphere.

If he had been too rough or too rigid, I would've had it in me to slow down. But he's perfect in every way. I swoon from the way he cradles me in his arms and the way his mouth presses against mine with gentle soft fullness, sucking and lightly biting as his fingertips slide down my neck…his touch silky smooth and reverent. He gives way to the building fire—flames licking my mouth, teeth scraping my chin, hands sliding into my jeans to cup my ass and pull me firmly against all that I desire.

"Ava, I want you. I've always wanted you." He bends his knees and thrusts his hardness right into me.

Fire and wetness mingle dangerously between my legs.

We're a wall of passion, and all the longing and unfulfilled desire now burns brightly between us. It's overwhelming and stronger than I could've imagined.

He pulls the neckline of my tank down below my bra, leaving my breast naked. He takes my nipple in his mouth, flicking the tip with his tongue.

My head drops back against the wall as I watch him. *Is this really happening?*

He devours me as he yanks down the remaining fabric, preparing my other breast for his touch.

I stroke the front of his jeans where his cock strains and we both moan loudly.

From this moment on, I'll never trust my instincts because I completely underestimated this man's attraction to me. I've never felt so desirable, so beautiful…so completely wanted in a man's eyes.

He moves to my other breast, and I take ragged breaths. I want more and my back arches, coaxing the soft fullness of my breasts towards him.

He responds with sensuous caresses and ravenous kisses, teasing and working me into a frenzy. Our groans of pleasure echo through the room.

I slip my hand under the edge of his shirt and rake my fingers across his stomach and up his defined chest.

With his sexy smile and wide eyes, his pleasure's palpable, and he lifts his shirt, encouraging me. I shower kisses across his chest, finally biting his nipple lightly, while tightening my grip on his cock.

He pushes his fingers through my hair and tilts my face up to meet his demanding kiss, while pressing our naked chests together. But this is no longer mere kissing, he's making love to my mouth. We moan, grind, grab and pull as the passion overtakes us. I become a wild animal. I bite his shoulder to keep from crying out when his teeth scrape my neck, and I slip my hands inside the back of his jeans to dig my nails into his ass. I writhe hungrily against him, and every one of his movements becomes more intense and powerful.

I need to tame this animal because what I really want is to make love all night on his big bed in Malibu with the ocean crashing just beyond us and the velvet curtains waving in rhythm with our movements as we tangle together. I want him to paint my portrait across the sheets as he strokes every part of me. Our passion will be color, light and texture combined.

But it's difficult to rein in the raw lust when it's simmered for so long. Max is too far gone.

"Ava," he says in a ragged, desperate voice, "I need to have you. I swear I'm going to take you here in this studio." He starts working on his belt buckle.

Despite my raw lust, my mind clears enough to see a flaw in the plan. I still his hand. "No," I say as I try to catch my breath. "Sean." I have no sense how much time has passed, but he could enter the studio with the new screen at any minute.

"Fuck Sean, he can watch. I don't care about anything but fucking you right now." His eyes burn.

The music that's been surging, moving toward a crescendo hits a sour note, and I freeze.

Fucking you right now... up against a wall...in a fucking hallway... in front of Sean.

Fucking art slut.

Reverence shifts on a dime to tawdriness. Making love morphs into a quick fuck. We're slipping down a slope and can't seem to stop.

"What about Adam's office?" There's an edge of desperation to his voice.

"Glass walls." My voice is losing its tone and inflection.

"Isn't there a storeroom with a door, a bathroom?" he asks frantically.

It's as if a yellow-green fluorescent light has snapped on revealing this for what it is, and I push him off me and step away.

"The bathroom?" I ask, trying to keep the hysteria out of my voice.

"What? What!" he barks.

I don't back down—instead I pull away even more as the passion falls away from me like a discarded cloak.

His anger blossoms like a high-speed shot of a flower opening in a science film.

"Really? Now you're going to be precious and self-righteous? I don't get you! I can never tell what you want. Is this a game to you? Your whole body was begging to be fucked a minute ago!" He steps back and yanks his shirt down.

"You're wrong...I didn't want to fuck, I wa—"

His face burns to a hot red. "I didn't want this to happen, either!"

"What do you mean *you* didn't want this to happen?"

His fury builds. "I! Did! Not! Want! This!" he barks staccato, grimacing. "I knew it would ruin everything, and I was fucking right.

Fuck it all!" He pivots and storms into the gallery, leaving me and my naked breasts in the darkened hallway.

"You didn't want me?" I whisper, horrified as I push my breasts back into my bra and pull my shirt down.

"You didn't want me." I repeat to myself with a mix of anger and confusion. As I say it a third time, I realize how true it rings. It's the only idea that's made sense the whole evening.

He didn't want me for anything but a fuck. And he'd never want *me*. Not the way I've wanted him to. The emotional tremors start in my hands and move across my body.

During an earthquake, it'd been recommended that you perch in a doorway or crawl under a table until the shaking stops. Later it was revised to say you should crouch next to the table, not under it, to create a little pocket to survive if the walls come down around you. But when the world is shaking, and one's mind is not sound, there's a natural instinct to run out the door…run to an open space so that when the glass explodes and your ceiling crumbles, you can sink to the earth with nothing but the sky and air holding you.

But there's danger, even in the open air.

I discover this as I grab my bag, shoot out the back door of the studio and into the open air of the parking lot. For as I lean forward, my hands frantically gripping my knees while desperately trying to take air into my lungs, I realize there are no safe pockets for me.

As I fall into my car and tear out of the lot, the sinking realization hits me that the damage from fireworks and earthquakes is often too catastrophic to comprehend.

Chapter Twenty / Ain't No Prince Charming

Life is the art of drawing without an eraser.
~John W. Gardner

I turn onto Santa Monica Boulevard, hell-bent on getting home, when the traffic comes to a complete standstill. This isn't unusual for this time of day in this part of the city, but in my current state of mind, it's tantamount to having needles stuck in my eyes. I slam the steering wheel with my fists.

My phone rings, and even though I'm sitting with nothing but time on my hands, the president could call and I wouldn't answer at this point.

I glance down—Sean. *Fuck!* He's probably discovered the scene of the crime and is wondering why I abandoned him. The last thing I wanted to do was screw things up for him too. I resolve to call him after I get home and calm down enough to speak coherently.

Traffic barely inches forward as the light goes from red to green to yellow and to red again. The blare of sirens confirms an accident ahead, which only makes the nasty traffic worse. My voice mail pings. I sigh and press the button to listen while I'm waiting. At least I won't have to talk.

"Ava, it's Sean." He sounds pissed, his voice tight and his words clipped. "I just brought the screen up and you guys aren't here. If you were going to go out, couldn't you at least have left me a note or something? That's messed up."

There's a pause.

"You didn't print very much, and—What the fuck?…*Why* didn't you wash off the screen before you left? This one's probably trashed now too!" His long-suffering sigh is loud and clear. "Call me right back and let me know what's going on."

The damage is done. Calling him back now or later isn't going to change that. At least Max was gone before Sean returned to the studio.

Max.

The thought of him makes my stomach sink. I'm still stunned by his blast of rage, and I feel completely raw. Part of me wishes I could turn the clock back and make sure our encounter never happened. We'd still be friends who could go bowling or get burgers at The Apple Pan. But the other part of me is steaming angry for how he treated me. Now there's nothing but the ashy charred remains of a friendship that meant a lot to me.

To top it off, I'm not even sure what happened. How did everything go so horribly wrong? I went from such a high with the way I felt in his arms as he kissed me with an intensity I've only read about in romance novels to the lowest low where we yelled hateful things at each other like a couple going through a bitter divorce.

A wave of sorrow and frustration washes over me, and I angrily wipe the tears away from my face. I'm mad at myself for missing the asshole so much already. But I continue to cry and watch the lights change— green, yellow, red, green, yellow, red.

Life is cruel.

Sitting there in a traffic jam, I watch the beautiful boys saunter down the street, fresh from the gym, handsomely buff. They don't call West Hollywood "Boys Town" for nothing.

I move forward about twenty feet. Green, yellow, red, green, yellow, red. I turn on the radio and flip through the channels, but everything agitates me, so I shut it off. After a few minutes of silence, my phone rings. Again, I let it go to voice mail and wait for the ping before I listen to the message.

"Ava, pick up your goddamned phone. I need to talk to you and find out what in the hell is going on! Fuck!" Sean is breathing hard and his voice sounds angrier, bordering on rage, and it freaks me out.

"So, I'm wrapping things up, and I walk into the gallery to leave some paperwork for Adam, and your boy Max is sitting in the middle of the room with his head in his hands. I ask him what he's doing and nothing…I mean he doesn't even look at me. So I walk right up to him, and he ignores me so I shout his name, and all he does is moan like he's been shot or something. What the fuck?

"Ava, I need to know, and I mean right now. What did this asshole do? You would never leave the studio like you did, and he's in this freaky state. If he did anything, touched a single hair on your head, I'm going to beat the crap out of him. I don't care who the motherfucker is. And if you don't call me right back, I might just do it anyway because he's freaking me the hell out. Call me now, Ava! NOW!"

The bile rises up my throat and I choke it down. The picture of Max broken down in the gallery is haunting, especially because since we've met, I've been the one to help him during his low times. I certainly won't be helping him now.

I wipe my tears and clear my throat. As my fingers fumble across the screen of my phone, I figure out what I can say to Sean to minimize the damage.

He picks up during the first ring. "Ava, are you okay?" he shouts, his voice a mix of fury and concern.

"I'm sorry, Sean. I'm sorry I left things like I did. That was so not cool, but Max really pissed me off, and I was afraid I'd say something to ruin the project. I just needed to get out of there for a while."

"You needed to get out of here for a while?" he repeats sarcastically. "What the fuck happened, Ava? The guy in the next room isn't sitting there moaning because you had a *little* argument. What aren't you telling me?"

"He's a crazy-ass artist. You know how unstable they are. We had an argument about the book and he got mad, and then I got mad and left. That's it, so don't beat him up—as much as I know you'd enjoy it—just get him out of there."

"And how do you propose I do that? He's ignoring me. Should I hoist him onto a dolly and roll him out to his car?"

"Very nice, Sean. No, just push him out the door. This is how he acts when he's really upset. He won't fight you." Although I'm not one hundred percent sure Max won't fight if Sean pushes him out, I hedge my bets.

"Argh! Okay, I'll try, but I'm calling you as soon as I'm done, and you better pick up the goddamned phone."

"I promise I will."

After I hang up, traffic starts to break up, and I actually make it down two streets in a row without hitting my brakes. I'm just a few blocks from home when the phone rings again and I answer.

"Ava, that dude is messed up. You should seriously stay away from him. I had to push him all the way to his car, and he looked like the world had ended. It was fucking creepy."

"What happened after that?"

"I went inside and wrapped things up. When I went to leave, he and his car were gone. He must have gotten his shit together enough to drive."

"Well, that's a relief." I sigh. "Look, Sean, I'm really sorry about all of this, and I'll make it up to you."

"I'm going to make sure you do. You'll be taking me out for drinks, wherever I want to go...even if it's a sports bar or strip club."

"Okay, whatever you want," I repeat numbly.

I don't know when I've been so grateful to be home from work. Riley greets me cheerily, holding three small hangers with tulle-laced confections.

"Look, Ava. Our latest princess designs." She beckons to me and holds up each of the miniature dresses, one at a time, for my viewing pleasure.

I dump my bags down on the living room couch and groan. "Riley, doesn't it bother you that you're shoving this princess propaganda down little girls' throats and teaching them they don't have to work hard and develop their intellects to grow up to be strong independent women? Instead, they should focus on dressing up pretty and waiting for their prince to come along and take care of them? I think companies like the one you work for are ruining an entire generation of young women."

Her eyes widen and she frowns. "Rough day, Ava, or is there another reason I get to be the focus of your bitch-fest?"

She pivots around in her platform shoes and marches back to her bedroom.

Damn! Riley didn't deserve that. I'll apologize later when I'm not so edgy.

I pick up the pink tiara from the table. The wires are strung with pink crystal beads and woven together in the shape of a crown. A medallion with the glowing portrait of a princess is glued to the front. I run my fingers over her printed face.

What's she so damn happy about? If there's anything I've learned today, it's that there ain't no Prince Charming... just crazy-ass artists who want to fuck you in hallways.

I sigh and walk slowly to my room, crawl onto my bed, pull my knees into my chest, and wrap my arms around them protectively. I wish I could believe that I'm better off without Max—that he's trouble no matter what. But part of me doesn't believe that. Part of me cares about him.

It reminds me of a universal truth. There's no better way to realize how much something means to you than to lose it.

I show up to work the next day with my tail between my legs, prepared to kowtow to Sean to make up for yesterday's transgressions. Luckily, he's in a generous mood, and other than making me promise to take him to his favorite sports bar Saturday evening, he's merciful and doesn't make me grovel. I'm grateful it's not a trip to his favorite strip club. To show my appreciation, I buy him his favorite drink, a venti blended mocha with extra whipped cream on my afternoon coffee run.

We work hard to finish the print job, not just make up for the time we've lost, but to convince ourselves that this lucrative project hasn't flown the coop. So far, we haven't heard from Max or Dylan, so we soldier ahead.

I haven't told Adam about the disaster. I'm not feeling like I can handle his disappointment on top of everything else.

As for Max, I suspect I won't hear from him, but what I don't expect is the idea of him, the physical manifestation of his impression, following me like a phantom all day. A flash in the corner of my eye has me looking to see if he's next to me, but it's only the edge of the printing press he leaned over the night before.

When I peer down the hall into the gallery, I almost think I see him standing silently, waiting. But it's the ghost in my shrinking mind… perhaps my attempt at denying my loss.

At five twenty, I take my things into the bathroom to change for my meeting with Jonathan at six. We have a tight window because Jonathan has another obligation at seven thirty.

I'm relieved the meeting will be shorter than expected. The idea of having to work on Max's book tonight is so horrific I'm almost numb, but the sensation may help me coast through the work ahead.

Hopefully, I can be professional enough that Jonathan won't notice anything's amiss. I get in my car and turn my radio up, giving myself a continuous pep talk all the way to his office.

"Ava!" His greeting couldn't be warmer, and the look of adoration in his eyes feels good, despite my conflicted emotions. It's such a nice contrast to the discarding and shunning of less than twenty-four hours ago.

We sit down at his table and catch up. When he's done telling me about his trip to San Francisco, he brushes his fingers along my cheek and squints as he examines my face. "You look tired, beautiful. Are you working too hard?"

I smile. "Yes, but I'm determined to get this book done on time."

"Well, you'll like my news then. I'm very happy with the last round of edits, and we have minimal work to do tonight."

I clap my hands happily, and he laughs.

"Let's get to it!" I say.

The words are now so familiar, I doubt I have any perspective left on whether the work is decent or not. But Jonathan seems enthusiastic, so I have a reason to be optimistic. Some areas have changes and there is some additional writing.

"Did Sebastian add this? It's really good."

He smiles. "Actually, I added that while I was waiting for the flight. But I accept the compliment."

We tear through chapter after chapter, and because the changes are minor adjustments, the work goes quickly. After we've scanned the last page, he closes the folder with a great flourish.

"Done!" His eyes light up. "Congratulations, Ava! Your first book is complete. I think it's time to celebrate."

I'm so pleased. And to think, a matter of months ago I was at an art show handling shipping and installation, and now I've written a book for Taylor and Tiden Publishing. It's hard to wrap my mind around the idea.

"I've brought something special to help us celebrate." Jonathan opens the mini-fridge at his bar. He takes out a bottle of Cristal champagne and grabs two crystal flutes out of the cupboard. He opens the bottle and hands me my glass, the champagne fizzing wildly. He lifts his glass to toast me.

"You know, Ava, I admire you. It took courage to take on such a big project, to deal with a very difficult artist and a demanding publisher, and handle it all with poise and determination. It took tremendous tenacity to follow it through to the end…even when the road got rough. As a result, you've written an exceptional work. You're really something, Ava Jacobs, and I expect see great things in your future."

I'm speechless and embarrassed from the unabashed flattery. That's the most incredible thing anyone has ever said about me.

He holds up his glass even higher, and I raise mine as well.

"To jumping in with both feet."

I grin. "Both feet." We clink glasses and take sips of the champagne.

I walk over to his window and gaze across the Los Angeles skyline. Dusk is falling, and the city is twinkling a pale platinum glow.

This stunning view, Jonathan's enthusiastic support…it's all so much to take in.

"I'm sad about one thing," I say, turning back to him.

"What's that?" he asks with a concerned expression.

"Now that it's over, we won't be working together anymore. I've really enjoyed our time together."

He picks up the bottle, joins me at the window and refills both our glasses. The champagne's decadently good and the buzz even better.

"What makes you think we won't be working together or seeing each other anymore? Now that I have a taste of you, Ava, I'm not letting you go."

I slowly turn to him. His expression is a cross between admiration and seduction.

His phone buzzes, and he scowls before striding to his desk to activate the intercom. "Yes?"

"Mr. Alistair, I'm leaving now. Remember you need to leave in twenty minutes to pick them up by eight."

"Thank you, Jacqueline. I'll see you in the morning."

He returns to my side.

"So little time," he whispers. He trails the tips of his fingers down my cheek and my neck and stops just above my breasts.

I decide that it's finally time to address the elephant in the room. "Jonathan, one thing has weighed very heavily on my mind."

"Yes?" He lifts his eyebrows as he studies me.

"This job's been so important to me, life changing. So I feel really uncomfortable that I allowed things to get unprofessional with you." I pause awkwardly. "Well…you know what I mean."

I see a frustrated look cross his face as he tips his head back. "Why do you blame yourself when I'm the one who crossed the line? We both know who initiated all of this."

"I've been a willing participant."

"That means we both consented to something that's become very important to me. From the moment I met you, I was wildly attracted to you and, yes, I was determined to get to know you better, but I worried about the ramifications too. I tried to convince myself that you're not a regular employee here at *Art+trA,* and therefore, it wasn't so egregious. I wasn't even originally going to be working with you directly."

"But you have the ability to make or break my career. Doesn't that make this wrong?"

"In a perfect world, yes. But show me a company where something like this hasn't happened. People that work together often share passions and their intellects, and they have the luxury of getting to know each other over time. My mother was an operating room nurse and worked with my father who was a surgeon, and they fell in love. It happens every day. Is it really so wrong?"

When he says it that way, it doesn't sound as bad as I've imagined. Are the champagne bubbles making my head fuzzy? Of course, I'm craving an excuse not to feel guilty or foolish.

After taking another sip, he sets his champagne flute down and steps up close to me. He rests one hand on my waist as he very slowly runs the other through my hair.

"Is it so wrong for me to touch you like this?"

I look up, wishing he'd touch me again. His gentle affection feels heavenly, his presence warm and secure, as if he'd always catch me if I fell.

His eyes search mine for the answer to his desires. He lightly brushes his lips across my forehead, before moving down to my lips. "Is it wrong for me to want to kiss you so much?"

I shake my head ever so slightly. He takes my chin in his hand and pulls me to him, his lips softly move over mine. I slowly open up to him and my heart pounds as everything moves forward. There'll be no looking back once the current sweeps us into its powerful arms.

This man is so tender with me and a complete contrast to Max yelling at me last night for not wanting him to fuck me up against a wall.

Somewhere deep in my heart, I know I'm using this to fill the hole that Max tore through me last night. I know it's wrong…a wrong that may become another regret in the morning. But none of the wrongs are compelling enough to make me stop when I've felt so undesirable all day. Jonathan's attention feels so damn good.

He slides his hand behind my neck and kisses me deeper. I surprise myself by kissing back with a surge of passion. I can feel his smile of satisfaction as our lips move together.

When the kiss ends, he trails his lips down my neck and strokes my cheek with his hand, while pressing his other hand against the small of my back. He looks down at me.

"Is it wrong for me to want to hold you in my arms? Is it, Ava?" His expression is even more intense as he pulls me closer. "Surely you know how much I want you."

He feathers his fingers down my neck, pausing several inches below my throat.

"I can feel your heart beat," he whispers. He follows by dragging his fingers between my breasts, then back up and drawing invisible little circles just above the edge of my blouse.

"Your skin is perfect, you otherworldly creature," he says with relish.

"I'm glad you approve," I tease.

"Approve? That is woefully inadequate for the way I feel right now. I'm enchanted…completely under your spell."

I kiss him along his jaw and then whisper in his ear. "You cast a captivating spell too."

"Oh, Ava," he says. There's reverence in his voice, and it makes me feel beautiful. His breathing accelerates and his color rises.

He pulls me closer and kisses me slowly as he explores my body with his hands. Everything is gentle, slow and sensuous. I feel worshipped. It's heady and I like it.

I need this.

"How much time do you have?" I whisper between kisses as I work my fingers through his hair.

He looks at me with eyes hooded with lust. "Time?"

"Before you have to leave?"

He gently releases me, and the cool air against my burning wet skin shocks me.

"Why, beautiful?" he whispers as he leans forward.

"I don't want to make you late," I say softly, too timid to look him in the eye. "And…I'm wondering what you have in mind right now."

"Don't worry, Ava, as much as I want to, I'm not going to take this any further tonight. It would be rushed and I want to linger…taste every inch of you."

I look back up at him and he gives me a sexy smile.

"Really?" I ask, amazed that he has such restraint.

He nods. "I have a very clear picture in my mind of our first time and I hope this fantasy will soon be realized. I want to sweep you off somewhere beautiful and take my time worshipping you."

For a moment, I'm reminded of Max. Why couldn't he say those words, or at the very least want our first time to be important? Here's Jonathan offering me the very thing I wanted from Max.

Jonathan pulls me tightly against him. I can feel everything as he kisses me deeply.

I glance up at the clock, remembering his assistant's warning. "Oh no."

He looks at the time, sighs and nods.

Our eyes lock while he pulls himself together. I don't know what he's thinking, but judging from his smile, it's all good.

As I smooth down my hair, I feel guilty. "I feel bad I've made you late."

"Believe me, it's worth it." He pulls me into his arms and murmurs softly, "Now that our project's over, I'm going to plan something special. I'll take you to Santa Barbara, somewhere fabulous, and we'll play all weekend."

"Sounds amazing." I love the idea of being treated so well. I can't seem to resist the sentiment that bubbles up inside of me.

To hell with Max. He doesn't understand what he could've had.

Santa Barbara, here I come.

Chapter Twenty-One / Taking Flight

Fasten your seatbelts, it's going to be a bumpy night!
~ Bette Davis, All About Eve, 1950

"Why would you assume she did something?" Riley demands angrily. "He's the crazy one. He always acts erratic and you know it."

Home from my meeting with Jonathan, I've walked right into an argument between Riley and Dylan.

Dylan's mouth is open as if he's about to argue when he sees me and quickly clamps his mouth shut.

"Hey guys. How are things going?" I ask.

Riley rolls her eyes, while Dylan gently kicks the end of the couch.

I sigh and put my things down. "Look, it sounds like your argument includes me, so why don't we all talk about it?"

Dylan looks hesitant, but Riley dives right in.

"Well, *art boy* has been on a rampage today. He blew off an interview, snapped at a gallery owner, and when the company showed up to crate and transport his final group of paintings for the Barcelona show, he turned them away and said they weren't done."

"Why did you arrange for the transport company to come?" I ask, turning to Dylan.

"Because, yesterday, he told me they were done." Dylan throws his hands up in the air.

Riley and I look at each other. Obviously, this is the aftereffect of my blowout with Max yesterday.

"Look, Ava, I've encouraged Max's friendship with you because he obviously cares about you and you've had a positive effect on him."

The irony of this sentiment doesn't escape me, since Max hasn't been supportive of Dylan and Riley's relationship.

"He's happier when you're around…calmer. And a calmer, happier Max is easier to deal with."

"Glad I can facilitate a happy Max," I say curtly. His tone implies that he cares more for how cooperative Max is than how he's doing as a person and it really irritates me.

Dylan ignores my snarky comment. "But on days like today, I'm really concerned. Did you notice anything strange yesterday? He was excited about the press run, but completely unhinged about something today. We're talking really extreme mood swings here, and I'm seriously worried. It's as if all the pressure with work has really gotten to him."

Even though I know some of Max's drama today is because of his anger toward me, I think of how worried Jess had become about Max. Jess and Dylan know him best.

"Can I ask you something, Dylan? When we were in New York at Max's show, I pulled him away from a bad scene. He was completely drunk and insulting Jonathan Alistair. Just before I got him in the cab, he snapped and…I don't know—it was like he'd sunk into a dark hole. He was so depressed and unresponsive, as though he'd shut the world out. Have you ever seen him behave like that?" I exclude his similar reaction last night for now. I watch Dylan anxiously and then look at Riley.

"Oh man, he used to do that when we were younger and it would freak me out. Then I went through a stage where it pissed me off because I thought he was doing it for attention. And now, well, I can't remember the last time it happened…around me at least." He shakes his head. "It's really disturbing, isn't it?"

I nod, agreeing.

"I had a chance to talk to his mom, Elizabeth, about it once when we were in college. I guess he's had episodes of extreme downswings since he was a little boy. The way she explained it to me is that it's not unusual with extreme creative talent or genius to be manic which means, high highs and really low, lows."

"Manic as in depressive?" I ask.

"I don't know," Dylan says, "I've heard a lot of possibilities tossed around, everything from in the Asperger's spectrum to manic depressive to Savant syndrome, but I never found out exactly. I think I didn't really want to know. Some of the ways it shows is in his complete obsessive focus with his art and his educationally-based information about every aspect of art. His level of talent, focus, and knowledge has that savant quality."

Savant? Asperger's? Manic depressive? No wonder he's been so difficult to figure out.

"He also has always lived inside his head and struggled dealing with people. When I first met him he was completely non-social, and could barely interact with other kids. All through high school, he didn't have regular friendships or even go on a single date. He would just draw and paint for hours and shut the world out."

I'm feeling worse for Max with each negative attribute that gets assigned to him.

"It also didn't help that he lacked the ability to censor his thoughts when he spoke. He's always had a short fuse, and when he snaps, it can get really ugly. Elizabeth had him in therapy, and doing all kinds of things to improve, and it has improved a lot over the years, but it hasn't been an easy road for him."

"Anyway, it's far more complex than I can explain here, but what I do know is that when Max gets over-stimulated, in an emotional way, he can shut down."

Riley looks over at me, alarmed, while Dylan continues.

"I do believe that Max's mind works differently than the rest of ours. He told me once that there are times where the pictures and emotions flashing through his mind are so overwhelming that he can barely function. It contributes to his brilliance in his work, but the personal toll it takes—let's just say that the price he pays is very steep."

Riley jumps in. "Maybe it's just that he's an artist. I thought all artists were a little crazy. But he always seems pretty social to me."

Dylan nods at Riley. "Well, some of it can be explained in that he appears to be unusually comfortable around Ava. But it's not just that." He walks over to the fireplace and looks up at my angel painting.

"The one thing I know for sure is that his girlfriend in college, Chloe, had a lot to do with his improvement. He'd never been able to be that close to a girl, let alone fall in love, and she drew him out and changed him. It happened over time, and it was a startling transformation."

I feel my heart drop as Dylan describes Max's adoration of Chloe. The depth of my pain surprises me.

"I thought when she left him that he'd revert back to who he'd been. And for a while, immediately after the break-up, he was worse than ever. But once enough time had passed, he became even more social, more aggressive about becoming successful. That's when his career really took off."

I look over to Riley.

Her expression is heavy with sadness.

"What, Riley?"

"Oh, I just realized the one girl he loved left him, and his mom, who adored him and helped him, died. His father isn't in his life, and he doesn't have any brothers or sisters. Dylan, I know you're his friend, but let's face it, you're in business together. Then there's Jess, but you've told me she's really tough on him. Who does Max have to really talk to when he's at the end of his rope? He's under so much pressure all the time."

She shakes her head with a sad pout. "I feel sorry for him after hearing all of this."

If she feels bad, she has no idea how confused I feel. His efforts to turn me into his savior makes sense now.

"Maybe you should try to talk to him, Ava," she says softly.

A wave of emotion washes through me. "No, I don't think so."

Did she forget what happened? After what he did at the studio, he's the last person I should help. Even if he has legitimate problems, it doesn't mean I should be the one to deal with them and try to fix him. This stuff's way over my head.

"Please, Ava," Dylan begs.

"I'm sorry, Dylan, but I don't think I'm the best person to talk to him right now."

Riley looks at me, but she doesn't seem surprised. She knows how angry I am about how he treated me.

Dylan drops his head and lets out a long sigh, but I stand my ground. After all, no matter what Max's problems are—he isn't so dysfunctional that he couldn't have contacted me by now. If he really cared about me, he could have at least apologized for the way he acted last night.

Later, I lay awake for a long time. Pictures of Max, flattened by depression and his body completely quiet while his mind is a brilliant blur—haunt me.

Even if I wanted to ease some of his burden, what kind of a price would I pay to provide relief to such a tormented man? The price is too high. The other resolution I come to is that I need some closure, if not with our relationship, at least with the book project. I just have to figure out how.

⟜⟜⟜

With closure in mind, the next morning I get up right after my alarm rings so I can print the final draft of the book for Max. I haven't decided how I'm going to get it to him, but I can always send it FedEx.

I can be professional enough to acknowledge that, even though Max agreed to stay out of the writing process, he deserves to see the book before it goes to press. I wonder if his erratic behavior is why his approval of the final draft wasn't stipulated in his contract. My inkjet printer chugs along while I shower and eat breakfast.

When I collect the pages from the printer, I'm satisfied with the pristine stack of pages without editing notes scrawled on them. I carefully set the pages in a folder and cradle it to my chest while I head to my car.

Work's quiet today. Sean's at the dentist, so I help Brian. It feels good to be around someone who's calm and happy. We work through the logistics of the orders, and as noon creeps up, he suggests lunch. We walk to the little Italian café on the next block.

Brian's stories of his dating life with Thomas are entertaining. The contrast of movie premiers and celebrity events with the quiet calm when they just hang out keeps things interesting for both of them.

I notice Brian watching me carefully and the corners of his mouth slowly turn down and his eyebrows knit together with a concerned look. It makes me sad because I know how much he wants me to be happy, and I can't hide that I'm not.

"What's up, Ava? You seem really down."

I nod and rest my chin in my hand.

"Let me guess…the Jonathan and Max juggle? It must not be working out too well."

I pause, trying to remember the last time we talked. "Oh, I'm so confused Brian." I sigh, my face sinking forward into my hands. "The thing with Jonathan has escalated. It's not just talk anymore." I give him a wide-eyed look.

"Hot! Do tell," he gushes.

"Let's just say the man knows how to make a woman feel sexy. We haven't slept together yet because of circumstances."

"Such as?"

"He wants to do it the right way and at the right time rather than in his office after one of our business meetings. He's classy like that."

Brian nods. "I like a gentleman. So when are you going to ride the pony?

"He wants to take me to Santa Barbara or something."

"Romantic…he must really be into you, Ava." Brian apparently isn't as surprised by my news as I expected him to be.

I sigh. "I wish I felt the same. Don't get me wrong…I really like him and he's skilled at getting me worked up. He knows how to treat a woman, but I'm not obsessed. I don't think about him that much when I'm not with him. It's just weird.

"He's certainly good-looking for an older man, and he's sexy. I think part of it is that I'm so flattered by his attention, and I look up to him, so he's been rather hard to resist. But if I'm honest with myself, I'll admit there's something I can't put my finger on. He's so smooth and a little mysterious. I have a feeling he has a side I haven't seen yet."

"Is that not in a good way?" Brian asks.

"I'm just not sure yet."

"So, what's the latest with Max?"

"We had a big blow out. It was really awful. I doubt we'll ever be friends again."

"Well, there's your passion." The honesty of his words cuts right to the bone.

"Yes, there's the passion, but at what price? As it is, the more I learn about Max, the more messed up he seems. So the smart thing would be to exercise my escape clause. The book's done, we aren't speaking, so we can just part ways."

"But?"

"The man's in my head all the time. I'm pulled to him. It just doesn't make sense. What a damn mess, Brian. How am I going to resolve this?"

"How did you leave things?"

"He stormed out, and we haven't spoken since."

"What if you talked to Max? You could tell him how you feel and why you think the argument happened."

How horrifying. I look up at the ceiling, trying to imagine having that conversation. Just the thought of it makes my insides flip-flop.

"What was your fight about anyway?"

"He wanted to fuck me in the studio and not in a romantic way." I grimace.

"That really sounds hot too. Sorry....Where were you?" he asks, his eyes aglow.

"I was printing when it started. Watching me print his art turned him on, and Sean was in the back burning screens. Next thing you know, we're up against the wall in the hallway, and he's all over me."

Brian's eyes narrow. "Mmm....Steamy. I know how attracted you are to him. Did you let him take you? Man, I would've."

"No, I pushed him off because I was worried about Sean walking in on us, and I didn't want to do it in the storage room or somewhere skanky like the bathroom. He got really mad, and now he thinks I gave him mixed messages. The whole thing happened so fast. I was shocked and confused, and I didn't know what it meant."

"Things certainly have moved along since our last discussion, you little hottie, you."

"I don't think I qualify as a hottie, Brian. All I can think about right now is that Max and I are no longer friends. On the one hand, I'm furious, and on the other...I miss him."

Brian gives me a long look as he pushes his plate away. "You know, Ava, some people expect love to be handed to them like a gift, love in a box...all tied up with big red bow. But it rarely happens like that. Sometimes it's rough and gritty, and you have to fight your way to it."

I link arms with Brian on the way back to the gallery. It feels good to lean into his strong, solid body. The Santa Ana winds have started to pick up, making my hair whip around my face, and I have to hold my skirt down so I don't put on a show for the passing traffic. Meanwhile, Brian's laughing and teasing me as only he can do.

Back at the gallery, Sean's returned from the dentist and is just heading to the studio, so I join him.

"Hey, while you were at lunch, the freak came looking for you."

"Max was here?" I ask, surprised.

"Yeah, and he looked like hell. I'm surprised he had the balls to show up here after his bizarre behavior the other night."

My heart pounds. "What did he say?"

"Not much, just that he *had* to talk to you. He wouldn't take no for an answer when I said not to wait. He looked frantic. I told him I didn't know where you were, and I hadn't seen you since your date with Jonathan last night."

Date? That's really helpful, I think angrily. "Anything else you'd care to share?"

"Oh, yeah, I also asked him why it mattered, since you'd told me you never wanted to see him again." Sean looks quite pleased with himself.

"Why in the fuck would you tell him that, Sean? I didn't say I *never* wanted to see him again…I said I didn't *think* we would see each other again."

"What's the difference? The fucker's long gone now." He smiles darkly.

"There's a big difference, Einstein."

"Well, I still think I did you a favor. You deserve better. I don't care how important his art is or what the fuck everyone sees in him. He stormed out of here like someone had stolen his car, his girl, and his best friend all in one day. What a dramatic ass…good riddance."

Now I'm overcome with curiosity about what Max wanted to say. That he finally had the guts to come here to talk with me weighs heavily on my mind.

As we finish the work in the gallery, Brian asks what I'm doing this evening, and I confide that, if I summon the courage, I may head to Malibu to take Max the transcript for his book. While I'm out there, if he feels like talking, we will. If not, at least I'll know that I returned the effort. I still don't want to be with him, but I may find the closure I'm craving.

He gives me a hug and wishes me luck.

Just before six, I get in my car. The Santa Ana winds are really howling and palm fronds from the towering palm trees dotting the streets litter the ground. Swirls of dust and city grit dance around my car, shimmering from the backlit effect of the late-afternoon sun. I sit for a moment, wondering what to do.

Do I go home and watch TV, or do I get on the freeway? I rest the palm of my hand on Max's folder—his story sitting on my passenger seat—and I close my eyes. One choice is easy, the other risky, but ultimately, isn't it worse never to know what could've happened? The invisible rope winds around my waist and begins the pull toward Malibu.

The drive's a slow blur because I'm compelled to relive the scene at the studio in my mind over and over. The what-ifs start. What if I hadn't stopped him? The pictures are so raw and vivid in my mind that my entire body is aroused and on fire. A part of me desperately wishes we'd had sex that night. To feel him inside me would've been intoxicating, perhaps satiating the desire that's simmered in me since the day I met him.

The sun blazes low as it slowly inches toward the horizon, and I lower my car's visor and squint to see the road more clearly. I picture the look on his face while things were still good that night in the studio…in his eyes a look of lust and wanting, desperate wanting. He wasn't holding back. He was ready to physically give me everything.

Damn. Why didn't I let go and give into my passion? We'd become so close lately. Finally being physical would've added another shade to our relationship.

But if we had fucked, would I have joined his collection of art sluts to be tossed aside? That would've been much worse and the idea is darkly crushing. My anger boils up again, deflating my useless what-if fantasies.

I'm so deep in thought, I almost miss Max's driveway off Pacific Coast Highway. My hands are shaking as I punch in the security code to the gate, and the memories of my last visit haunt me. Yet the MOMA crisis that brought me here the last time ended happily, so maybe it's a good omen for tonight.

When I get to the bottom of the road, I stop in the driveway. There's a rental car parked behind Max's Porsche. A surge of panic shoots through me. It hadn't occurred to me he'd have company. The desire to turn around and head home has weighed on me the entire drive over. Now, I just want to get this over with. I'll give him the book and leave. It's still early evening, so I figure the worst is I'll interrupt a dinner.

As I walk along his garden path, I notice the front door is wide open. I look in, but don't see any sign of Max. I do notice an open bottle of tequila on the side table along with an abandoned shot glass on its side. There's a sweater on the floor just beyond the table.

This type of foreshadowing is heavy-handed and irritating in stories I've read and movies I've watched. In those cases, I turn the channel quickly or close the book and push it onto my nightstand. But tonight seems ripe for a train wreck, and I'm troubled enough to not be willing to turn away.

I take cautious steps into the foyer. What hits me first are the sounds. The moaning and indecipherable words slam into me, rendering me breathless.

'Oh no! Anything but this…anything but this, Max!' my mind wails. I clutch the folder tighter to my chest and try to contain my exploding heart.

I continue forward until I've entered the main room. A tableau from a European porn film unfolds before me. The French doors are wide open with the ocean crashing just beyond. The sun, sharing its last rays of the day, skims over the scene, casting sharp outlines of light and darkening shadows.

The girl is blonde, the palest of yellows, which is striking against her tanned skin. I marvel at the way she's folded over the table, her ample breasts pressed almost flat while her head is arched back. Words fall out of her mouth, and in my stupor she could be speaking Swahili or Albanian for all I know. The fact that her skirt is pushed up over her hips and her panties are missing is not surprising, but expected.

The first thing I notice about him are his hands. One has her peroxide mane wrapped around it, and he's pulling hard, as evidenced by how far her head is jerked back. The other hand is halfway between her hip and her ass, and the shadows indicate that his fingers are digging into the flesh.

My gaze travels up to his face and I gasp quietly.

He's ugly. I didn't think it was possible, but his beautiful features are twisted with hate and anger as he looks down on his golden goddess.

His jeans are pushed down low on his hips and the gathering of fabric around his knees is a symphony of folds and shadows. I'm angry that he doesn't wear a shirt, as if the thin layer would provide a shield of armor in case the whore pressed up against him.

I'm stunned to finally hear his voice. "Fucking say it, Sheila. What in the hell do you want from me?" I can hear the tequila in the slur of his words.

"I want *you*, Max! Fuck me hard. I need it so bad!"

He lets go of her and starts to undo his belt buckle, but he pauses.

"What are you waiting for, Max? Fuck me already!" the blonde goddess yells.

Okay, I'm done here. Yes, completely done. I'm shocked and numb. I really understand the potential benefit of the depressive shutdown thing right now. But that would not be good. I need my legs moving to get me out of here immediately.

I'm in the shadows, so I take a silent step just far enough forward to deposit the folder on the table. I'm not even sure it's a good idea to leave the book now. I just know I can't have it in my possession another motherfucking second.

I step back and turn to my prize, the front door, my gateway out of this hell that's burning me more with each second's passing.

A fierce wind slams one of the French doors hard into the wall and I automatically turn toward the sound. The curtains whip up. For a moment, they are white flags suspended over the room.

Goddamn the Santa Ana winds.

And in the final act of my humiliation, the folder peels open in a horrific slow motion, and the pages take flight, dozens of slender white birds furiously soaring all over the room. Several of the pages fly up against me and wrap around my waist and legs, and I reach down to tenderly peel them off and set them free.

The ugly face now turns toward me, and the expression morphs to a deeper shade of fury. His displeasure that I'm an audience to his tawdry show is quite evident. I quickly calculate that timing-wise I'm at an advantage being mere steps from the door, where he's on the far side of the room and has the blonde one to deal with. She doesn't look like she's in the mood to share, so any attempt he makes to move toward me could be greatly compromised.

And I can tell from the look on his face that he'll be coming after me. Of this I'm eerily certain…so I must plan accordingly. I must think clearly, even though I'm fairly convinced that I'm losing all semblance of sanity as each moment passes.

I exercise my timing advantage as I bolt for the door, turning back only once to show him both the disgust and devastation shadowed in my eyes. And despite his alcohol-induced stupor, I hope he understands; one more unspoken truth shared between us.

Chapter Twenty-Two / All that Matters

When you trip over love, it is easy to get up. But when you
fall in love, it is impossible to stand again.
~Albert Einstein

When another blast of the Santa Ana wind pushes me out the front door, some pages of the book follow me into the garden. One page careens into the koi pond, and it sickens me to see my efforts become fish food. My ridiculous miscalculation, where I bend down and retrieve the soggy page, gives Max just enough time to reach the front door before I've completed my exit. I've underestimated how fast he can move when properly motivated.

"AVA!" His howl tears through me. His jeans ride higher up on his waist now. His expression's wild and frantic.

For a moment, I look at him. The limp wet sheet of paper caught in my fingers is steadily dripping water on my shoes. I let it go, hearing the faint slap as it hits the terracotta tile of the walkway. My bearings recovered, I bolt for the garden gate.

He charges after me, catches my wrist and, just before I make it through the gate, he pulls me back inside. My heart pounds and I refuse to look at him.

"Ava!" His voice is commanding, but as soon as he's spoken it seems he has nothing to say beyond my name. He grips my wrist so tightly that my hand starts to go numb. I look at my car and will it to come to me. I'd really like to do a Batman move and fling myself inside my supercharged car and blast out of this fucked-up situation.

I can hear his ragged breath as he waits. God only knows why he's waiting or what he expects me to do.

"Why did you come, Ava? Why did you come?" His tone is desperate and sounds remarkably sober.

"Because I wanted to talk to you," I reply, still turned away. My voice sounds lifeless.

"What did you want to say?" he asks frantically.

"It doesn't matter anymore and don't worry, I won't be coming back." *You bastard.*

"Don't say it doesn't matter!" he yells.

His fierceness scares me and I curl up inside.

"It's all that matters." His voice cracks with emotion like it's a revelation.

"Max?" the blonde goddess says.

I look over his shoulder at her calling out to him, and then look back at Max. He grimaces. I look away again as tears stream down my face and I refuse to look him in the eye. I won't give him that.

"Shut up, Sheila!" he roars.

"Ava, please tell me why you came," he pleads.

"You shouldn't tell her to shut up—*she's* all that matters now. I'm finished here. Let go of me." I swing my arm down, loosening his grip, and rush to my car.

My hands shake so much I can't get the key in the ignition, and as I fumble I hear an angry howl and a crash. There's a shattered potted plant in front of his garage door now and he screams again.

"It fucking matters, Ava!"

I finally get the key in, start the car, and quickly back out.

CRASH! The sound of pottery hitting a wall is so dramatic and B movie that it's jarring and I'm grateful his target is the wall and not me.

"AVA!" There's a pause and then more pottery, soil and plants crash to the ground. "It's *all that matters!*"

I floor the gas and tear up the driveway as one more crash and his howl echo around me.

"AVA!"

It isn't until I'm on Pacific Coast Highway and accelerating straight ahead that I realize I'm not breathing. My lungs ache as I suck in as much air as possible. I'm sure I'm not steady enough to be driving. The sun has dipped below the horizon, causing the sky to quickly darken, but all I can think about is getting as far away from Malibu as possible.

When I'm no longer gasping, I can focus again. The damage from seeing Max with Sheila and Max seeing my reaction seems irreparable. The rage-filled side of me is sure I never want to see him again. Yet, now that everything's final, I have to face that not seeing him again is heartbreaking.

Max has broken my heart. And perhaps through all of the events that led us here, his heart is broken as well.

This hits me full-force as I drive up the canyon. When I get to the highest point of the hill, my tears turn to sobs and I pull over on the desolate road, too devastated to drive. My car feels like a cage, and I throw open the door and jump out, wanting to feel the solid ground under my feet.

I step over to the edge of the canyon and look at the inky black sky, moonless and calm now that the winds have died down. The stillness and silence make me feel completely alone in the world, which only amplifies my agony. Despite my fury over what I left behind in Malibu, I torture myself by allowing better memories of Max to seep into my mind.

The times he took me to his favorite places are when I saw glimpses of the real Max. We seemed to grow closer with each experience, which lead to that fateful night in the print studio. I'll never forget his passionate expression and his whispered words as his body and his heart leaned toward mine.

"I've really tried Ava, God only knows how hard I've tried. But I can't fight it anymore...I don't have it in me to deny how I feel anymore."

I'd never felt such passion, and as my fingers skim over my lips, I relive what followed...the kiss that I'd waited my whole life for. I let out a deep sigh. I thought we were destined for a great love, not a showdown on an emotional battlefield.

My tears continue to fall as my gaze trails down to the canyon below. Void of light, it's a black abyss, much like my heart in this aftermath. If only I could float down and surrender to the darkness. Surrounded by silence, perhaps I would be spared the ugly voices in my head and the ragged stutter of my broken heart.

Feeling pathetic, I sink down on a nearby rock and cry until my tears run out. I wonder if I'm capable of holding it together long enough to drive home. A rustling in the nearby brush, followed by the sorrowful cry of a small animal, snap me out of my stupor. I'm not the only creature suffering in the universe.

My grandmother used to tell me that no matter how our rough circumstances are—large or small—life moves forward and we have to figure out how to carry on. I find the strength to climb back in my car and drive home.

❦

Two horrid and hazy days later, I'm lying in bed, staring at the wall and willing myself to get up and make coffee. The phone rings. It's Jess, which is a surprise, considering she never gets up early on Sunday.

"Hey, Ava." She sounds tense, and I hear another muffled voice in the background. "Listen, when was the last time you talked to or heard from Max?"

"Friday night. Why?" A bad feeling settles in my stomach.

"What was his mood like when you talked last? Was he okay?"

She's scaring me. "Why, Jess? What's going on?"

"Answer me, Ava," she snaps. "Was he okay?"

"No." I take a deep breath.

"Fucking hold on."

"Dylan!" she yells. She's louder than I expect, even though it sounds like she moved the phone away from her mouth.

"Please, tell me what happened," she asks me.

"We had a fight and I left."

"Fuck! That's just what I was afraid of."

She speaks to Dylan again. "They had a fight. She hasn't heard from him either."

"How upset was he? I really need to know."

"*Very* upset, and I'm getting *very* upset now too because you aren't telling me what's going on. Is Max okay?"

"Listen, can you come out here?"

"Come out where…Malibu?" I'm freaked out. What the hell's going on? My heart sinks. Max's house is the last place I want to go right now.

"Yes." Jess sounds frustrated. "No one's been able to reach Max since Friday night. He didn't show up for a lunch meeting with Dylan yesterday. When Dylan still hadn't heard from him, he drove out to Malibu. There's no sign of him."

"When I got to Max's house on Friday evening, he was with that blonde, Sheila. Maybe you should call her?" I know it's not likely they're together, considering his reaction to her that night, but it's worth a shot.

"Sheila?" she snaps. "He was with that idiot? Okay, we'll try to reach her, but could you still come out here?"

"You know, Jess, I've been through enough crap with Max. I'm done. I really don't want to come out to his place when I'm trying to forget him."

"Please? I'm scared something bad has happened. When Dylan showed up, he thought Max had been robbed. His front door was wide open, and there was broken shit like the place had been trashed. But all the stuff robbers would take like TVs and cameras were still here.

"Dylan couldn't find him, but his car is parked outside. And the paintings…Ava, I'm so worried. I've never seen anything like this. You have to come here and see what I'm talking about."

My heart pounds in my chest. The fear in her voice compels me to set my own reservations aside. "Okay, Jess. I'm on my way."

Chapter Twenty-Three / Missing

When painting, an artist must take care not to trap his
soul in the canvas.
  ~ Terri Guillemets

When I pull up to Max's house, the state of his house is even worse than I imagined.

There's broken pottery, dead plants and potting soil everywhere. Max's garage door and walls are dented and scratched from multiple impacts. There's considerably more damage than I remember from before I drove off Friday. In the heat of his fury that night, Max must've kept throwing things.

I gingerly step over the shards and enter the front garden. Even though the sun's burning through the fog, it's still quite cool, and I shiver as I look around.

More pages from the book have blown into the yard, decorating the garden with the wandering pages. Several are perched in the trees, captured by branches. A few are in the flowerbeds and others float on top of the koi pond like a fine layer of snow. The sight of it humiliates me and fills me with hopelessness.

One of the dining room chairs is on its side on the lawn, a fallen soldier undoubtedly surprised to be part of the melee. I breathe a sigh of relief to see it's nowhere near the tree as the image of a noose dangling from a branch comes to mind.

Jess stands in the doorway to the house and looks battle-worn. I've never seen her expression so bleak and my nerves instantly fray.

"Where's Dylan?" I ask, not knowing what else to say.

"He's in the studio. We'll go see him in a minute. Come on." She motions me into the house.

Broken glass litters the floor and the stench of alcohol permeates the air.

"Watch your step," Jess warns.

There's a scar where the glass hit the wall—probably the bottle of tequila. The sweater that'd been tossed on the floor is no longer there. White pages are scattered all over the room.

The dining room table is on its side and the remaining chairs are askew. One of the sheer white curtains has been ripped off the wall, the rod hanging at an odd angle from its uprooting. It's as if a savage animal tore through the house.

Could Max have that much rage?

A framed picture is smashed on the floor and there's a dent in the plaster where it collided before falling on the tiles. Jess carefully picks it up. It's a photo of Max accepting an award amid the shattered glass.

"The Whitney Biennial. Damn, Max," Jess whispers and narrows her eyes as she stares at the broken mess that framed one of his successes. She gingerly sets it on a nearby side table.

"I don't even know how to process this," I say.

Jess shakes her head. "It's complicated. Let's go to the studio. I want to warn you…Dylan's really upset, so take anything he says with a grain of salt."

So he's going to blame this all on me? I wonder.

To avoid facing the chaos inside, we weave between the palm trees along the side yard until we reach the front of the studio.

Jess grabs my arm to stop me before I go in. "I have to warn you…this may freak you out. But I'm here, okay?"

Am I wearing my heart on my sleeve? She's scared for me. Am I that transparent? I take a deep breath, ready for more chaos, and slowly step inside.

At first, I'm surprised by the quiet cleanliness of the studio. Nothing's smashed or overturned, and it's as pristine as I remember it. But the look of accusation on Dylan's face just before he turns away is intimidating.

What?

I look around the studio again, searching for the piece of the puzzle I'm missing. And then it hits me like a ton of bricks. Three large paintings are leaning against the wall. Are those the paintings that were supposed to be on their way to Barcelona? They're gorgeous—all color and emotion. Or at least they *were* gorgeous until Max defaced them.

Across each canvas, a large letter has been slapped across the face in dripping black paint. It's savage—the most brutal form of graffiti to deface something so beautiful with so little regard.

"No," I groan, reaching for the paintings, as if I can undo the mess with a wave of my hand. I stumble forward and Jess catches me. Max has crushed me with his final message scrawled across his work. My eyes move left to right, painting to painting.

A-V-A.

One letter per painting, each one a cry in the dark, a surrender, a loss.

If there'd been any lingering doubts about Dylan's theory that Max was obsessed with me, there aren't anymore. Replacing them is a feeling of anguish that, if I'd understood the depths of Max's feelings, perhaps I could've handled everything differently.

"I'm fucking tempted to just send them to Barcelona like this, damn it!" Dylan spits out, as he paces back and forth in front of the paintings.

"I don't think so. You don't want to leave him open for ridicule," Jess says.

"What the fuck was he thinking, Jess? He knew these paintings were late."

"Obviously, he wasn't thinking. That's the problem."

"Can't he fix them?" I ask.

"Well, we'd have to find him first, wouldn't we?" Dylan says, exasperated.

"And so far, we have no idea where he is." Jess's defeated expression and the hopeless tone in her voice surprise me.

"Did you reach Sheila?" I ask Jess.

"Yes, but she wasn't very helpful. She said she hoped she never saw the fucker again. Before she hung up, she said she left Friday night right after you; she didn't know about the rest of what happened around here."

The jealous part of me is happy to know she didn't stay and party with Max after I'd left.

"Dylan, what about that art restoration guy? The one you used last year after the rain damage at your place," Jess says.

"I've already called him and he's on his way. Hopefully, he can fix them. I'm going to try him again to see where he is." Dylan steps into the garden with his cell phone.

"Now do you see why I called you, Ava? You had to see all this to understand the depth of it," Jess says gently.

I nod but I'm confused. Is this an obsession or something more?

Jess shakes her head. "Remember my party in New York? I had an argument with Max that night because I wanted him to stay away from you. He's too messed up for a relationship right now."

I study her face. I know she's right...he's a mess...and now he's a missing mess.

"I see now that he tried to avoid falling for you, but in the end, he couldn't help himself. Max is a force of nature. Once he focuses on something or someone, I've learned to just get out of the way. There's no stopping him. And now that he knows he's ruined everything..."

"But Jess, none of us can know for sure what he's thinking."

"I have two more things to show you." Jess leads me to his desk and carefully opens a large folder. On top, there's a computer printout. In the margin of the print-out I notice that he's doodled my name a number of times in different sizes and styles.

"This doesn't mean anything. He could've been talking to me on the phone while he was doodling," I argue.

"Really?" she asks with raised brows like I'm deluded.

I give her an exasperated, wide-eyed look and let out a long sigh.

She gently lifts the paper out of the folder and holds it up me. "It's a love poem, Ava."

I take it out of her hand to examine it more closely.

The printout is of an E. E. Cummings poem, "Somewhere I Have Never Travelled, Gladly Beyond." My breath catches—he couldn't possibly know it's one of my favorite poems. My gaze drops down to the last graph and I silently recite it to myself.

> (i do not know what it is about you that closes
> and opens; only something in me understands
> the voice of your eyes is deeper than all roses)
> nobody, not even the rain, has such small hands

"Oh, Jess," I whisper. I press my hand on my chest to keep my heart from unfolding.

She rests her hand on my shoulder to steady me.

"But Jess…all this time I thought he had no romantic interest in me. Sure, he'd flirt, but more often than not he'd treat me like a buddy. I didn't know what his intentions were until the night of the printing, and even then I thought he only wanted sex."

"I know, babe. And now you know you meant so much more to him. Here's the last thing…look at this." She turns back to the folder and tenderly peels back a sheet of parchment paper. There's a piece of heavy watercolor paper with a drawing of the photo he emailed me from the day we went thrift store shopping for paintings. It's exquisitely detailed with accents of soft pastels.

He's rendered me far more beautiful than I am, and for a moment I'm transported away from our current crisis and my heart soars. It takes my breath away that such a beautiful piece of art was created in my likeness. But more than that, this drawing was done when things were good between us. Unlike my angel painting, which was *my* gift, this drawing was for him. It's quietly beautiful, not the rage-filled scrawl of my name on the paintings that stand before us.

This drawing holds the truth of how Max once saw me, and I ache now for all that we've lost.

Jess points out something in the bottom corner and I lean in closer to see. Handwritten in small letters Max has written: *My Ava...*

Overcome, I rush out of the studio and down to the beach. Tears fight their way down my face as my mind races. I need to get away from all of this, both the drawing Max created, and the paintings he destroyed as he pulled me into his heart and ripped me out again.

When I reach the shore, I stop, close my eyes and picture Max's face, from his brilliant eyes to his perfectly-sculpted jaw. When he smiled, he was too beautiful. Everything about him was too much, perhaps more than I could ever handle. His presence was so commanding that, even when he was quietly standing, I was drawn to his energy.

Now I understand that he was powerfully drawn to me too.

In my heart, I know I won't be at peace until Max is found and gets help. So I make up my mind that I'll be a force of nature too, if that's what it takes to bring Max home. Only then can I know what the next chapter of our gothic romance novel holds, or if the cover is closed forever, forcing us to move on with our lives.

I look to the horizon and brace against the gale that curls off the ocean, carrying part of its mysteries and the stories from its depths yet to be told. I wish my words could travel with the current to places near and far, where answers linger in hallways and nestle in corners, waiting to be revealed. I close my eyes and whisper into the wind...

Max...where are you?

Coming Soon

The Trilogy

Book II~The Unveiling January 2014

Book III~The Masterpiece March 2015

For Work of Art release alerts and teasers sign up at
RuthClampettWrites.com

Also by Ruth Clampett

Animate Me

Mr. 365

Many thanks to those of you
that take a moment to leave a review
~it is much appreciated.

Acknowledgements

Big love to my Home Girls: Alex, Cheri, Lisa and Judy.

Hugs and high-fives to my Lost Girls: Erika, Dawn and Susi.

Endless gratitude to editors Angela Borda, Aviva Layton, Janine Savage and Janell Parque: it's that fine line you tease me with between sweet torture and sublime satisfaction that keeps me coming back for more.

My bookcover Mod Squad: Photographer David Johnston and Designer Jada d'Lee... you are image magicians, artfully rendering while coaxing me down the right path. You always lead me to exactly where I wanted to be. A million thank you's would never be enough.

Michael Senich you make a delightful muse. Thank you for always putting a smile on my face.

Thank you Flavia Viotti Siqueria and Meire Dias of Bookcase Literary Agency whose love for my passionate artist really lit the fire under Work of Art. Thank you for believing in me.

I'm grateful for the savvy guidance and enthusiasm of Neda Amini, the passion and visual stylings of Elli Iris, and the wonderful support and encouragement of Suzie and Kellie.

Love and appreciation for sweet friends Azu and Laura, and beta CJ who were by my side at the beginning of Maxfield's journey.

And last but not least....thank you to my fic friends, readers, reviewers, bloggers, Tweeters, and fic promoters....I'm so grateful that we're together on this thrilling ride. Tighten your seat-belts...the fun has just begun!

About the Author

Ruth Clampett, daughter of legendary animation director, Bob Clampett, has spent a lifetime surrounded by art and animation. A graduate of Art Center College of Design, her careers have included graphic design, photography, VP of Design for WB Stores and teaching photography at UCLA. She now runs her own studio as the fine art publisher for Warner Bros. where she's had the opportunity to know and work with many of the greatest artists in the world of animation and comics.

The Work of Art Trilogy is Ruth's third publishing endeavor, following *Animate Me* and *Mr. 365*. She lives in Los Angeles and is heavily supervised by her teenage daughter, lovingly referred to as Snarky, who loves art and visiting museums as much as her mom.

Connect with Ruth:
RuthClampettWrites.com
https://twitter.com/RuthyWrites
For book stuff:
https://www.facebook.com/RuthClampettWrites
For a more general stuff:
https://www.facebook.com/RuthClampett
http://instagram.com/Ruth_Clampett

www.ingramcontent.com/pod-product-compliance
Lightning Source LLC
Chambersburg PA
CBHW020747250626
47155CB00003B/961